Something
Might
Happen

Something Might Happen

A   N O V E L

JULIE MYERSON

LITTLE, BROWN AND COMPANY
BOSTON • NEW YORK • LONDON

First American Edition

The characters and events in this book are fictitious. Any similarity to real persons, living or dead, is coincidental and not intended by the author.

Library of Congress Cataloging-in-Publication Data

Myerson, Julie.
    Something might happen : a novel / Julie Myerson.
        p. cm.
    ISBN 0-316-77984-9
        1. Police — England — Fiction.   2. Female friendship — Fiction.   3. Murder victims — Fiction.   4. Married women — Fiction.   5. England — Fiction. 6. Grief — Fiction.   I. Title.

PR6063.Y48S66 2003
823'.914 — dc21

2003046094

10 9 8 7 6 5 4 3 2 1

Q-MB

Printed in the United States of America
Text design by Meryl Sussman Levavi/Digitext

For Esther Freud –

who understands about the place

Something Might Happen

Chapter 1

PEOPLE THINK WHEN SOMEONE IS STABBED THEY JUST fall down on the ground and die. Well they don't. When Lennie is found on that morning in the car park on Pier Avenue, they can tell from the mess that she dragged herself around for some time before she gave up.

Quite some time, in fact. Maybe even as much as a quarter of an hour. Crawling like a baby on her hands and knees, grabbing and swiping at door handles and bumpers, fingers tacky with her own blood. Then at some point slipping down and losing consciousness there in the nettles by the Pay & Display machine. They say they can't be certain about when it was, the precise moment that her heart stopped — but they can assure us that it was immaterial. She wouldn't have seen, wouldn't have known.

The one good thing, Mawhinney says, is that her brain would've shut down as her lungs filled up.

But I don't want the details. One moment or several? A curdled sigh, a spattered red breath, brown saliva clotting in her mouth? All I care about is that they're right, that it was quick. All I need to know is that her heart was not still beating when her attacker moved back in and cut it out.

Early October and four in the morning and no wind at all, just the blackest darkness, so dead and dark and black that if you stopped to think about it, you might find you couldn't breathe. All the lights out. And then all of them on, one by one — pop, pop, pop — the world reviving, turning large and transparent.

Something's happened.

He rings me at the deadest time, sleep holding me down. Since the baby that's how I've been, a dead person, trying to surface. Still I grab the phone the second its ringing hits my dreams.

Tess, he goes, Tess — and straightaway I can tell his voice is all wrong.

What? I say, struggling to sit up and focus. What is it? What's going on?

I'm —

The silence crackles.

I'm sorry, he says.

What do you mean, sorry? Why?

Oh Tess, he says and he sounds like he's going to cry.

Al, I go, for fuck's sake — what?

She's not here.

What?

You were right. She hasn't come home.

She hasn't?

She's just — I don't know where she is — she's not here.

Outside, a dark whoosh of wind in the poplars. If it was light you would see them bending. You get that by the sea — sudden changes, things getting crushed and flattened. I used to like it. It used not to scare me at all.

Next to me in the bed meanwhile Livvy is lying on her back in her white sleeper, snaps done up to the chin, mouth softly open and arms flung back. A swirl of blackish hair on her head. Mick funnily enough is lying in a similar babyish way but on his front — black matted hair pushed up, hands bunched into two hot fists. Dreaming of a fight is what it looks like.

Tess, he says, what am I going to do?

Call the police.

I've done that.

You want me to come?

He says nothing. Liv snorts. When did I feed her? I slide my fingers under to feel her nappy. Damply heavy with pee. I must have fed her in the night, in my sleep.

I'll come, I tell him. Wait for me.

I get out of bed, change the baby, get dressed.

In one way it is not a surprise. In the beach hut that night, the feeling is cold and hard, painful and unsettling. I shouldn't have let him come. It shouldn't have to be complicated.

I take the tumbler of wine from his hands. Take a sip. Put it down on the wooden floor which is slippy with the years of sand falling off our bare feet.

You should get back, I say. But he doesn't move. He just looks at me.

She'll be in bed. She'll have gone to sleep.

No, I say. It's not that.

What, then?

He reaches forward, half grinning, tries to take his drink back. I stop him.

The truth is, he's lazy. Whatever he gets from me, he imagines he can't get from anyone else.

It's not that, I say again. Batting him away.

He settles back in the old deckchair and looks at me. His old jeans, his big feet in their salt-stained boots. A bleached tidemark where he has walked in the edge of the sea. He looks at the joint in his hands — his rough, furniture-maker's hands — tips off the ash.

For God's sake, Tess, he says at last, I wish you'd calm down.

I sigh.

You're even making me jumpy, he says. What the fuck is it? Why're you in such a state?

I say nothing.

He shrugs, smiles. He likes to think I'm this uptight person. He thinks he's won.

I'm scared, I tell him and he leans forward.

What are you scared of, Tess?

I don't know.

It's not true though. I think I do know, even then.

The thing is, she is not the type to have something happen. She has everything going for her. Beauty, talent, kindness. She even sometimes goes to church.

It's the one thing she and Alex argue about, the only thing. It's not God, she says, just something bigger, greater than her. She needs to feel there is a larger Good out there.

You might think she's this good and pliable person but actually she's not, she's dogged and fixed. She's the strong one. She does exactly as she pleases. When we first came here, she was the one who said it would all be fine, who believed most certainly in the dream we had.

The only thing I have more of than her is kids. Double the amount. People ask me how I do it, as if there's some kind of trick to having four. But it's easy. I do it for myself. I can't help it. There's nothing to beat walking down the street on a sunny day with them all clean and happy and no one crying or fighting behind you and knowing just how it all looks. A perfect mother with her perfect life.

These are the facts. That she dies on a Monday night in October, some time between eleven and midnight, following a PTA meeting at the school on Marlborough Road. That she gets to that meeting around seven and it ends around twenty to eleven — later than usual, but then it is Lucy Dorry's first time as Chair and most people who can, stay on for a drink after.

That they reckon, anyway, that she reaches her car around 10.45, but that she never manages to get into it. She never even makes it around to the driver's side. Her keys are found lying on the ground just beneath the passenger door. All the paintwork around the lock is scratched furiously and the nails on her right hand are ripped and bloody and broken.

Both of us, with our perfect lives. She can't believe it when I tell her I'm expecting Liv. At thirty-eight!

You're saying I'm past it?

No, she replies and I notice the flicker of a frown in her eyes. Just the thought — and she shudders — of going through it all again.

I can't wait, I tell her as boisterously as I can. And it's the truth, I can't.

And work?

I can do that too, I say. Because I've already decided that I'll have to.

She turns and looks at me with eyes full of something, but what exactly I can't tell.

I wish I had your guts, she says. And your energy.

Which makes me laugh because, in my book, it takes guts and energy to deny yourself these things. And Mick and I have never been good at limiting ourselves, at sitting down and planning. In fact, none of our kids were planned exactly — or that's what we always tell people, laughing at ourselves. Just one big happy haphazard family. That's the story we tell ourselves.

And I am over the moon about Liv — from that first mysterious morning when the simple act of stirring the hot milk into Rosa's instant oat cereal makes me turn and hold myself, perspiring, over the sink.

When I tell Mick, he does nothing. He doesn't move. He is sitting there at the table and I bend and whisper it in his ear and maybe I expect that he will pull me to him, but he doesn't move a single muscle.

You're not pleased?

He looks at me.

I don't know. I'm not 'not' pleased.

Oh great.

I fold my arms and feel the buzz of my blood, my heart.

It's a shock, that's all.

We haven't been using anything.

I know, he says, I know, but I thought —

You thought what?

That we were being careful.

I laugh.

I suppose I thought it was very unlikely, he says.

His voice is small and tight. He sounds like a little boy who's been jumping again and again out of the highest tree and then the very last time has forgotten to bend his knees when he lands and has got himself hurt. Cross with the tree, cross with himself.

I've just chucked in my job, he reminds me, as if I didn't know.

Well, I tell him, this is good. You can be the nanny. You can do some writing.

He doesn't laugh.

With a new baby? I hope that's a joke.

But when he sees me looking at him and half laughing and half about to cry, he does get up and come and put his arms around me, bends his head to mine. I smell the blackness of his hair, the familiar day-old smell of beard, of husband.

So, he says.

So — what?

So we'd better get on with it then.

And that's it, that's all. That's the beginning of our daughter Olivia.

The last person to see Lennie alive is John Empson, PTA Treasurer and Chairman of the Christmas Lights. I know John well. His bookshop is next door to the clinic and he gives me discounts. In return I gave him ultrasound for nothing when he tore the ligaments in his knee. It's how we live in this place. You give what you can and you get back what you need.

On that night, John walks with Lennie as far as the junction of Marlborough Road and North Parade. It is bitterly cold by then, the kind of rough, sea cold that goes right through your clothes and hits your bones. A light rain has started up and Lennie is hurrying, they both are, and since she only has on a thin cardigan and no umbrella, she holds her papers up over her head.

Like this, John says later, using his big, grey hands to show the police. As if they could protect her, he says, terror and disbelief cracking his voice.

John and Lennie chat briefly about this and that — about how glad they are to have Lucy on board, about what should be done about the frustrating delay to plans for bike racks outside the caretaker's office (despite the money having officially been raised) — and so on. Then, because John is heading back to the High Street on his bike, he zips his big green waterproof and they separate, each making a dash for it.

In any other town perhaps, he might have seen her to her car, but not in this one. No one expects that here. This town really is a safe place, everyone knows that. Even in winter, even after dark, it's a place where, once kids know how to cross a road sensibly, they can pretty much go around alone.

What happens next is Alex says sorry to Gemma Dawson, who popped over from Trinity Street to keep an eye on the kids when he went out. She's only supposed to have been there for ten minutes or so, until Lennie came back. Gemma says that's OK. She imagined the meeting had gone on longer or that they'd all gone to the pub or something. She wasn't bothered. And she was watching TV and she lost track of the time anyway. Monday's a good telly night and it makes no difference to her where she watches it.

When Gemma's gone, Alex stands for a moment in the front room. Turns off the gas fire. Picks up Gemma's empty

Coke glass and the TV guide. Then, after checking the boys are safely asleep in their beds, he opens the front door and, leaving it ajar, goes a little way down the lane with a torch.

He's not that worried, not yet. Alex is practical. He doesn't worry until he needs to. But it's not like Lennie — she isn't the type to take off and go somewhere without telling him. That's him — he's the one who does that.

In October the night dew gets so heavy it feels like rain. You can smell woodsmoke and, yes, if you breathe in hard enough, the larger smell of sea. Alex looks but he doesn't know what he's looking for. He shines the light into the black tangled hedgerows, lets it move across the pale grit of the road — not perhaps wanting to think of why he is doing it, but doing it all the same.

Well, I couldn't just sit there, he tells me later. I had to get up and do something and I didn't know what else to do.

He sees nothing, hears nothing.

He thinks of leaving the boys asleep and setting off on foot up to the school but knows Lennie will think that's irresponsible. What if a fire starts? What if Connor has one of his dreams and wakes in a panic to find the house empty?

In the end he goes back in and calls the Farrs. Geoff answers — no, it's fine, they're not in bed yet. He gets Maggie. Who sounds surprised. And then worried. She can only confirm what Alex realises he already knows. That Lennie left the meeting an hour ago — at least an hour in fact, since she wasn't even the last to go.

Alex feels his stomach start to slide. He holds off calling for as long as he can bear it. Then he rings the police. And me.

*   *   *

He is standing outside in the drive when I get there. Next to him, a police car — sour stripes in the fuzzy dark. The dirty moon of the porch light shining, not yet dawn, not even close — the lane still grey, the hawthorn hedge a smudge of black at the bottom of the lawn.

I heave Livvy's seat up over one arm. She's getting heavy, the plastic digs into my arm, rubs against my hip. For a second her eyes flick open, unseeing, then back shut again.

You should have called, I tell him.

I did.

No, I mean sooner — straightaway.

He looks blank.

What could you have done?

I can't bear his face.

Been here with you —

He rubs his eyes.

I feel bad enough getting you up now —

Oh Al — don't be stupid, I tell him, shivering.

And Mick —?

Mick's asleep.

He looks at me.

Tess — I mean, how could you have known —?

I didn't, I tell him again, I don't —

But — what you said?

I shake my head.

You know what you said.

I've no idea why I said it, I tell him.

Tess —

OK, I say, I felt afraid.

What d'you mean afraid? Of what?

I don't know, I tell him, I mean it, Al. I don't know what of.

We stand in silence for a moment. I hear the crunch of footsteps by the back door. Police.

Do you think she has left me? he says.

I try to laugh.

No, I say. No Al, I don't.

A policeman comes out of the house and nods at us.

I watch him cross the gravel to the car and lean in to speak into the radio.

Lennie would never leave, I tell him, though it's only as I say it that I know it's true. She never would. Not just go.

The policeman comes over.

All right? he says.

Alex takes a quick breath.

We're going to the school.

You'll call me?

I pick up Liv's seat. He nods.

They're going to search the creek and the marshes, he says. If they get nowhere at the school.

Pure terror on his face.

She wouldn't go anywhere, I tell him again. Not willingly. I just know she wouldn't.

Sometimes there are things that I know.

Sometimes at the clinic, treating a patient, I feel my fingers slip in between the usual rhythms and catch something else, something I wasn't looking for. It might be something I don't want to know — superfluous to the treatment. It's possible in my work to have too much information — to have it all come flying so hard at you that you lose focus.

What bollocks, says Mick as he sorts the washing on the kitchen floor. What sort of things, anyway?

I don't know, I say, just things.

You mean if someone's going to move house or get divorced or win the lottery?

No, I'll say. For fuck's sake, Mick. You know I don't mean that.

Well what then? If they'll live or die?

I'll flush.

I don't know.

And he laughs. Not because he doesn't understand, but because of the opposite: he thinks he understands too well. I can't surprise him any more. All these years together and what is there left to discover?

So I keep quiet. When I pick up on Ali Ledworth's pregnancy long before the doctors do (two tests in a row come back negative), I say nothing about it at home. And when poor Janey Urbach is knocked down in Bury on a one-way street by a car going the wrong way and suffers appalling spinal damage, I know better than to mention to Mick that the last time I treated her I felt something — a heavy weight hanging over her — as unmissable as a cloud blotting out the sun on a hot day.

And when I tell Alex I feel that Lennie will be OK, it's a lie. I don't. Not at all. Ever since that moment in The

Polecat her presence — normally solid and resilient and un-remarkable — has been unfurling and undoing itself, snag-ging, tearing, falling apart.

Anne Addison types out the minutes from that night's meeting. She tells me it feels almost wrong, putting down on paper what amount to Lennie's last words, her last recorded comments — made only an hour or so before she died. She types them up and copies them, but does not cir-culate them yet, out of respect for the family, she says.

There is a report on the Quiz Night — Lennie recorded as saying she's disappointed by how little was raised and querying the amount spent on food. Maybe we should just get people to bring stuff next time? she suggests. Nothing fancy, just maybe quiches and baguettes and cheese and maybe a dip or two?

One or two people disagree. They feel that, for the price of the ticket, a hot meal is expected. Lennie's shrug is not minuted of course, but I can see it, clear as anything — her sitting back, blonde head bent, picking intently at her nails, deciding not to push her comments any further.

Lennie is good — better than me — at knowing when to shut up. Which is a good thing because there's always a bit of trouble at these meetings. There's always someone dis-gruntled, someone who resents the way someone else says something, someone who refuses to cast a vote.

There's a brief discussion about the Carnival Parade, which is going to be the last week of June along the sea front. Last year I took this on, but this time Lennie's agreed to do it. Someone suggests a competition at the school to design a Carnival poster — Maggie says great, she has a book-illustrator friend who would judge it. Maybe his publisher would even donate prizes? I know there would have been a murmur of pleasure at that. But Barbara Anscombe, who likes to get her oar in, ignores Maggie and says the post office should also be approached — see if they'd be willing to provide balloons and maybe smaller prizes for runners-up.

Then there's the usual argument about who the proceeds should go to. Barbara says Marie Curie.

What? Again? says Sally Abrahams, whose son is on his gap year in Nepal. Shouldn't we be raising awareness of something beyond the town — Christian Aid, Action Aid, something a little more multicultural?

Cancer affects people in all cultures, says Barbara firmly and Polly Dawson points out that many people in the town know someone who has died of cancer, though no one dares look at John who lost his wife so recently.

But Lennie agrees with Sally, that it might be nice to have a change. She knows, for instance, that the WI in Westleton are raising money for African farmers (a snort here from Barbara) — and what's to stop them going back to Marie Curie at Christmas?

All of this, except Barbara's brief snort of derision, is minuted by Anne Addison.

Later, shocked, baffled, interviewed by police, everyone who attended the meeting agrees that Lennie behaved quite normally, that there was nothing strange or different about her behaviour at all. A bit tired, perhaps, they all concede, but then who isn't tired on a Monday night after a day's work followed by feeding the kids before rushing out again?

At a quarter to ten, the meeting is declared closed and Lucy, Lennie, Polly, Sue Peach, her daughter Sophie and Maggie lay out a selection of crudités, tortilla chips and dips. Bottles are opened, paper cups pulled from their cellophane.

Sue lets drop that she's thinking of doing an Open University degree, now that her youngest has started full-time school. And Lucy says something along the lines of how terrific and that if she had her time all over again she just knows she'd study with a whole lot more passion.

And Lennie laughs and says, Ah but isn't that what being a student is all about? Taking life for granted? Living in the moment and for the moment and with no sense of what the future holds?

Everyone — Sue, Maggie, Polly, Sophie, Charlotte, Sally, Lucy, Barbara, John, Anne — remembers this comment of hers. They all mention it in the police interviews. No one can bear to think that, less than an hour later, the person who made it is dead.

Chapter 2

WHEN YOU LIVE RIGHT BANG UP CLOSE TO SOMEONE, IT can be hard to get far enough back to see them clearly. Or maybe your eyes do look, but your brain can't take it in. Like you never notice your own kids growing, or your own baby getting proper hair.

When Alex tries to give the police a physical description of Lennie, he gets confused. He goes almost crazy trying to think what she had on — earlier for instance when she screamed at Max about the state of his room, or kicked the washing-machine door shut and swore because it hurt her foot, or made the boys' tea in a hurry and upset Connor by slightly burning the frilled edges of his second fried egg. He knows she did these things, but he can't see her doing them.

This shocks him.

Like she'd already gone from our lives, he tells me later.

You were in a panic, I say. It's not your fault. You couldn't think.

I say it but I know it's meaningless. And he just looks at me — just screws up his eyes and rips the skin from the ragged side of his thumbnail and I know what he's thinking: he's trying to imagine the last time he saw her, trying to retrieve it from the deadest, most faraway part of his mind.

He tells the police he thinks she may have had on a red shirt, a shiny one.

Satin? they say.

He nods.

Something with a sheen anyway. Satin or silk, he says. Is there a difference?

Al shuts his eyes.

And jeans, he says. Jeans and slip-on trainers, blueish-grey ones, the type with the knobbly sole —

After clothes, they ask him about other things. The state of his marriage. He tells them it's fine, it's normal — no, no rows recently, not that he can think of. Nothing major anyway. And does Mrs Daniels have any history of depression or other illness such as seizures or fits?

No, Alex tells them, relieved that this part at least is completely true. Never, no. Lennie's a fit and healthy person, never ill, never down, nothing like that.

He explains that she's a potter, a ceramicist — that she's just had an exhibition in London. That a couple of big stores have bought her stuff — that she's doing well. They ask him what he does and he tells them he makes furniture. And maybe he smiles because he knows how it must sound. The potter and the furniture maker in their cottage by the sea. They ask him how his business is doing and he says, Good — thinking it a strange question — good enough, he says. Trying to stop his stupid hands from shaking so hard.

She would never go off without telling me, he adds then, hating the small whine of helplessness in his voice. But they seem to accept this and he relaxes. It's only when the officers step outside for a moment that he finds himself overwhelmed by the lingering tang of their aftershave and rushes to the downstairs toilet to be sick. A quick, odourless and painless throwing up, like a dog or a baby.

Almost six. I crouch on the edge of the musty sofa and feed Liv by Alex and Lennie's gas fire in the half-dark. She's not hungry — just gums my nipple in a kind of half-dutiful way, then relaxes her lips and lets it slip away off her tongue. You think that babies are these fragile little creatures, at everyone's mercy, but they're not. I know that and Liv knows it too. She knows what she wants from life and she's learning the knack of how to get it.

I pull my bra back up and replace the pad and at that moment hear the upstairs toilet flush and then Max's voice saying something cross. Then the creak of the stairs.

Not just Max, both of them.

Where's Mum and Dad? Why're you here? Is it a school day? Connor wants to know, one hand in his mouth, the other down his pyjama bottoms.

Mum broke down somewhere, I tell them, and Daddy's had to go and pick her up and sort out the car —

He can't fix cars, says Max straightaway.

No, I say, I mean, get it to a garage or whatever.

But Max looks suspicious.

So — you mean she broke down and stayed in the car all night?

No. I think she stayed at Maggie's, I tell him.

That's weird, he says, frowning.

Is it?

You know it is. Why wouldn't she just walk back here?

I search for an answer but it's not necessary, I've lost him. He's already switched on the TV and is holding the remote and staring intently at the screen.

Are you allowed TV in the mornings? I ask him. He shrugs and turns it off, chucks the remote on the sofa. He's a good boy really.

He won't be long, I say.

How long? Connor asks. How long will he be?

He pours himself a bowl of Coco Pops. Some have spilled on the table and he leans over and thumbs them straight into his mouth.

I ask Max to get some milk and he does.

Not semi-skimmed, says Connor quickly.

Yeah, yeah, says Max, ignoring him.

Just normal milk, says Connor, looking anxious. No lumps.

I love these boys. I love them just about as much as my own — my Nat, my Jordan, my Rosa, my Liv. When they were born, I was the third person in the world to hold them — after Lennie, after Al.

Connor pulls up his T-shirt with a basketball player on and looks at me.

Look, he says.

What? Look at what?

At this.

He stretches backwards. So skinny I can see right through him — through to the blood that threads between his little snappy bones. Nipples so tiny, like an afterthought that you can't believe in. A network of pale blue and mauve. Goose pimples.

You're cold, I tell him. Haven't you got anything to put on? Where's your pyjama top?

I don't like it, he says. And I'm not cold.

He stares at me and shivers, still holding up the T-shirt. He has got it, all of Lennie's whiteness — her creamy skin and hair, a real, milky blondeness you think you can taste on your tongue.

Connor, I say, what am I supposed to be looking at?

This, he says, indicating a small, scrubby mauve tattoo on his breastbone. Already coming off.

And this —

Pulling his elbow round to show me the snake tattoo curled there, It's not real, he says. It soaks off.

He rubs at it, frowning.

Wow, I say. Great.

It's from a comic.

The Beano, supplies Max, mouth spilling cereal.

Has Jordan got one? Connor asks me.

Um, I don't think so.

Jordan's too old for *The Beano,* Max informs him.

Shut up!

Mum's getting a real tattoo, Max tells me, keeping his eyes on my face. On her bum.

Connor whips around, to see if he means it.

She is! Max insists, laughing now. Connor relaxes and his eyes rest on Liv.

Why's she here?

Because she's too little to leave behind.

He gazes at her thoughtfully. Like Lennie too he has no eyebrows — just a ridge of white-blonde hair. And where are the others? he says. Where's Jordan?

At home asleep, I tell him. Why aren't you asleep? It's dreadfully early.

Something made me wake up, he says. I don't know what.

Liv makes an upset noise and I pull her out of the seat and lay her on a blanket on the floor. It's not the cleanest — stained with old Ribena and covered in dog hairs. Liv lies there, almost happy for a second, then suddenly and inexplicably not so happy — kicking, fast and angry and breathless. Building to a wail.

I pick her back up and she pants furiously, rescued from herself.

I want Mum, says Connor.

Shut up, says Max in a vicious monotone.

Shush, Max, I say, be nice.

I'm not nice, Max says.

I do, says Connor, I want her. Where is she?

Sweetie, I say and touch his head.

I joggle Liv up and down to keep her quiet. Every time I stop she takes a breath, ready to cry, so I joggle her again and the breath subsides unhappily.

Max gets up and windmills the air with an extended right arm, practising his bowling technique. After that, he hops around the room on one leg, hugging himself, the sleeves of his pyjamas stretched right down beyond his wrists.

OK, I say, do you want to see what's on TV?

No, says Max.

Can't you go now? asks Connor with a little wail in his voice. Can't Mummy get up?

Didn't you listen? She's not here you stupid fat moron, Max tells him, lunging suddenly and shooting a hand from a flopping sleeve just long enough to pinch him hard on the thigh.

Quickly, Connor slams his hand into Max's face. The TV remote control falls to the floor and the casing splits off.

Now look what you've done you little bastard, says Max.

He's not allowed to say that, says Connor.

He looks at me to see what I'll do and then when I do nothing he begins to cry and so does Liv.

OK, I tell them, I'm going to sit down and see if I can feed Liv. Who wants a chocolate biscuit?

They're for Saturday, Connor says helplessly.

Never mind. I'm in charge. Have one now.

What, in the morning? says Max, eyes fixed on my chilly, half-bared breast. But he gets the packet and helps himself to one anyway.

Outside, the sky is losing its thickness and blackness. Soon, if you were to go upstairs and stand in Lennie and Alex's wide, bare bedroom you'd be able to make out the two rigid funnels of smoke rising from the Harriman's Brewery.

Mick rings. Behind his voice are all the ordinary sounds of our house: Rosa shrieking, Fletcher barking, Nat shouting at him to shut up.

Mick shouting at them to be quiet.

What's going on? he says. I tell him I don't know.

Where's Alex?

You mean you haven't heard anything?

No.

I take a breath. It's hard to know what to say with the boys listening. Mick knows what I'm thinking.

Don't, Tess, he says, it'll be OK.

Silence. Max is screwing the Yoyo wrappers into a hard, green foil ball.

Shall I come and get the boys, then? Take them all to school?

I don't know — I begin.

I've got to take this lot.

I don't know, I say. I mean, should they go to school?

Come on, he says, of course they should go. What else are they going to do today?

I catch Max's face watching me, then turning to see if he can flick Connor on the back of his head with the ball. Livvy begins to cry: a slow, spiralling wail.

In his heart, or so he tells people later, Alex already knows. It can happen. That the usual rules melt away and you just find you know things. Facts queue up and slide, unasked, into your head, ears, heart.

Or, maybe it's true. Maybe Lennie's pain and dying does somehow get to him across the car park, over the tangly dark of Bartholomew's Green and down into Spinner's Lane. Or, more likely, is it just that when the worst things happen, time isn't the same any more? It twangs and collides and you can't any longer tell the hot and dirty moment when you knew from the clean, sweet, cold one when you didn't.

Alex's father killed himself when he was twelve and Alex was the one who found him there on the landing with the inside of his head pouring black stuff on the carpet. He always holds this fact up as a blanket — a protection against anything else happening. You can see why. Shouldn't he be safe now? Hasn't he had the worst? Hasn't he?

Alex is in the police station for a very long time. The longest hour of his life, he tells people later. Finally two police officers come to find him. One is called Mawhinney. He's not from here — that's how he knows it's serious. He's a black-haired, slightly European-looking man with big thick wrists and straight dark hair poking up beneath the collar of his shirt. A funny name, he'll remember it. It's about to be dawn but the air still holds the cloaked-off smell of night. Dim and quiet. Despite that, in the black conifer between the police station and Flook's newsagent's next door, a single blackbird is singing its heart out. Alex keeps hearing it, poor fucker, coping with the whole dawn chorus alone.

Slowly, through the tiny square of window, the light grows less dirty, shrubs and telegraph wires get more distinct. Alex remembers this. He tells me later that he remembers every detail of that room, that place, every sound, every smell. As if his body is on high alert: unable to stop itself from taking everything in.

And he is sitting at a table and smoking. And he hasn't touched his tea which tastes horrible, of the machine, but he has a pack of freshly opened cigarettes in front of him.

I keep trying to give up, he tells the duty officer behind the desk. And then something happens and I start up all over again.

The officer thinks what a nice fellow Alex is. Just an ordinary chap, friendly and approachable. A good guy — the type you'd lend money to, or trust with your wife and kids. He'll remember this fact later, when friends ask him about this terrible night, this terrible case. How can there be a God, for Christ's sake, he'll say, when the worst things always happen to the most decent people?

If Alex could think at this moment, he might be thinking the same. Instead, Oh God, oh God, he goes when he sees them coming in, Mawhinney and the other one. Oh, he goes, oh God, oh Jesus Christ.

Mawhinney holds out his hand — a forthright hand, used to facts and upset and awful things. Alex quickly stubs out his cigarette. Holds himself very still.

He wishes they didn't have to tell him what he already knows.

No, he says. Touching the suddenly foreign-feeling skin of his cheeks, face, eyes, with his hands (the hands that already feel cut off from him, like the hands of another person), No, please God no —

The words make little sense though he understands every one of them. Your wife. Has suffered. Some sort of violent attack. Has not survived.

Has not. Suffered. Violent. In a different order, the words might not spell the end. No, says Al. Please God no — he says it again several times.

One of them puts a hand on his arm and Alex lets him, even though he doesn't like being touched by strangers and especially not by men.

He asks if they could light him another cigarette. The younger one grabs the pack while the older one — Mawhinney — keeps his hand on him. And though he can barely take the cigarette when it is held out to him, so badly are his hands shaking, still he somehow manages to smoke it in long, trembling gasps.

*　　*　　*

Mick comes by with the dog and the kids. Everyone shouting, leaves lifting, trees bent over by the wind. The sky is white. Jordan has no coat on, just his frayed school jumper.

I ask him where his zip-up fleece is and he shrugs in a shivery way. Mick thinks I fuss too much but I hate the idea of my kids being cold. Jordan is nine, a year older than Connor, but just as thin. All our boys, Lennie's and mine, are thin. Rosa and Liv, on the other hand, are padded and rounded — big girls with a layer between them and the world.

Look at him, I say to Mick. He's freezing.

Mick stares at me and doesn't seem to take in what I say.

He is, I say. He's shivering.

Yesterday was warm for October, but not last night and not today. Here at Lennie's, even with the gas fire on it's not enough. I've just turned the heating right up.

Fletcher is pulling and jumping and trying to get the lead in his mouth. It's what he does. Mick loops the lead over the gatepost and yells at him to sit and stay. Louder than usual. The dog looks upset and sits and then straight-away gets up again, happy, expectant.

There was no bread! Rosa bursts out. For the packed lunches!

That's enough, Rosa, Mick tells her.

I was only saying —

Shut up, he says.

Rosa scowls.

I mean it, he says. Do I have to say it again?

I tell Rosa to shush. The sun shoots out and sends a wet, piercing light up over the brownish lawn, the path, the bins.

Mick — I say, but he doesn't look at me.

I'm taking Max and Con to their gran's, he says.

OK.

Suddenly Max is there at Mick's elbow. What? Aren't we going to school then?

That's right, boy, says Mick. He touches Max gently on the arm, but looks down at his keys.

Why? says Max. What's going on? Where's Dad?

Why is he missing school? Are we all missing it? Jordan asks quickly.

No, says Mick, Not you. Look, you lot —

Why not? asks Nat immediately.

What? Oh great, snaps Rosa. So they get to miss school and we don't?

She folds her arms and looks horrid.

Mick turns and fixes her with a terrible stare and her eyes turn furious.

Just give me a reason why that's fair, she demands.

You shut up right now or I'll give you more than that, says Mick.

Watched by all of us, Rosa bursts out crying. Mick looks like he's about to hit her but he doesn't. He does nothing. Lets his hands drop to his sides. Rosa thinks she's won.

Happy now? she asks him through her tears.

Mick and I look at each other.

What's going on? I ask him.

He says nothing.

You better tell me, Mick, I say.

He touches his face.

Come on, let's go inside, he says.

The bin men find her. The dawn refuse collection. Pitch dark at first, then grey sea, bleached early morning sky. Seagulls wheeling and squealing and hanging, steadying themselves in the air over the same piece of ground.

She is lying on her front, one arm under her, the other thrown out, concealing the worst of her injuries. That's what we are told. That she is still wearing her red satin shirt and cardigan but her jeans and pants have been pulled right off one leg and caught around her right ankle. That though there is no sign of her having been assaulted, her sanitary pad, with its modest brown smear of blood, is lying there on the concrete next to her.

My knees feel weak as water. All the muscles that normally hold me up have lost their zip, their strength. Mick tells the children to wait in the garden. He knows they won't venture out of the little wooden gate. Somehow we walk together over the hall mat, him ahead, him taking me. Our feet slip a little, moving over paper — letters that have come for Alex and Lennie. We don't pick them up.

What? I ask him. Mick, please tell me, what?

I can smell his body, the worry on him, the heat. His face is dark with whatever it is.

He pushes me into the sitting room and shuts the door.

I think I say please. Or tell me. That's what I say: Tell me, Mick. As if it was that easy.

And my teeth are shivering in my head, like I'm so cold I can't hold my jaw still, which is silly really. And even the ends of my fingers have gone hot and fizzy. I'm afraid.

He takes my hand. His own fingers are cool.

At first they think (or hope) she might be drunk or asleep — though, even at the height of the season, drunks, and especially ones with their underpants ripped off, are unheard of in this place. Then they see that the visible arm is too long and all splayed out at the wrong angle. And in the same moment they realise that the dark puddle in which she lies half submerged isn't mud as they thought, but blood.

One of the men dials 999 on his mobile.

There's normally a very small, half-hearted police presence in the town, but it doesn't wait around for murders to happen. Several more cars and an ambulance are summoned at once from Wrentham and Halesworth. Within twenty minutes there are sirens, winking lights, crackling radios, as police park diagonally to block the road and then proceed to tape off the car park and the adjoining areas. The electric milk van is stopped and told to go back round the other way, along North Road. The tide turns. A series of black groynes point up like fingers at the sky.

After perhaps half an hour, a small yellow and white tent is erected. It flaps about in the early morning wind that comes off the sea. Yellow tape is strung between the posts of the car park. No one is allowed to cross it — only one or two police are let through and even they have to be cleared by the grey-haired man in a white jacket who arrived ten minutes earlier, looking tired-out and carrying a small nylon bag.

Paramedics stand around. Grim faces. Confusion. What are they waiting for? Is someone just injured or are they dead? At last a police officer walks briskly forward, head down, talking into his radio. They immediately let him through the tape. His breath is a cold cloud and he looks at no one.

He pulls a coat on over his neon jacket, which glints oddly in the bright sea light. He is followed by two police-women, one of them frowning hard and carrying something small and heavy. The wind blows the clouds apart and everything is lit up and sparkly-yellow in that split second. Far out to sea is a perfect little boat with a brown sail. You can tell the wind is strong because of how the boat scuds along. Eager and fast. It looks like it's going to be a lovely day. That's what it's like the morning they find Lennie — everyone says that, everyone remembers it. An especially lovely day for the time of year.

Someone has died. The whisper goes around. A woman's body has been found — attacked and left for — yes, a female, someone from here — no one knows who. No, they haven't said. Yes, dead.

No one says murdered, not yet, not then.

A good soul from one of the B. & B.s on North Parade appears with several mugs of tea — by which time a crowd of dog walkers and delivery people and shopworkers has gathered. A couple of chambermaids from The Angel, shivering in their black. People speak quietly to one another. Someone's mobile phone starting up and the culprit walking away, guilty, to answer it.

Meanwhile, three or four hefty gulls alight on the concrete wall by the bins — in case such an improbably sudden crowd means food.

Oh Tess, he says.

Have they found her? Even as I speak the words, something in my throat settles and hardens and the answer bubbles up.

Yes, he says, they have.

I wait and then whisper, And —?

I'm afraid they have, he says again.

It's — bad?

He takes a breath. There's sweat on his face, and on mine.

I think she's dead, he says. He takes a breath, corrects himself, No. I mean — she is — oh Tess — she is dead.

Dead. Lennie is dead. The air around my head blooms into a massive, soft silence. Everything stops and my ears are velvety with it.

Tess?

I am about to answer him but instead the floor comes zooming up to meet my face.

It's OK, I can hear him saying, it's OK.

With my head between my knees and him holding me, I breathe. Big, hurting breaths, in and out. Down there in that other world, I notice things — the bare patches on Lennie's blue carpet, the crumbs and dust bunnies beneath the edge of the sofa. Two rubber bands. A piece of Lego and next to it something sticky, dulled with fluff, a spat-out fruit gum perhaps.

Deep breaths, Mick says and him saying it reminds me of us in labour, having our babies. The most together we have ever been. Except that right now this moment I have no memory whatever of having Liv.

How? I ask him, and he tells me. He tells me what has been done to Lennie. After a few moments, he asks me if I am OK. He asks even though he knows the answer. It's not his fault. It's only because he loves me.

And outside the wind has dropped and the kids are all standing just as we left them. Such good children — so quiet, all of them, no one touching or nudging anyone else, not a cry or complaint or a yowl of anger from anyone. You would not know there were five children huddled out there on the damp porch step.

Chapter 3

MICK DROPS OUR KIDS AT SCHOOL AND THEN DRIVES Max and Con on to Alex's mother Patsy in Halesworth. Alex has already told Patsy. She knows. She says she'll have the boys as long as necessary. No one knows how long Alex'll have to spend with the police.

Mick asks Patsy if she's sure she'll be OK? She tells him she's fine. She's taken 4 mg of valium on her GP's advice and a neighbour has come in to be with her.

Have a drink, Mick says to me, have a stiff drink.

I stare at him.

I'm OK.

Go on, he says. I mean it — you'll feel better.

Have you? I ask him.

I'm driving.

I'm OK, I tell him again.

What are you going to do?

I don't know. Tidy up here then come home.

You'll walk?

Yes.

I watch the children pile into the car, oblivious and ordinary, hands and feet scuffing, shoving their rucksacks in the back, getting Fletcher to jump in afterwards.

We've told them nothing, Alex will do it, he should be the one. For a moment or two all I see is their small white faces in the back window. And Connor especially — smiling, tilting his head back in a naughty-happy way, looking just like Lennie.

The air around Liv's head smells of milk. Her mouth is open, one small fist pushed up hard against her cheek. I know that if I were to pry it open I'd find sweat, fluff and grit from where she lay on the blanket on the floor. I stay for a moment, just looking. Checking. I always do that with my kids. Check them. I even still do it to Nat, yes even now, even though I can tell from the strange, large, folded-up shape of him that these days it's a pretty redundant thing to do.

After I've looked at her, I put away the cereal packets and rinse the bowls in the sink — then put on Lennie's rubber gloves and rinse the sink as well, swishing it around with my fingers. Next to the sink is Lennie's hand cream, the pump-head clogged with greasy pinkness where she's used it. A sparkly hair clip that she wore recently — when? why don't I remember? — with two of the sparkly bits come off.

The phone rings. I jump. It's only Mick.

Tess, he says, you're to get out of there. They're going to seal it off. You're not to put your fingerprints on anything else — a forensics guy is coming over any minute now.

Tears come to the back of my throat.

But — if I'm not here — how'll he get in?

He has a key. Tess, I mean it — just leave. Now. That's what they said. They don't want fingerprints everywhere. Just get out. Just pull the door behind you and come home.

You've already dropped the kids?

Yes. I thought you'd be back. Shall I come over and get you?

I try to understand how much time has gone since Mick left. More than I think. Shock pulls everything tight around you.

No, I tell him, I'm coming. I'm coming now.

We live about a four-minute walk from Lennie and Al. Down Spinner's Lane, across the Green and up Victoria Street to the row of little cobble-fronted cottages by the church. To get there you pass the doctor's surgery, Pratt's newsagent's and an Antiques & Curios shop that belongs to Margie Pinnerman but is hardly ever open. The rest is residential — silent, pebble-dashed semis and then the older, more desirable cottages with names like Sailor's Stash and Ebb Tide. More like a bunch of racehorses, Mick remarked when he first saw the names painted on their proud little plinky-planky china plaques.

Our street is quite different from Lennie and Al's. The cottages in Spinner's Lane have larger gardens and uglier fronts and look out over the marshes. But ours have white-painted walls with ragged hollyhocks bursting out over the tops and through the cracks. Our gardens are more like yards — just enough room for a bike perhaps and a row of washing — but inside our houses are bigger than they look, and from our tiny bathroom windows you can see the sea.

It ought to be easy. To go and get my coat, my little, sleeping baby, creep out, close the door behind me. But the cats — Lennie's two angry tabbies — circle me, mewing loudly. I don't like cats, something Lennie will never understand. She can't understand that a person could be afraid of a small furry thing.

But I know where she keeps the food so I get it from the shelf by the back door and pour some onto a plate, make a kissing noise with my lips like she does.

And they come, slowly, tails stuck up in the air. The one with the white patch on its face looks at the food, then back at me, disgust on his dreamy cat face. Then they both sit back and start washing.

The moments fall away and whole seconds go by before I notice that a man is in the room. A stranger, a man, about thirty years old with lots of darkish hair and an odd, quiet face. Standing there and looking at me.

My heart clenches and then dips.

Oh!

Sorry, he says quickly, I really am so sorry.

He says it but he's almost smiling. I am grabbing at the edge of the counter, hot and trembling.

I didn't mean to make you jump. I should have knocked. It's just —

I say nothing.

The door was open, he says, looking more helpless now. And I was told the house was empty.

I'm — it is. I'm going, I tell him.

Oh look, don't feel you have to — he says, but he's looking all around him at the room. Which already isn't Lennie's room.

Are you police? I ask him, because he doesn't look like it.

That's right. Sorry.

He nods.

You're the forensics guy?

I'm Ted Lacey, he says, I'm — I'm called family liaison. I'm here to —

I fold my arms tight against me in case he tries to shake my hand.

I'm with the police, he begins again, but I deal with —

The family.

Right, he says quietly, keeping his eyes on me. Yes.

Tess, I say, I'm Tess. A friend of —

He blinks.

Yes, he says. Yes. I know that.

And he just stands there.

Are you OK? he says at last.

I'm fine, thanks.

He looks at me.

Is that your job? I ask him. To ask if I'm OK?

No, he says and shrugs, looks away.

I smile. I don't know why.

Look — he begins, then stops.

I daren't look at him. He's so young. Something about him makes the room tilt.

Maybe I look dizzy.

Why don't you sit down? he says.

No, I tell him, I'm fine. I just need a cigarette.

He watches as I pull open Lennie's kitchen drawer.

She has a secret supply, I tell him without knowing why, of cigarettes.

He says nothing.

I find them quickly, hidden between the clingfilm and the roll of sandwich bags. Also, a pink plastic lighter with the Virgin Mary on. A present from Barcelona, it says.

We did give up, I tell him. At New Year.

Oh, he says.

But we keep them here. Just in case.

He looks at me and the way he does it makes me feel funny.

I'm going home, I tell him. Now. In a minute.

OK.

It's just, I tell him, my husband wouldn't want me smoking.

He looks down at the floor. I see how shiny his shoes are. Definitely not from around here. I offer him the pack. He shakes his head. He hasn't moved.

I flick the lighter and the flame whooshes up too high over the Virgin's head and then goes off.

Shit.

I drop it. The cigarette too.

Fuck.

He reaches forward, bends down, picks them up for me. I look into his hair, which is black as anything and dense and shiny.

He watches me fumble all over again with the lighter.

Shall I do it? he says at last.

OK then.

I put the cigarette between my lips and pull back my hair which is falling everywhere and he lights it for me. I suck it quickly in and let it hit me hard all over before I weep.

And at home, there's Mick, standing lost in the middle of something in the room where he can't settle or do anything, which is how I feel too. And he's been crying.

I ask if he's heard anything from Alex and he says no, he hasn't. He's still with the police as far as anyone knows.

My head feels hot.

I can't believe it, I say.

Tess, he says.

Who? Who would do it? Who would do such a thing to someone here in this place?

This is a safe place — that's what I want to say.

Mick sits down heavily on the sofa, putting his hands in his eyes, trying to stamp out the tears with his fists.

I don't know, he says.

Poor Al, I say. Poor kids.

Go and lie down, he tells me. I mean it. Take Liv and just go and sleep.

I can't.

But you've been up half the night.

So have you.

Not as long as you.

I'm afraid, I tell him. I'm afraid of lying there and not being able to sleep and then I'm afraid of going to sleep and having to wake up and — go through it all again.

I begin to sob. He comes over and puts his arms around me, rests his chin on my hair.

We've got to tell the children, I say.

Of course.

Well how, for fuck's sake?

We'll just tell them.

What, tonight?

It'll have to be tonight. Otherwise they'll hear it from someone else.

He takes his arms off me and away and steps back. The front of his shirt is now wet from my face.

I love you, I tell him.

He says nothing. I ask him if he thinks Patsy will have told the boys by now.

I don't know, he says.

He stands there, arms hanging down by his sides. He has on a very creased shirt with a huge greasy mark on the front. It must be the first thing he picked up off the floor in the other world that was this morning.

He looks at me.

I don't know, he says again.

* * *

You'd think it might be impossible to sleep but once I get in there onto those chilly, milk-stained sheets with the baby in beside me, I fall into an easy, dreamless place. I wake to find the sky white and the pillow and the corner of my mouth wet, a ball of tissue clenched in my hand.

You'd think there would be wailings of sirens outside, or at least the sound of something going on, but there's nothing, same as usual, just the comforting purr of the wind in the pines.

Liv has woken already and stayed silent and kicking, small huffing breaths — careful wide-eyes watching the ceiling. Fairies, Rosa always says in that authoritative voice of hers. She's watching fairies.

I pull her over to me and I kiss her. Not for any reason, just because I always do. For a single quick second the kissing makes me forget what has been happening. I breathe her in, she smells of new piss. The earthy sweetness of it makes my throat fill up.

Downstairs, Mick is sitting blankly on the kitchen sofa with the phone book open on his lap and a bottle of whisky on the table at his side. Also, some slices of cheese in a plastic wrapper and no plate. I am amazed Fletcher hasn't had them, but he's asleep against the door jamb, paws together, dead-dog style.

Has he rung?

No.

I look at Mick carefully. He looks about eight years old, skinny and tired.

You managed to sleep?

A little.

Good.

I go and sit softly by him, Liv on my lap.

What're you doing? Who're you ringing?

He stares ahead of him as if he has to listen a long time to take in the words. Then he puts his hand on my knee.

We have to do something about the roof, he says, as if it's obvious.

What? I say. You mean now?

Since Mick left the paper and has been at home, he's made a special effort to keep up with DIY. Getting all those jobs done that nag at you. It's his way of being more than just a house-husband. And last week some time, Jordan's ceiling developed a long brown zigzag and started oozing water. But it's been dry since then and I've forgotten it.

He jabs his finger on the page to mark a place and looks up.

Don't you realise, Tess, he says, Jordan's ceiling is bust. It's about to cave in.

Oh, I say, trying to think back to the other life, the sweet life of yesterday when we had this as a problem.

It won't go away just because of —

No, I agree.

And there's more wet weather on the way.

Oh darling, I say and I try to look at him but suddenly he's not there, or at least I can't see him properly.

Chapter 4

THE THING ABOUT THIS PLACE IS, IT ISN'T ON THE WAY to anywhere. It's the end of the road, a dead end — creek, sea and river on three sides, the road going up to the A12 on the other. Apart from in the height of summer when the holidaymakers descend, a stranger would be noticed right away.

Certainly, no one here lives in fear of crime. Pat, the local copper, is too busy untangling the kids' kites that get stuck in the dog rose and gorse that slopes down from the promenade to go chasing criminals. And the last time a panda car came flashing up the High Street was when poor Ellie Penniston fell off her bike.

Even our vandals are considerate. When the donations box was stolen from the Sailors' Reading Room, the culprit went out of his way to return the box. And when the Conservative Club, the United Reformed Church and a couple of small lock-up businesses on the harbour were all broken into in the space of a single night, it was assumed it must be someone from the new council houses down beyond the pier which look out over Might's Creek.

All sorts are housed there, Barbara Anscombe complained at a heated local residents' meeting. Travellers, even.

One of the happiest and most picturesque seaside towns in all England, that's how our town is referred to in the booklets *Best of Suffolk* and *Coastal Rambles* that you can pick up at the Tourist Information Centre on the High Street.

The town's most pressing concerns are quaint and small. Such as what to do about the graffiti on the public toilets off North Parade. Or, should a second Thai takeaway be allowed to open in place of Caroline's Orthopaedic Shoes in the High Street? And how to make people take notice of the Clean Up After Your Dog campaign? (Free doggy bags are provided by the local Society but still there are individuals who do not use them.)

And then, that night in autumn — the coldest October night for ninety years according to the *Bugle*. He binds her wrists with nylon twine. He hits her twelve or maybe fifteen times on the chest, neck and head with something blunt and heavy — possibly one of the larger lumps of shingle from under the pier — before he uses the blade on her.

*   *   *

The day of Lennie's death ends with a dozen officers in white gloves crawling on hands and knees to search the whole car park — now emptied of all but a handful of cars — including Pier Avenue and the area beyond the beach huts where the dunes roll down to the sea. They have to get it done before high tide, so they move methodically yet quickly, aware always of the creeping water and the fading light. The area is still taped off and no one is allowed in. At one point a Labrador slinks under the tape and comes bounding up to them joyously licking and pouncing. The owner calls it off quickly, mortified.

Nothing whatsoever is found.

Straight after school we tell the children. We sit them down and tell them that last night a bad man came along and hurt Lennie so badly that she's never coming back.

Is she OK? Nat wants to know.

Mick looks at me.

I'm afraid she died, Nat, he says softly.

Rosa takes a breath. She's been killed?

That's right.

She and Jordan both burst into loud, immediate, shocked tears. But Nat just bends his head and gazes at the floor. I watch him and I know that the odd half-smile, half-grimace on his face is from fear and shock. He can't look at anyone, he won't join in.

It's easy to comfort Rosa and Jordan — I throw my arms around them and I cry too. Meanwhile Mick sits beside Nat and rubs a point between his shoulder blades and Nat lets him for a while and then shakes him off.

Was it a gun? Jordan wants to know. Mick looks quickly at me and then says in a small, tight voice, Yes, boy, yes, it was.

Nat looks up despite himself.

What was anyone doing with a gun? he says, shocked. I mean, around here? Isn't that illegal?

Well, says Mick, yes. Of course. But there are lots of questions they can't — I mean, they don't know everything yet.

Did she die in hospital? Rosa asks. Did she know she was going to die?

I squeeze her hand.

We hope not, I tell her. We really hope not.

Jordan cries again and I hold Rosa's hand in one of mine and his little, cold and slightly sticky one in the other and he soon stops. I listen to his breathing. No one says anything for a moment or two.

We love you all very much, I tell them, and this is the hardest thing that's ever happened to us. Now what you've got to do is try and help Max and Con.

How? demands Rosa, her voice cracking with grief and fury. How can we help them if they don't even have a mum any more?

They've got a dad, Nat points out with unnecessary vigour.

Mick ignores him.

You've got to be very, very kind, he says. I mean it, guys. They're going to be sad and upset for a very long time.

And shocked, I add.

Yes, he says, Mummy's right. Shock takes a very long time to get over.

Will they still come round here? asks Jordan anxiously.

Of course, boy, says Mick, cupping his fingers around Jordan's bony knee. Jordan gives a little sob of relief.

Of course they will, I say. They're going to need us, they all are, Alex too.

I don't want to be horrid, but I'm just so glad it wasn't you, says Rosa suddenly and she puts her forehead on my arm and weeps into my sleeve.

Oh darling, I say.

Well, begins Mick, but he doesn't finish.

We sit in silence for a long time after that, just the five of us and Liv on her blanket on the floor. After a while Fletcher hears the strange sound of silence and comes padding over, slapping his tail from side to side, shoving the fish-fur of his nose into everyone's hands.

He doesn't know, Rosa observes.

No, I say.

Is there anything you want to ask us, guys? Mick says after a moment or two.

Jordan gives him a quick look.

Have we missed *The Simpsons?* he says.

*   *   *

Mick and I go in the kitchen and listen to the sound of them all laughing at the TV in the next room. Three lots of laughter, then silence, then more bubbling laughter again.

They're laughing.

Mick shrugs.

I stare into the fridge and then the cupboards one after another and try to think what to make for their tea. He meanwhile sits in the big chair and holds Livvy on his lap, looking at her as if he's never seen her before, as if she's someone else's child, or something that is supposed to be a child but doesn't look quite right. Eventually Livvy gives a little gasp of dissatisfaction at being held so still.

Of course they are, he says, picking up the phone with his free hand and using his thumb to press redial — trying Alex again. Of course they're laughing. What do you expect?

I rub my eyes, pull out a pack of quick macaroni.

I wonder what I do expect. The thought hangs there fuzzily.

They're just kids, Mick says, a tiny crack showing in his voice. Kids compartmentalise. It's not real to them yet. But it will be — it'll sink in.

Mick knows about kids. Or at least, I know about them as a mother, but he understands how their heads work. Before he went into journalism, back in London, he was a teacher and he worked in a rough school and dealt with the toughest kids — eleven- and twelve-year-olds who'd had no breakfast and had to be frisked for flick-knives and razor blades before they even started lessons. One time a kid set fire to the toilets during PE and Mick had to put it out and in doing so suffered burns all over his hands. He still has the scars — great shiny streaks where the hair never grows. Monster hands, Rosa calls them.

When he first started on the paper, everyone warned him to watch out for the editor who was a difficult, moody and unpredictable sort of man. But Mick just laughed. He never had any trouble from the guy. Not after dealing with all those kids.

At teatime, the children eat their macaroni cheese without complaint. Nat drinks his cup of milk without investigating it for lumps. Rosa even asks for seconds. She squeezes ketchup all over what's left on her plate and mixes it in till the sauce turns a glossy pink.

She's playing with her food, Nat points out, tipping back on his chair.

Nat darling, I say, let it go.

Yes, but —

Nat, says Mick. And Nat sighs and kicks at the table leg.

We decide to leave them thinking Lennie was killed with a gun because it's somehow cleaner. Guns leave small neat holes in people — or that's the impression kids get off the TV. People with guns do it from a safe distance. They don't come after you as you lie in a car park bleeding to death. They don't rip your heart out.

Later I hear Jordan kicking a beat-up tennis ball around the empty dining room with Fletcher. It's the dog's favourite game and one which makes him go absolutely, religiously still. The way they do it is, Jordan kicks the ball across the room till it hits the skirting board and bounces off — and that's the dog's cue to move, to dart for it and grab it before Jordan can.

Jordan and the dog have a collection of these tennis balls — balding and dirty and bit right open some of them, by Fletcher's sharp teeth. We are always finding them — stuck behind radiators, in the clean-laundry basket, in the tangle of wires behind the TV.

Which would you rather, Jordan mutters to the dog as he drops the ball, be shot by a gun or chased by a shark until you wet your pants with fear?

At ten the kids are finally in bed. We are still sitting there in the room that's gone cold and dark and quiet. And at last there it is, the sound of him at our back door.

Al!

I jump up from my chair.

We never bother locking our door, not until we go to bed, and even then just with the one turn of the key. He knows this and comes straight in. Behind him, the man I met at his house, the family liaison man.

Well? Someone says, but it's not Mick and I don't think it's Al either because he just stands there and says nothing.

I put my hands to my face. I'm shaking all over and I feel sick. Seeing him makes it real, brings home to me what has really happened. And her absence. Normally if something had happened, Lennie would be here by now. We'd all be here together.

But Mick knows what to do. He goes right over and

clasps him around the shoulders, pulling him in — at the same time nodding to the other guy who hangs back in the shadows. Maybe he introduces himself to Mick, but I'm not sure.

Alex looks worn out. When Mick lets go and steps back, he moves across the room to me and puts out his arms and holds my head tight against him.

Don't, he says. Don't speak.

His fingers are on my face. And I don't know what to do, though I smell him — his exhaustion and confusion and grief and the breath that hasn't eaten anything in a long time.

The boys? Mick says then. Where are the boys?

Still at Patsy's, Al says. I took them back there. It's OK. They're — I mean, I've — been with them.

You told them?

Al shuts his eyes for a quick second.

Mick pulls out a bottle of whisky.

OK, he says, a drink.

Lacey refuses but Alex sits down and has a glass just like it's any other day. At our kitchen table. Keeping his coat on — the coat that sits on him like a husk.

He looks at his drink but doesn't drink it.

Con was sick, he says. Everywhere. All over Patsy's fucking sofa.

I take a breath.

I suppose that's to be expected, Mick says.

Yes, says Lacey in a low, quick voice. It's the first time he's spoken and we all look at him. He looks down, as if he'd prefer not to have the attention on him.

I mean, he says, all kinds of reactions are normal, especially with young kids and —

He doesn't finish.

This is Ted, by the way, Al says, as if he's suddenly remembered his manners. He's been so great — you wouldn't believe it, how he's looked after me today.

Lacey gives a weak smile.

He's done all this before, Al says in a harder voice.

Lacey shakes his head, rests his elbows on his knees and clasps his hands together.

You know, Alex tells him, this is my home from home. These two lovely people are our best friends, our oldest mates, everything —

He breaks off.

I look over at Lacey. Blotting my eyes with the sleeve of my jumper.

Ted's sticking by me, Alex says, been with me all day. He's even going to stay over. Are you sure about that, Ted — that you want to stay over?

Lacey says, I think it's best —

You see? Al says, looking at us as if it's all a bit of a joke — probably because he's in shock.

Where will he sleep? I ask Al, and he looks at me.

In the studio, he says. He means Lennie's studio.

Great, Lacey says.

Good, says Mick.

*   *   *

Alex says that what Lacey needs right now is a photo.

Of her, he says, taking a mouthful of whisky, a nice little snap.

He spreads his hands on the table and studies his knuckles.

You don't mind? he says, only I can't face —

I squeeze his shoulder.

Hey, I tell him, I'll get it now.

Lacey stands up and looks at me.

It's for the press, he says.

Oh.

I'm really sorry, he adds, to have to ask for it now.

I tell him it isn't a problem, I'll get it. In my hurry to move towards the stairs I kick the chair and disturb Fletcher who comes wobbling up out of sleep. Stretching, yawning, shaking himself, claws clicking on the stone floor.

Give me two minutes, I say.

In our house, in our family, I am the archivist. I am the one who can produce evidence to show that we were all here and happy together. But it can be lopsided, this evidence. So, there are loads of photos of Nat as a baby, and plenty of Rosa too, in all situations, all moments of life. Fewer of Jordan and then, as poor Liv was born, they tail off altogether.

I think I have one hazy faraway one from the day she came into this world — and then nothing at all until the one where Lennie is holding her up in the garden of the pub at Blackshore and she is wearing the faded paisley hand-me-down sunhat that all of our kids have worn at one time or other. Also, because Mick took most of the pictures, he is more absent than he should be, too. But not Lennie and Al — they're in nearly all the pictures. A measure of how much they've always been here with us in our lives.

Fletcher is loudly lapping water as I open the little door and start upstairs.

I'm halfway up before I realise Lacey is right behind me.

Sorry, he says softly. Just — wait a moment.

I stop and turn.

It's just — I didn't want to say it in there. This photo, it's going to be all over everywhere, in the papers and on TV and so on — what I mean is, he and the children will be seeing a lot of it —

Oh, I say, thinking how helpless he looks.

It needs to be current, obviously, he says, and it needs to be — well —

How they'd want to remember her?

Lacey takes his eyes away from mine.

Yes, he says, that's right. Thanks.

That night, the first night of our knowing that Lennie is dead, I sleep a strange sleep of amazement. Amazed that I can sleep at all. Again and again in the blue darkness, the fact of what has happened slips over me. Icy, amazed, over and over again.

That's what I was most afraid of — of waking up and having to think about it. I can't. I can't think about her. I can't think about the car park.

Livvy sleeps right through. Only the second time ever. I ought to be pleased but it scares me to death. At 5 A.M. I poke her to check she's still breathing. She is.

Mick brings me coffee. I mention to him about Liv.

He says, For God's sake, Tess, she's shattered. Leave her. Let's enjoy it while it lasts.

Enjoy. The word wedges itself in the air between us.

The school is closed while the police make enquiries, but the kids know better than to say they're glad. They watch TV downstairs while we drink coffee and wait for the phone to ring. If I can just get through the morning without crying, I think.

The man called Mawhinney comes round to have a word with us. They're making house-to-house enquiries throughout the town, he explains. Though obviously, he adds, he would have wanted to talk to us anyway, because of our relationship with the family.

He says he's sorry to have to do this when we're still feeling so raw and having it sink in, but he needs to ask us both exactly where we were on the night it happened —between eleven and, say, eight in the morning.

I blush hot to my hair, but Mick doesn't hesitate. He takes my hand and squeezes it. He tells Mawhinney that he and I were both in bed.

We were exhausted, he tells him, really shattered. That's why Tess didn't go to the meeting. She's on the PTA and she should have been there but she just couldn't face it. I wouldn't have let her go. I think we went to bed at — well at a guess — ten, ten thirty.

Mawhinney listens.

Would that be earlier than usual then?

Mick pinches at his nose with his thumb and finger as he thinks about it.

Pretty early for us, yes.

Something unsaid floats past me. In my hand the balled-up tissue is coming apart with dampness. Bits of it sticking to the sides of my fingers like skin.

Mawhinney turns to me. I can see he is trying to be kind, to make it easy. I wonder if he has a wife and kids at home and if he goes home and takes a beer from the fridge and tells them all about his day.

Is that right? he says and you can see by his eyes what he expects me to say.

Yes, I tell him, yes, that's right.

Then I remember a sudden, true thing: that I had to stay awake to feed the baby. I tell Mawhinney this, though my heart bangs crazily as I say it.

He listens without much interest.

Oh yes, says Mick just like it's not important at all, so you did, I'd forgotten that.

I glance down at Mawhinney's little notebook. He hasn't written anything down.

We're bringing her feeds forward, I explain, or trying to anyway.

My voice sounds reasonable. I hate myself.

Why did you say that? I ask Mick once Mawhinney has gone.

He looks up from the floor where he's kneeling on newspaper and cleaning Rosa's brown school shoes.

Why did I say what?

About us being in bed at ten thirty?

He goes on dabbing polish in with the cloth, working it carefully into all the cracks and creases. He breathes through his mouth as he does it, his tongue touching the inside of his top lip. That's what he does when he concentrates. Mick's good at concentrating. He says that's how you make the smallest jobs satisfying.

Because we were, he says carefully.

I swallow, taste polish in the back of my mouth.

You were, I tell him. I wasn't.

He sits back on his heels in an unsurprised yet exasperated way.

Oh for fuck's sake, Tess —

I wasn't.

You wanted me to tell him that?

I gaze at him. Sometimes his confidence amazes me.

I thought you'd tell the truth, I say.

Well I was in bed, he says. And as far as I know you were too. As far as I'm concerned I was telling the truth.

He says that but his eyes narrow. He's angry.

But I got up, I tell him. You know I did. You know I got up.

He says nothing, picks up the shoe.

Don't you want to know where I went?

He hesitates and I don't like the look on his face.

You're saying I should stop you?

No. I don't know.

You can't have it both ways, Tess.

He laughs then. He laughs because he knows my position is ludicrous. You can't make someone want to know things. Just like you can't force someone to be jealous or upset or aroused. They either are or they aren't and that's it. There are no halfways.

But I love him, I tell myself. I do. I would never, never want to be married to Alex — thank God I didn't stay with him, we'd have been hopeless together, fatal, lethal, always knowing what each other wanted and getting there quicker, wanting it first.

Now, every clock in the house is ticking, but each one says a different time. Mick's job is to wind them up. He's the one who likes antique clocks, the noise and the work of them, not me. If it were up to me, I'd have something modern: fierce red digits glinting in the dark.

The thing about Mick is, he thinks it's clever not to rise to things.

I'm not trying to hide anything from you —

That's what I tell him, but he shrugs.

I know, Tess. I don't think you are. It still doesn't mean I need to know.

It's your life, he says when I don't reply to this. Your life, your time.

No, I say as carefully as I can. Don't you see how maddening it is when you say that? It's not. It's our time.

He laughs.

What? What's funny?

He doesn't answer, just laughs again. Then turns away and begins the thing of buffing the shoe. He does it hard. Rosa's feet will shine. Not that she'll notice.

I went to The Polecat, I tell him. That's all.

He gives me a quick look.

Fine.

Fine?

Lucky you're still alive, he says and his voice is small and dull and tight.

He places Rosa's shoes perfectly straight on the mat by the back door and folds the newspaper and stuffs it in the recycling. He recycles every piece of paper in the house, Mick does. Sometimes he recycles things before I've had a chance to read them.

I think he's going to leave the room then, but he doesn't. He comes over. Holds me for a quick moment.

Let's not do this, he says. Please, Tess. Not now.

I kiss the bristles on his cheek.

I don't want to do anything, I tell him.

He sighs.

I thought this was what you wanted anyway, he says. I thought it was the whole point?

What? I say. The whole point of what?

Of everything. Of what you say you want in life?

I don't know what I do want any more, I tell him.

He pauses and looks at me.

It's not relevant to any of — this — where you were.

Is that why you lied?

I didn't lie. I just told them what I knew for certain.

But don't they have to — look at everything?

He touches my face, my cheek, my jaw. I shiver.

You tell them then.

What?

Tell them where you were.

You think I should?

No. I don't. Where would it get you? What's the point of confusing things further. For God's sake, Tess, I was only trying to help you, keep you clean.

Clean?

Out of it. Uninvolved.

You think I should be grateful?

Don't put words into my mouth.

Chapter 5

IT TURNS OUT THE CORONER NEEDS TWO PEOPLE TO identify the body — another person, an independent witness who knew Lennie, as well as her next of kin. Bob, her dad, is struggling to get his doctors' permission to fly over from Philadelphia. But he is eighty-one and frail with a poorly heart and the journey itself will be hard enough.

Mick says he'll do it — go to the morgue with Alex. At first I try to persuade him out of it. It should be me. He's never seen a dead person and I have. I cut up plenty when I was training.

Those were strangers, he says. This is completely different.

Is it?

Tess. For fuck's sake. You know it is.

Anyway, he tells me, he wants to go — he wants to do this for Alex. And for Lennie. He means it, but I am tempted to remind him of how little more than a year ago just the sight of Livvy's reptilian shadow on the ultrasound almost made him pass out.

When I hear that Lacey is going with them, I feel better. In all these hours, Lacey's barely left Alex's side. Mick says that's the whole point of what he does — to offer continual support, twenty-four hours a day.

When Alex comes and sits in our kitchen — hunched at our plate-strewn, crumb-covered kitchen table still wearing his rough and musty-smelling coat and rolling cigarettes with shaky hands, now Lacey comes too. They make a strange pair — Alex with his pale face and fair unwashed hair and visible grief, Lacey smaller, darker, younger, mostly silent and watching.

Mick says that's how he's trained to be — to make himself invisible, so that he doesn't inhibit any of us, so that he doesn't intrude. He accepts my offer of a cup of coffee and then just sits there in his smooth, dark London clothes, elbows on his knees, watching us all. Maybe he's looking for clues. Maybe he's thinking that by finding out how we all live, he can somehow work out how Lennie died.

He's not a detective, Mick says.

I say I think he seems far too young to have such a terrible job and Mick agrees.

I couldn't do it, he says, but I think he's good. He's a good guy. I like him.

*   *   *

Alex tells us that new details have emerged from the post-mortem. He says they suspect the killer used a lino-cutter. He says that Lennie's sternum was cracked open, her ribs forced apart like the bars of a cage. The vessels that pumped blood from her heart were severed in a surprisingly methodical way, the organ lifted out intact. Though the initial attack was frenzied, uncoordinated, the subsequent surgery on her torso was carried out with chilling accuracy and cool.

The fucker knew what he was doing, in other words, he says.

I take a breath and catch Lacey's eye. He holds my gaze then looks away.

Mick lowers himself into a chair, his face bloodless.

But how can they possibly be so specific? he wants to know.

The angle and depth of the cut, says Alex simply. He looks at us and shrugs and his voice doesn't wobble or falter. It just stays exactly the same.

Meanwhile other things have come to light. We know now that her underclothes were partially pulled off. That she wasn't sexually assaulted. That the bludgeoning to her head was so frenzied that large fragments of her skull lodged in her brain causing extensive haemorrhaging. Which means her assailant would have been covered in blood. It would be impossible, the police say, to inflict those kinds of injuries and on that scale and remain unbloodied.

He probably left in a car. Police say they want to trace

the owner of a silver Fiat Uno that was seen on the junction of Hotson Road and North Parade around the time of Lennie's death. Anyone who knows anything at all should come forward. They appeal again and again for help from anyone who was in the pier end of town on that night.

You wanted my mummy to die, Connor tells Rosa as they sit together on the low, flinty wall at the end of Spinner's Lane.

Rosa is shocked. She calls him a liar. He calls her a bitch and throws a handful of gravel at her. She throws a handful back and then runs sobbing all the way home, leaving her anorak behind on the wall.

You know he didn't mean it, I tell her.

He did! Rosa sobs. He did, he did! He called me a bitch!

I know better than to try to hug Rosa, but I touch the biscuity top of her head.

Poor Connor, I say.

He called me a bitch! Don't you even care?

Rosa —

She pushes me off.

Leave me alone, she says. Get your hands off me. If you're going to side with him. You only care about him.

I never know what to do with Rosa — she has all of Mick's surly cleverness combined with the pouchy beginnings of breasts already (and she's only eleven) plus a frighteningly clear idea of what she expects from the world. Mostly it lets her down.

Sometimes I think we would be closer now if I'd never

had Liv. Having another baby made me go down in her estimation. It's true — she despises me for it.

It's an alien, she told me when she saw how the baby's fast-growing body turned my navel inside out. You've been taken over.

It's just all a bit much when you're her age, Lennie suggested. She's too young and too old for it. She can't see what's in it for her.

I laughed. There were times back then when I couldn't see what was in it for me either. But Lennie was right. She was better at working Rosa out than anyone else. Poor Rosa. Just as she was learning to do cartwheels and handstands and to make her own body bright and ruthless and elastic, there I was, slow and large and weighed down.

When Liv was born, Lennie gave Rosa a kitten. She named it Maria. She said it was the best present anyone had ever given her.

All I have left of Lennie, Rosa says now as Maria's warm white weight spills through her fingers.

I tell her that Connor must be very mixed up right now.

Just think of how he must be feeling, I say.

Well, he should think of my feelings, she replies.

You don't really think that, Rose.

I didn't want Lennie to die, she says.

Baby, no one thinks you did.

He does. He thinks so —

No, listen darling, that's what I'm saying. Connor's eight years old and he's lost his mum.

Almost nine, says Rosa.

What?

He's almost nine. And I've lost my — friend.

OK. Nine, I say, but that's a terrible thing to have happen to you. Think of how awful you're feeling. Then multiply it by a thousand.

Rosa stops crying then and grows still and silent. After some minutes she takes my hand and feels my fingers, my two rings, the soft, fleshy pads under my nails. She asks me where Lennie is right now.

The question takes me by surprise.

You mean where's her body?

Yes.

Well, it's in a morgue, I tell her carefully. That's the place near the hospital in Ipswich where they look at her to see how she died.

But they know how she died —

More or less, yes.

Rosa frowns.

So — what — aren't they going to bury her then?

Eventually, yes of course they are. Or cremate her.

Rosa slips one of the rings off my finger and puts it on her own. This is a favourite thing of hers to do. The ring sits lopsidedly on her thin little finger. She spins it absently round.

Who'll decide? she says.

It'll be up to Alex.

Rosa shudders.

I wouldn't want to be underground, she says. But I wouldn't want to be burnt either.

You mustn't think of it like that, I tell her, taking back the ring and easing it onto my own finger. You're not you when it happens.

No, but — what? Just a body?

That's right.

Oh, well, I wouldn't want my body to be burnt or underground then. It's the same.

It won't be your body. Because you won't be you.

But I will be me! Rosa insists. My body is still me —

Not in that sense, not in the feeling sense.

It will be for me, she says firmly.

You can't possibly know that.

But I do!

No you don't, I tell her as gently as I can.

Rosa says nothing. Then, Yes I do, she whispers.

I take her in my arms and hold her tight enough to feel the fizz of her heart. She doesn't fight me this time.

Now Nat knows things. He knows about Lennie's heart, and he knows she wasn't shot. He's heard stuff. At school, in the street. Kids of twelve read the papers. Details are going round. Mick calls him downstairs and shuts the door.

We're talking about a very, very disturbed person, he says, looking him all the while unflinchingly in the eye as he always does when he's telling something serious to the kids. A sick person. Someone badly in need of help.

A psycho? Nat asks a little too eagerly.

Well, psycho's a silly word they use in the movies, Nat. Real life is mostly a lot more boring and nasty and banal. But if by psycho you mean someone who is so inadequate that they get some kind of kick out of killing someone in this terrible way, then yes I suppose so, a psycho.

Will he get life? Nat asks. Swallowing.

If they catch him, Mick says, yes, I'm pretty sure he will.

I bet Alex wishes there was the death penalty, Nat says, and his eyes bunch up in sympathy. I bet he wishes this was in America.

Mick looks at him patiently.

Not for a sick person, Nat, he says. It's not right to kill a sick person.

It's never OK to kill, right? says Nat and this time he looks at me.

Never, I agree.

Nat pauses and fiddles with a rubber band he's picked up off the table.

But what if they don't catch him? he asks, stretching the band between his fingers.

This time Mick looks at me.

They're going to try very hard to catch him, I say.

Do you think he's upset? I ask Mick, once we hear his feet thudding back up the stairs.

No, he says, getting himself a drink out of the fridge.

What? Not at all?

Not especially, I don't think so, no.

He roots around for a beer. They're all at the back. When he has it, he grabs the bottle opener, rubs it on his jeans, looks at me.

I think he's just put it away.

Oh.

Don't worry, he adds. It's perfectly healthy.

Is it?

Not everything has to be talked about, Tess.

He tilts his head back and sips as if nothing was wrong. I look at him.

Really? I say, I'm surprised. You never used to think that.

Didn't I?

No.

Are you sure you know what I used to think? I mean, you always assume you know what I'm thinking, he says more gently.

Do I?

I bite my lip.

I don't mean to — assume things, I begin, then I backtrack. Anyway, don't you assume you know things?

I don't think so.

You don't? Of course you do.

Mick shrugs, puts the beer down on the table.

I don't know. I don't give it much thought. I mean, I don't think like that. I get on with life instead.

He says it like that, as if it's perfectly normal and true, but there is a kind of pain and tension in his face as he says it and it occurs to me that, for perhaps the first time ever, there is pain between us, too. Why? I don't think it's about

Lennie, not really, I don't think you can blame that. No. I actually think it's about us — him and me and how we are together.

Later, when I let it back into my head, the idea shocks me. I decide it cannot be true. It must just be that all the grief and shock has got mixed up and seeped into our feelings about each other. If someone you care about dies violently, it infects everything. Anyone would agree with that.

I know what Lennie would say about this. Don't be stupid, she'd say. You're going through a difficult time, that's all. Don't generalise or say or do things you'll regret. Just hang on in there and wait for it to pass. Because it will. It'll pass.

A man rings from the coroner's office. For a chat, he says. He apologises for disturbing us, but explains that he is supposed to take Mick through what will happen that afternoon at the morgue — how much he'll see, what it will be like, etc.

Mick takes the phone and walks slowly into his study and shuts the door. He's in there for a few minutes. When he reappears, he looks tired. He tells me that the man said that only Lennie's face will be visible, that the rest will be covered by a sheet.

There aren't any marks on her face, he says. Nothing visible apparently, not even any bruising.

He stands there and looks at me and scratches at his arms.

Was it supposed to make me feel better, do you think?
he says.

I don't know, I say.

I mean, couldn't Lacey have told me all that?

Would you have asked him?

He sighs.

I don't know. I mean, maybe not.

Later, when he's gone, I take the chance to cut Rosa's
toenails. She makes such a fuss that I am forced to bribe her
with a bag of Doritos.

What do you want to do, Rosa yowls as I grab her slim,
white foot and prop it on my knee, torture me?

Yes, I say to shut her up.

Even though it's only five — way too early to drink — I
pour myself a glass of wine, a big one.

You never cut the boys' nails, Rosa complains as she
crams her mouth with Doritos.

How do they get shorter then? Tell me that.

Rosa giggles.

What d'you think happens? You think they just drop off?

It's discrimination, she says happily. You just want to
get me.

I smile and drink my wine in big, quick gulps, feel my
edges soften. Rosa wipes bright orange Dorito dust from her
mouth and onto her jeans. She sneaks a glance at me as she
does it. Normally I would shriek at her, but I don't, I barely
notice. I feel strangely untouchable, as if I've slid sideways

into someone else's life. It's a good feeling. After some moments, I leave the room and walk upstairs.

I put Liv down and curl up on the sagging, Marmite-stained kids' sofa with Jordan. We watch *Tomorrow Never Dies* and I let him zap forward to the action bits, even though this is something he's not normally allowed to do. You either watch the whole of something, Mick always tells the kids, and watch it properly, or you do something else useful instead.

This, apparently, is how Mick got somewhere in life and it's a position that, on the whole, I agree with. So Jordan can't believe this waiving of the rules.

Are we being slobs? he asks me hopefully.

You bet.

Do you like Bond?

I love it.

No. I mean him — James Bond? Do you actually like him?

He's great, I say, and, exhilarated by my attention and approval, Jordan turns and pats my face tenderly. His fingers smell of heat and cheese.

I love you, Mummy, he says.

Yeah, yeah.

You're so beautiful — I mean, you look so young.

I laugh.

I mean it — you only look about thirty-five, he says and I kiss the soft skin next to his eyes where the freckles spill over so enthusiastically you can't believe he will one day be a man and shave and have serious, grown-up thoughts.

Mummy needs another drink, I tell him and he pauses the video so I can go to the fridge to replenish my glass. But he rewinds a little before he pauses it. He doesn't want me to miss anything.

In the kitchen the windows are black and battered with rain. The fridge is white, the wine bottle yellow and cold. I put my hands on it, feel the chill. It goes straight to my heart.

When I return, Jordan is kneeling up on the sofa, waiting.

What would you do if a baddie came in now? he asks me urgently as I set the wine down on the carpet and he unpauses the film. He watches me, watches my face, waiting to see what I'll say. On the screen, a Chinese girl is swimming underwater (again), black hair waving in the gloom.

I'd call the police, I tell him.

Yes OK, he says impatiently. But what if they didn't come?

They would, I say — surprised that Lacey's serious face slips into my mind — they would come.

But, he insists, I mean, what if something happened to them on the way?

Oh Jordan —

Or if they didn't hear the phone?

There are people whose special job it is to answer the phone, I tell him. So if you dial 999, of course they answer and they come.

Hmm, he says, more or less satisfied.

But he's missed one of the fights — they shot at the Chinese girl when she came out of the water — so we have to wind back. As he holds the remote up and concentrates on the screen, I slip my arms under his and feel the snap of his little chest, the warmth of his neck, his baby hair.

You smell like a rabbit, I tell him.

But he's not listening, and before I can stop it happening, the room blurs and tears come.

By the time Mick gets back I've got Jordan into the bath. Then climbed the stairs to watch the sun go down over the creek from Nat's shambles of a room at the top of the house.

It's a violent, chemical sunset — smouldering as if something poisonous has been chucked across it. The colours are sharp and exhausting — or is that three glasses of wine on an empty stomach? Just watching it takes the breath out of me. I watch for a long time. It feels like the first time I've looked properly at anything since Lennie's death.

After that I sit down and try to feed Liv, but she's in a wriggly, fed-up mood. Maybe I shouldn't have had the wine. And soon after, there's the sound of the front door, keys dropped on the shelf. My heart sinks.

He comes in bringing with him the smell of outside, plumps heavily down in a chair with his jacket still on.

Well, he says.

I wait and he looks at me.

Well?

He was wrong.

Who was?

Him. The guy who phoned.

Oh.

Yeah. I mean her face was clean, but —

I feel the blood creep down my body.

But what —?

Yeah.

He takes a breath, pauses, blinks hard.

Oh darling, I say.

He is not exactly crying. He takes a breath, a gulp, covers his eyes.

What he omitted to tell me, he says in a strangled voice, is that the top of her head is fucking well gone.

No —

He doesn't look at me.

There's nothing there, Tess.

You could see?

Mick shuts his eyes and the blood rushes to my head.

There was a sheet over it, he says, but yes, you could see.

Liv begins to cry. I try to put her back on the nipple, teasing her mouth open with my fingers. But a curdled lump of milk slides out of her mouth and down into my bra, making everything wet and cheesy.

I grab the cloth.

I'm sorry, I tell him.

What do you mean? It's not your fault.

Look, I begin.

He pushes both fists into his eyes.

Don't always try to make things better, he says, I mean it, Tess. Leave it, OK?

OK.

We sit in silence for a moment. The room swerves. My bra is cold and damp against my skin. I feel a little sick.

Have a drink, I tell him. I did.

I did, I think, and it worked.

Clearly, he says.

We watched a whole Bond film, I tell him, Jordan and me, all the way through.

You're drunk, he points out.

Yes, I agree — and I hold my baby tight and close my eyes and the room whistles brightly and then just fades away.

Chapter 6

OUR TOWN IS SURROUNDED ON THREE SIDES BY
marshes — Bulcamp Marshes, Angel Marshes, Tinker's and
Woodsend and Buss Creek. Now they're beauty spots
where birdwatchers go, but a long time ago, people
drowned there. There are all sorts of stories.

Ellen Bloom aged 20 months, beloved daughter of Chad
and Susannah, stumbling down the mud flats after dark.
Rosa once found Ellen's little stone, strangled by ivy and
splattered with lichen, in the graveyard at St Margaret's.

Or, the young man who forced himself on a local girl
and then tied a brick around his foot and drowned out of
shame. Or the girl who, rushing to see her secret lover, took
a fatal wrong turn and was sucked down like a leaf. Two
seconds of bad luck and your life closes over your head.

The most recent is poor Anne Edmondson's son Brian. Many in the town still remember him. A clever lad and keen sailor, all set to read engineering at Leeds University. The plaque's inside the church. Brian John Edmondson aged 17 years and a good swimmer. Departed this life August 10th, 1958. No one knows why he just went out there one still summer night and drowned.

People say that if you drive down the old Dunwich Road at night and dare to stop the car and turn off the engine, you'll hear things.

Oh yeah? Alex and Mick say when Lennie and I come home and tell them this. You mean the fucking owls and wind in the trees.

I used to laugh too. Until Roger Farmiloe who pumps the petrol at Wade's garage told me he'd heard crying out there. So had his dad. And his uncle Peter too — fifteen years in the Merchant Navy and would laugh in your face if you said you believed in ghosts, Roger said. And yet.

In fact many brewery workers and darts players, farmhands and van drivers, people who you'd think might scoff or know better, have wound down their windows on dark nights and been so scared that they've driven back into town in a blazing hurry and refused to go back, not even if you paid them, or so they've all said.

Yes, says Mick, but after how many pints at The Anchor?

None, I reply. Roger said his uncle Peter was stone-cold sober.

This cracks him up.

That's harder to believe than all the fucking ghost stories put together, he says, laughing.

Lennie's death is good for trade, with both police and reporters in town. Both hotels are immediately full and the coffee shops, delis and snack bars have queues forming outside at lunchtime. Linny's The Outfitters even considers opening up the room at the back and laying on some kind of cold, takeaway food, something it has not thought of doing since back during the summer of the Queen's Silver Jubilee in seventy-six.

Even Somerfield runs out of bread and meat halfway through the week and has to be restocked. And The Griddle stays open till seven each evening serving its famous cream teas and exotic ice creams, instead of closing as it normally does at half past five, though Ann Slaughter is heard to complain that Mei Yuen's next door starts frying at five and the smell puts people off their tea.

The photo that I gave to Lacey appears on TV as well as on the front page of the papers. I think Mick took it on holiday in France a couple of years ago when we all went away together and liked it so much we thought we'd always do it except we didn't, we never did it again.

In it she is wearing a striped pinkish T-shirt and she's smiling and screwing her eyes up against the bright sunshine and her hair is that little bit longer, strands of it caught in the wind across her face. She's not tanned — Lennie was too fair to tan — but she looks well and happy, standing there next to her boys. Of course the papers cut Max and Con off — they wanted just Lennie. So there she is, oblivious, alone and smiling.

And suddenly, there she is, all around us, even in Curdell's newsagent's on the High Street. It's too much for some people, to see her beaming out at them like that from the racks. Too close up and personal. One or two get all shaky or have a little cry when they go in to buy cigarettes or their lottery ticket. Some mums won't even take their kids in the shop but leave them outside instead, by the fishing nets and buckets and spades and windmills, next to the Wall's Ice Cream sign that flaps in the wind in the place where people usually tie their dogs.

On the Friday I go back in to work. Though everyone understands why I've been postponing appointments, I can't leave the clinic shut for long. I have a number of older patients who rely on me.

It smells cold in there — we have a constant problem, with the damp. I turn on the heating and water the plants, stuff some towels in the washing machine and turn on the computer to look up the appointments. As it crackles into life, I realise that Lennie's e-mails from just a few days ago will still be on it. Not wanting to see them, I go straight into the diary.

I've been there about twenty minutes when there's a knock on the door at the front. It's not the door we use. Patients come in through a side door in the alleyway they call

Dene Walk. I lift the front blinds and see that it's Lacey. Surprised, I indicate to him to go round to the side.

Sorry, he says when I open the door in my white coat, jeans and clogs with my woolly jacket still on top, I should have phoned —

No, no, I say. It's OK.

Have you got a moment?

He looks past me into the room. I step aside to let him in.

As I apologise for the cold and explain that the heating system's old and takes a while to get going, I feel myself blushing. If he notices, he doesn't show it.

You work alone here?

I've done less since the baby. There used to be a partner. But he left and went back to London. Making tons more money there.

You're busy?

I shrug.

There's enough to keep me going.

No, he says, I meant — today.

Oh, I say, colouring furiously again. No one's in till this afternoon — I mean, I cancelled all the earlier appointments this week. It's the first time I've been in — since —

He nods.

I just came in to get things — organised.

I offer him a chair and he sits, looks around him.

What's the smell? he asks me.

I frown and sniff.

Oh. I don't know. Lavender? I use a lot of oils.

He looks at me.

Do you? What for?

Massage, I tell him. Soft-tissue work.

He seems to think about this. And then, I'm sorry, he says. About the other day. The morgue.

Oh, I say, it wasn't your fault.

Was he OK?

Just upset, I tell him. What about Al? I haven't seen him.

Lacey looks at me.

Eucalyptus, he says.

I feel myself smile.

The smell —

Yes. Quite probably.

Just then Liv gives a gasp from under the desk. I normally put her down on a small mattress on the floor behind the filing cabinets.

Lacey laughs in surprise.

You've got the baby down there?

I laugh back and squat down to pull her up against me. She smells hot and fusty, of sleep and piss.

She gazes at Lacey and then she smiles. So does he.

You're honoured, I tell him. Mostly she cries when she sees strangers.

Am I a stranger?

Well —

She's seen me before, he points out.

OK. But not very much.

He stands up then and I'm thinking several things — how hard he is to talk to, how awkward and how this awkwardness makes me shy. And also that he seems to be about to go and I don't even know why he came, what he came to say.

Look, he says abruptly, do you want some coffee or something?

Coffee?

Yes.

He coughs a little cough of embarrassment and my heart races. I glance down at Liv and flush again.

We have coffee here, I say.

No, he says. No — I mean out somewhere.

I laugh.

I haven't got long.

Come on.

All right, I tell him, OK, fine.

Outside it has turned into an OK day. Warmish and lightish, almost not like autumn at all, but late, lingering summer, the last dregs of brightness.

I put Liv in the buggy, tuck the blanket in around her and clip her in. Her small white fingers flutter a moment on my wrist and I feel almost happy.

So, he says as we wheel up the High Street. Where to?

No idea, I say.

Come on, he says, you know this place.

OK, I go. Follow me.

We head for the front, the prom. Up past Curdell's and the grocer's and The King's Head and John Empson's and Somerfield. Across the marketplace, wheels joggling on the cobbles. He doesn't speak. I glance at his reflection in the dark windows of Pam's Florist's. I feel him beside me but I don't look.

The Whole Loaf Deli has its shades down as if it's lunch. Hard to tell if they're open or not. Outside there are two people with large woven shopping baskets.

Do you know, I ask him since he has already brought it up, how soon they'll release her — the body, I mean?

You mean for a funeral? he says and I nod.

He hesitates, pushing his hands through his hair.

No, he says, not really. It could take a while.

We've reached the Sailors' Reading Room. He glances uncertainly down the steep and narrow steps to the prom. The metal handrail is splashed in places with birdshit. One or two pink poppies still bloom in the gorse.

Can you help me lift it? I ask him.

What, all the way down there? That's where we're going?

It's worth it, you'll see.

He takes the other side of the buggy and helps me down, me in front and him behind.

You know, he says once we reach the concrete esplanade at the bottom and put the buggy down, how Alex feels? About her heart?

I flush with surprise.

What? What about it?

Getting it back, I mean.

I stop the buggy and turn to stare at him properly. The wind drops and my head feels suddenly warm and light.

No, I say, I don't. What do you mean?

That he doesn't want to bury her without it?

Oh, I say. He hasn't said that to me.

Oh, well I'm sorry. I thought he might have.

No.

Lacey seems flustered. Again he pushes his hair back from his head — a pointless thing to do since it springs straight back.

I think, he says slowly, hesitating, I mean, I don't know how to put this, but I think Alex may have unrealistic ideas about what I can do —

You?

With regard to bringing it back I mean. Finding it.

I take a breath.

Well, you can't can you? I say.

He looks at me again.

Look, he says. Do you mind me talking to you like this?

No, I say without even thinking.

Despite this, he seems to hesitate.

It's just — I can understand it — he doesn't want to bury her without it.

But he'll have to?

He looks away from me, at the beach, the sea.

I think so. Yes.

I press my fingers on my mouth, stopping a rush of tears from coming.

Have you said that to him? I ask Lacey.

What?

That he'll have to.

No, he says and I turn my face away into the wind. I don't want to cry in front of him.

I'm sorry, I tell him as we continue on along the prom, it's just that I can't really think about it for very long, any of it —

I know, he says. It's OK. You don't have to.

I'm sorry, I tell him.

Don't be silly, he says.

I look away from him and try to think. The tide is out — a distant frill of brown — and the shingle shines all over with smallish creeks. I love the beach best like this.

Some little kids are running and shouting and building something in the sand exposed between the bumps of shingle. They have swimming costumes on even though it's October, but they dash around in the jagged, goose-pimpled way of kids by the sea, waving their spades and shrieking.

You're used to this, though, aren't you? I tell him.

We stand for a moment and watch the kids — their small, curvy backs and tense, startled little legs. A dog is barking and barking at the far-out waves the way Fletcher used to when he was young and crazy, and a woman is hanging wet towels on the railing of one of the beach huts.

Used to what?

I mean this stuff — dealing with it, the really terrible stuff.

I know he's looking at me.

He says, It's my job. To support people — the victims and their families. But I don't think anyone gets used to it.

Do you stay in touch with people? — I mean, after-wards?

Not always. Mostly not. Sometimes they just want you out of their lives.

Oh?

They want to start again and not be reminded. That's fine. It makes sense.

But, I say, what about you? Don't you ever get — at-tached?

He smiles. Doesn't answer.

Or them, I insist. Sometimes they must get attached to you?

If they do, he says, it's fake. That's what you have to re-member. It's only because you're with them for twelve or fourteen hours a day. You have to withdraw — carefully.

How? I ask him. How do you do that?

It's called an exit strategy.

He smiles again and looks at me.

It's not as bad as it sounds, he says. It's just a job.

You must be very strong, then, to do it.

Not especially, he says. Just a good listener.

Al doesn't talk much, I point out suddenly though I don't know why.

No, Lacey agrees, he doesn't. Where's this coffee, then?

In the buggy Livvy gurgles and bats at her toy.

Estelle's is the next one along, I tell him.

What's Estelle's?

The Tea Hut. Look, down there.

OK.

The best place.

If you say so.

I do.

The day after Lennie died, they had Estelle on the local TV news. They showed her putting hot water in the big metal teapot, looking sad, looking out to sea.

She said, This is a very rural community and everyone knows everyone else and we are all so very shocked that such a terrible crime could happen here in our midst.

At Estelle's you can buy just about anything. Windmills and air mattresses and pocket kites and buckets and spades, the lot. When they were younger, the kids would nag us for the little packs of paper sandcastle flags, the ones you can get for 35p. They'd swear to us that they couldn't build a sand-castle without them — and then we'd find them later, dis-carded and crushed and sandy at the bottom of the nappy changing bag.

I park the buggy and Lacey goes over and buys two mugs of coffee filled the way Estelle always fills them, to the brim. He brings them over carefully, picking his way be-tween the big white plastic chairs.

We came here all the time, I tell him, pulling my coat up around me, Lennie and me, you know. Even in winter.

Jesus, he says, looking around him, I can't say I really see the point of this place in winter.

Oh, winter's the best, I say, vaguely disappointed that he should say such a thing.

I try not to think of Lennie and me, huddling on the

shingle in our jumpers, with a mug of weak Earl Grey from Estelle's, taking it in turns to watch the kids. When the beach is empty, you can let them run and run till they're no more than tiny black specks heading for Blackshore. As long as you can still see them, they're safe, you can relax. And then if the sun slides out from under a cloud, a moment of pure yellow heavenly warmth, before the grey returns.

Lacey is looking at me.

Can I ask you something? he says.

What sort of thing?

Well — ah, OK, it's this. I need to know what sort of a relationship Lennie and Alex had.

You can tell he finds this a difficult question to ask because he looks me straight in the eye as he asks it. His gaze doesn't wobble. I feel the blood hit my face.

Goodness, I say. You mean their marriage — were they happy together?

Lacey nods. That sort of thing, yes.

But — I hesitate — I mean, shouldn't you ask Alex that?

Oh, well, I have.

And?

He shrugs, looks down at his knees.

As you yourself said, he doesn't talk much.

But — why ask me?

Come on, he says. She was your friend, wasn't she? Women tell other women things.

I think hard. I think about what to say.

I'm sorry, he says. I've embarrassed you.

No, I tell him quickly, no, of course you haven't. I understand — that you have to ask these things.

Lacey puts down his coffee mug and scrapes his chair back a little on the concrete. Shoves his hands in his pockets, waiting.

It's just, I say, it's difficult. So soon after.

He says nothing, waits, looks at me.

Do you think you were a good friend to her, Tess? he asks me then. And I notice two things: that it's the first time he's used my name and also that the question bothers me more than I thought it would.

I take a breath.

Not always, no, I tell him.

He looks surprised.

Do you mind telling me why?

It's personal, I tell him. And I don't think it's relevant.

Relevant to what?

To — this.

It could well be, he says.

I don't think so, I tell him.

Isn't that for me to decide?

I look at him then. He's leaning forward, wrists on his knees, the way he did when he was listening to us all in our kitchen at home. I look in his eyes and try to discover what he's expecting to hear.

Is it part of your job, I ask him, to question me like this?

Yeah, he says, you know it is.

I make an exasperated noise and he laughs. Not seeming to mind that I haven't answered him.

OK, he says at last. OK, forget that. Tell me something else instead.

What?

I don't know. Anything. Whatever you like.

Afterwards, we walk a little way together along Pier Road — claustrophobic with its leylandii and dwarf conifers, porches crammed with dead geraniums. I always think that and I think it now. But if I cut across the playground and the churchyard, it's the quickest way back to the clinic.

By the phone box on the corner I stop.

I'm going through there, I tell him, indicating the grassy field with its swings and slides and big old tyre which hangs above a bark-chip-strewn expanse.

The church clock is striking. Eleven already.

Oh, he says. Right.

I'll see you, I tell him. Thanks for coffee.

Take care, he says and he looks at me.

You OK? he asks me.

I'm fine.

Thanks for your time, he says. Maybe we can do it again?

Maybe, I say uncertainly. Then a thought occurs to me. It was random, wasn't it? I ask him suddenly, my heart racing. Just a random, horrible, vicious thing? She was just in the wrong place at the wrong time —

He stares at me.

Hey, he says, why'd you suddenly say that?

I don't know. It's just — been in my head.

There's no such thing as random, he says slowly, not really. Not in that sense.

I shiver.

Meaning —?

Tess, there'll be a reason, a kind of logic to it —

You think he's local? Someone we might all know — someone living right here in this town?

Is that what you think? he asks me quickly.

You're the expert, I say and he gives me a sober look.

No, he says, I told you. Not in that way. I'm not much of an expert, not really.

I leave him then. In the playground a couple of mothers — I don't know them — are sitting at the picnic benches near the climbing frame, chatting and watching over their toddlers who are picking up handfuls of the bark chips and chucking them at each other. As the gate swings shut behind me, I hear squeals of laughter, then the sound of someone crying and then — very faint and only in blotted snatches — the sound of someone practising the organ deep inside the walls of the church.

Chapter 7

FOR DAYS AND DAYS, PEOPLE HAVE BEEN LAYING FLOWERS in the car park. Even strangers from Reydon and Wangford — people who didn't even know her — have brought bouquets and laid them there. The pile is growing. It feels like it will never stop. If you go near the pier, it hits you. The decayed sweetness of freesias and roses wrapped in cellophane and blown on the wind.

Alex isn't comfortable with it. He says it's not what Lennie would have wanted and anyone who knew her agrees. On Sunday morning, Canon Graham Cleve lets it be known that Lennie's family would far rather people made a donation to one of her favourite charities instead. But no one takes any notice. The flowers keep on piling up and Winton's, the bigger florist's in the High Street, stays open till 7 P.M. four days in a row to cope with the demand.

Two national papers run obituaries of Lennie — proper longish obituaries that talk about her with a serious kind of respect, as if she was someone you'd have heard of. In the world of ceramics she was on the way up, though, as Alex likes to point out, they still wouldn't give her a show of her own in London.

The photo they use is the one taken about three years ago by one of the local papers. In it she is bent over a glossy wet pot, strands of hair falling in her face, fingers and apron squidgy with clay. Because she's concentrating, the expression on her face is unsettling — savage, almost. It's a different Lennie from the one we knew. Certainly I never saw her look like that.

Someone from the Crafts Council is quoted as saying that, Leonora Daniels was a welcome breath of fresh air in ceramics, relying as she did on her instincts rather than following the whims and vagaries of fashion. Bollocks, Alex says. He's sure this person never even met Lennie, let alone had anything good to say about her when she was alive.

Meanwhile everyone in the town has their own small thing to add.

She was so normal, Peggy at the dry-cleaner's tells me when I go to pick up the curtains. There was no side to her, no side at all.

She was ever such a nice person, one of the dinner

ladies at the school tells the *Gazette*. I hardly knew her but she always went out of her way to say hello.

Almost a week has passed and the whole town knows that no killer has yet been caught. Daphne Ellison, who works on the till at Somerfield, tells me that everyone she meets is talking about security. People who never thought twice about leaving their doors on the latch now double-lock them, even during the day. More than once, she's seen the locksmith's van parked in Cumberland Road or Skilman's Hill or next to the cottages at Woodley's Yard.

It's sad really. You don't want to give into it, she says, the fear I mean. But it's all right for me, I've got a husband. What can I say to my poor old mother who lives alone?

Now everyone supervises their kids closely. Mick won't let Nat go out alone to the playground and he's not allowed to hang around on the Green with the other kids like he used to. In fact, plenty of people I know won't venture out across the Common or do the marsh walks alone now, not even to watch the sun go down or exercise their dogs. And certainly no one would dream of going near the pier, or hanging around anywhere in the town after dark.

I bump into Alex at the school gates. He looks terrible — pale, unshaven, used-up, glittery-eyed. Some days he lets us call for Con and some days he doesn't. He'll only accept so much help, even from us. He says he's still trying to be a normal father, and I can sympathise with that.

Naughty girl, he says, once I've shouted at Jordan to come back for his PE kit and waved him goodbye.

What?

I hear you've been hanging out with Ted Lacey.

I blush straightaway and hate myself for it. I should know better. I should know Alex better.

I try to look him in the eye.

We talked, I say, yes. Why?

And, he says in a mock-accusing voice, you had coffee and went for a walk.

I look at him. I can hear the dryness in his mouth. I wonder vaguely, helplessly, if he might be ill.

Are you all right? I ask him.

He smiles.

Perfectly fine. Why? Don't I look it?

No, you don't actually. You look — terrible.

We start walking, away from the school, and he rubs his face. I see that his hands are shaking.

Have you eaten today?

Yes, Mummy.

Al —

Well for Christ's sake. What the fuck do you expect me to say?

I touch his sleeve and he pulls away.

I never see you any more, he says.

I look at him.

What? I say. But you see me all the time —

No. I mean alone. I don't see you alone any more.

I stop.

You don't need to see me alone.

Don't I?

What's this all about? I ask him: Seriously — what's the matter?

You know what the matter is. Seriously.

No, I say. I don't. I mean today — this — what's it about?

He shrugs.

I glance down at my watch.

Got an appointment? he says.

No.

What, then?

Moments later.

I was thinking, I say.

What? He gazes at me greedily. What were you thinking, Tess?

You really want to know?

He rubs his eyes, yawns, looks at me. Waiting.

I don't understand why you never told the police — about coming to the hut. On the — on that night.

He looks exasperated. But says nothing.

Mawhinney has no idea, does he? I say. That you were there?

I look at him hesitating.

How do you know that? he says quickly.

Well it was obvious, I say. From — by the way he spoke to us.

He touches his face, glances at me.

And you said nothing?

No, but — I don't understand why you haven't told him, I say.

Don't you?

No, I say again, I don't.

A thought seems to occur to him.

Mick still doesn't know — that I was there with you?

No, but —

He relaxes. Licks his lips.

It's fine, Tess, it's OK.

But —

Just leave it, OK?

No, I tell him. It's not OK actually and I can't just leave it. No one's telling the truth here, not even Mick.

He laughs and makes a face.

You don't say? Not even Mick.

You know what I mean, I tell him.

It's not a question of the truth, he says. It's just that we don't need to confuse things.

It's lying, I insist. You're all lying. So am I.

I haven't lied, he says and his voice is suddenly pinched and hard.

By omission you have. By not telling the police everything.

Oh for God's sake, grow up, Tess, Alex says and he snaps off a branch of elder as we turn the corner into Woodley's Yard.

I'm silent for a moment and then I turn and face him.

Well — I may tell them, I say.

He brushes my cheek with the elder twig. It's scratchy.

Ow, I say.

What you do is your business.

Exactly, I agree. Yes.

Except that Mick will have to know I was there with you
on that night.

I think about this.

It's fine, I say. He isn't really very interested. Plus we
were just talking. There's nothing to hide.

Isn't there?

I look at him and feel a sudden surge of anger.

No, Al. There isn't.

He stops and takes me by the shoulders. Puts his face
near mine. The grip of his fingers is too hard. His nails dig
in a little.

How about this then? he says.

He kisses me, hard, on the mouth. He's trying to do it
properly but it doesn't work. There's something crazy and
awful about how hard he's trying. Like he's trying to cram it
in. I taste the tip of his tongue, feel the chin bristles, the
sourness, the sad unwashedness of him.

I push him off. My cheeks are burning.

For God's sake, Al — what're you doing?

He smiles stupidly. But his eyes are burning.

Giving you something to hide, he says, smiling as if it's
all a big joke.

I look at him and I'm trembling.

You're sick, Alex. You're ill. I mean it. You need some help.

He throws his head back and looks at the sky. Says
nothing.

I mean it, I say again. I'm not just saying it, Al. I think you are.

He spreads his arms out like a bird, fingers splayed.

I'm fine, he says. Never better. Don't give me a hassle, Tess. Don't be so touchy.

He begins to walk off, away down the lumpy, lush grassy path that gives into Spinner's Lane.

It's just a kiss, Tess, he sings back after me. Just a little harmless kiss. What's a kiss, for Christ's sake, between old friends?

I stand there, watching him. In the hedge there are blackberries, clusters of them covered in cobwebs. The sky crackles above me.

It's not real, I hear him say, from far away now, none of it's real. It's not happening. It's just another thing on the TV —

I smell the wind from the sea.

A murder mystery, he calls. A suspense thingy —

I taste salt in my mouth like blood.

I love you, Tess! he shouts. You know I do. I always have and I always will. Lennie knew it too.

That's the last thing he says before he disappears from view behind the hedge.

Lennie knew it too.

It's not true. I start walking the other way. I am sick with shame.

At home, I look around for Mick and can't find him anywhere. The kitchen smells of washing powder, coffee, dog.

A pile of tomatoes has rolled off the table onto the floor but fortunately Fletcher hasn't touched them. He doesn't like tomatoes. Nat says they're poisonous to dogs. He read it in a book of dog facts. The trouble with Nat is, he'll read all about dogs but he won't take Fletcher out for a walk.

I shout for Mick.

Liv is asleep in her rocker on the floor, fat-cheeked and peaceful, lips wet with spit.

The back door is open onto the yard. I can smell cigarettes.

Mick?

He's out there, standing looking at the bare fence and holding a cigarette carefully between thumb and finger. He sees me and doesn't move, just smiles.

You're smoking, I say.

That's right, he says. Ten out of ten for observation.

I look at him.

You've smoked, he says.

Yes, but —

Well, then.

I stand there for a moment, say nothing.

What's the matter? he says.

I'm extremely worried about Alex, I tell him at last.

Oh?

Yes — I take a breath — he tried to kiss me just now.

Mick holds the cigarette away from him and tilts his chin and laughs loudly.

Why? When did you see him?

At school. Just now. Coming back.

Ah. Sweet.

No, I say, staring at him. Mick, I mean really kiss. Snog.

Mick laughs again, more coldly.

Was it good?

Mick —

Did you kiss him back?

He flicks his ash onto the scrubby flowerbed where Nat and Rosa like to set fire to blades of grass with a magnifying glass and where Jordan once grew a sunflower.

Mick, I say, what's the matter with you? Al's really weird. He's in a state. I was shocked. I mean, I don't know why he's doing this —

Oh, come on, says Mick, look at the poor man. Give him a break.

And you — all you want to know is if I kissed him back? A joke.

Mick screws up his eyes and takes a last drag of his cigarette.

Well it's not funny. I think he's cracking up. Seriously, Mick, I'm worried about him.

Well — Mick looks pretty unmoved — I'd leave it. He'll get over it. He's very stressed just now.

I stare at him.

You don't mind?

He shrugs.

I'd mind if it meant anything, of course I would. But it doesn't. It's absolutely nothing. Insignificant.

Thanks, I say.

You know what I mean. Poor old Al.

But he was talking in the strangest way, saying odd things.

What sort of things?

Just — I don't know — stuff. It didn't make sense.

So, he says, stubbing his cigarette out on the peeling metal garden table, what is it exactly that you want me to do about this?

Mick, I say, I'm just telling you.

I know.

So — be a bit nicer —

Sorry. I didn't mean not to be nice.

Couldn't you talk to him?

And say what?

I don't know.

We fall into silence. Mick sits on the edge of the table. Fletcher comes padding out, sniffs at the concrete paving.

Maybe you should talk to Lacey about it, Mick says, if you're really worried.

I couldn't do that, I say straightaway.

Of course you could. He knows Alex, he's with him, he knows about this stuff.

No, I say. I just couldn't. You talk to him.

I think it's better coming from you —

Well, I can't, I say, I just can't. I don't want to, OK?

OK, says Mick. Well, leave it then.

*　　*　　*

At dusk, the High Street changes. It's taken over by kids in nylon clothes, kids whose parents we don't know, who live in the rows of pebble-dashed semis down beyond the marshes, with their scrubby, barren back gardens and kitchens that smell of frying.

They clutch their cans and hang around the video shop or the Chinese takeaway — or else sit smoking on the swings in the playground, leaving their empty cigarette packets at the foot of the infants' slide or kicking up the bark chips with their trainers.

But mostly they just stand at the bus shelter where the odour of cleaning fluid only just masks the smell of piss. The timetables behind the glass are yellowed and old. There are two buses a day, three on market days. But the kids never get on these buses. They don't go anywhere. They just stand and wait.

Popping out to get milk before Somerfield closes, I catch sight of Lacey standing at the bus shelter, talking to a bunch of them. He is talking and they are listening, awkward, one or two of them kicking with their feet at the wire litter-bin outside Curdell's.

Lacey doesn't see me. I hurry past and down Bank Alley before he has a chance to turn.

Lennie's dad sits in the big pine chair in our kitchen and tells me how he's always been planning to come over to visit Lennie and his grandsons but has never been given a clean enough bill of health to fly.

This time, he says, I thought it might be different. I was

hoping they'd just give me a bunch of pills and say, Get your-self on the first plane, Bob — just look after yourself is all.

While he talks, Bob doesn't look at me, but plucks away at the sleeve of his jersey. With Al and the boys, he didn't break down, not once. Then he came over and stood in the middle of our kitchen and just wept. Because he doesn't know us, Mick said. He doesn't feel he has to be strong.

Bob used to be a lawyer.

In Manhattan. But I've been retired for twenty-two years now, you know — twenty-two years!

Twenty-two years is a long time, I tell him.

He explains that he retired young, so he'd have time to do all the good things — the stuff you dream of doing.

He gives a bitter laugh.

What a joke, he says. My wife, Maya, she died a year later. A year almost to the day.

I tell him how sorry I am to hear that.

Anyway, he says, Lennie did make it — she did come over with the boys — what? — six years ago now, maybe seven. Certainly it was when Connor was still in diapers —

Max remembers it, I tell him, he definitely does, he still talks about America.

Bob brightens. Does he?

Then his face falls.

But the damn doctors, he says. My heart, my blood pres-sure, all that crap. So I never got to come and see where she lived. Not till now —

He pauses and his eyes fill up again.

And, you know? It's such a beautiful place!

It is, I tell him, I know, that's why we all came here, it is.

For a moment, Bob puts his head in his hands and is silent. The clock on the dresser ticks.

Oh Christ, he whispers. Oh Jesus, oh Christ.

I touch his shoulder.

I wish, I tell him softly, I wish there was something I could do or say.

He takes a breath.

There's nothing, he says. Just letting me be — just letting me sit here in your lovely home, you know? That's enough.

I turn around and put the kettle back on.

You're a lovely person, he says, you know that? A lovely girl.

Not that lovely —

Oh yes, I mean it. If I was a few years younger —

I try to laugh.

You were a good friend to her, he says, I know you were. I could tell, you know, I could — from the things she wrote, the things she said —

I loved her, I tell him.

She should have gone into the legal profession, he says. Would have made a superb lawyer, she would.

Well, I say, she was a great potter —

She was?

Yes. Always selling her stuff, you know —

Really? Bob says doubtfully. But you make great money in the law, you know.

Yes, I tell him, but it's a big thing, what she did. You

should be proud. It's not at all easy — to make a living from art.

You're an artist? he says.

No, I smile, I'm an osteopath. You know — I fix backs and necks and knees, that sort of thing.

Bob looks forlorn.

I don't have any trouble with mine, he says.

Well, that's good.

It's about the only thing, he says, that doesn't give me trouble.

You should eat something, you know? I tell him. A piece of fruit? Some cheese?

He shakes his head.

I wish you would.

Bob says nothing. Then he asks me if I realise how fat Lennie was as a baby? So fat that they worried at first, him and Maya, that something might be wrong with her. But the doctors reassured them that she was healthy and she was.

A sweet, fat baby. Never any trouble to her mother or me, he says. A placid little thing she was, always smiling, always happy. She was enough for us. We never even thought of having more kids, never even got the idea into our heads. Maybe we should've — or maybe we even did, I forget now — but anyhow the time just went and, well, Len was enough for us. She filled up our time.

Later, when Bob has gone back to Alex's, Lacey rings. I have this small problem, he says. Just that Lennie's dad needs to stay in the studio and I can't get a hotel room till tomorrow night.

You can stay here, I say at once before I've even thought about it. Hating how my voice sounds twittery. Hating as well the feeling of not being able to breathe.

He pauses. He sounds nervous.

Look, he says, you're not just saying it? You've really got room?

It's fine. The boys can shuffle up.

Thank you, he says. You really are sure?

Of course I'm sure. I wouldn't offer otherwise.

Well, thanks very much. It's just for the one night, OK?

Don't worry about it, it's fine.

We ought to make Nat move out and put Lacey in there, but frankly Nat's room is too much of a mess.

Nat's room's stinky, says Rosa without looking up from her drawing. I mean it. It really smells.

Yeah, says Jordan, of farting. It smells of all the farting he does.

Shut up, says Nat.

That's enough, I tell him.

Make him clear it up, says Mick. He ought to anyway.

No, I say. It's too much hassle. It's a week's work, anyway. Lacey can go in with Jordan.

In the bunk bed? asks Rosa. Really?

With me! shrieks Jordan immediately. I'm not having police in my bed.

But as he says it he thinks about it and his face changes.

Actually, he says, cool. I'll do it.

You're doing it anyway, I tell him, whether you think it's cool or not.

He can go on the bottom. He can't touch anything though, Jordan says, thinking of his Warhammer stuff.

Nat sniggers. What's he going to want to touch of yours, poo-head?

Nat, says Mick, shut up. That's enough.

I think he's nice, says Rosa, still concentrating on her sketch pad. I do. I really like him. Connor says he's going to live with them.

Mick laughs.

Of course he's not, I tell her gently, poor man. He has a home and family of his own in London.

Rosa looks up, interested.

Does he? Has he got kids?

I look at her and realise I have no idea. I know nothing about Lacey except that he comes from London and is on transfer or whatever they call it.

He can't have, Nat says, or he couldn't be away from them this long.

He could, says Rosa. Some dads go away to work. Don't they, Dad?

Yes, says Mick and I know what he's thinking. He's thinking: yes and some dads even work.

He looks too young to have kids, I tell them, but he might do. We should ask him maybe.

*   *   *

At the clinic, I tear a hole in the rough blue paper on the bed so that June Sedgely can put her face in the gap.

Are you cold? I ask June, who says she's sixty but I guess is closer to seventy-five.

Not really, says June in her thin, polite voice. I pull the string to turn on the electric wall heater. My fingers are freezing.

I'm sorry, I tell June, my hands are awfully cold.

June laughs agreement as I touch her.

I work my fingers up and down June's spine.

There's a little inflammation, I tell her. The connective tissue doesn't feel right —

You can tell all that, June says, just by feeling?

I smile.

Not always, I tell her. I can't always feel it. But I can today.

How's that baby of yours? June asks me. She has kids of her own but none of them have produced a grandchild for her. It's a sore point. We've discussed it.

Big and heavy, I tell her. She's growing fat.

She's a good feeder?

I'll say.

June tries to nod her head and I feel the movement up and down her spine. A spring, a tremor.

And that poor man, June says. How's he coping?

Alex? He's doing OK.

Not what I've heard, June says, her voice muffled by the blue paper. I've heard he's gone a bit crazy. Insisting on making her coffin all by himself.

My fingers stop.

Really?

It's what I've heard. Jan Curdell told me. She heard it from the woman at the farm shop. I don't know how she knows —

I'm sure it's not true, I tell her.

You haven't heard it?

No, I say firmly.

Oh well, says June, and you'd know.

She sighs.

Those poor kids, she says. It's unthinkable.

Yes, I tell her, it is.

Lacey's already there when I get home, sitting in the kitchen with Mick while he peels potatoes for supper. Each of them has a glass of red wine and on the table is an open bag of crisps. Mick has on his thickest jersey with the zip front and no socks. Lacey has loosened his tie and taken his jacket off — the first time I've seen him without it. His hair sticks up as if he's been running his hands through it. I don't know what they're talking about but when I come in they stop. From upstairs you can hear the kids — pounding of feet, the frequent shrieks of complaint.

Livvy's lying on her mat on the floor, gazing at the back of the sofa. I kick off my shoes, pull her onto my lap. Kiss her four times on the soft, wide moon of her forehead — four fast kisses to make her laugh.

She does. She squeaks.

In the quick pocket of silence that follows, I can feel

Lacey watching her, the way people watch babies when they're embarrassed or tired or don't know what to say. I don't look at him. I hold her away from me, hold her up under her sweet, fat arms, and then zoom her back for another four kisses. Up and in, up and back. She does her cartoon giggle. He watches her, watches me.

Mick grabs a handful of crisps.

So, he goes, how was work?

Oh, I reply, OK.

You sound fed up.

No, I say, I don't think so. Not fed up. Just tired.

I look at Lacey and he smiles at me. I think what a nice smile he has — expectant, careful, kind. And then the kids come down.

What's for tea? asks Jordan, sniffing the air.

Rosa eyes the crisps while holding her kitten nuzzled against her shoulder.

Maria peed on the beanbag, she says. It wasn't her fault.

Get everyone to wash their hands, Mick says.

Can I have a crisp? says Rosa.

No, says Mick. Wash your hands.

From now on, Nat says, the little ones are banned from PlayStation. I mean it.

I wish he wouldn't say that! We're not little! screams Rosa.

The kitten wriggles away and jumps to the floor. The cat flap bangs and before anyone can grab his collar, Fletcher rushes at it with a great long skid across the floor, barking loudly.

Why can't I? says Rosa, back on the crisps. Can't I even have one?

Crisps are for grown-ups, I tell her.

Oh great! she says. I get it — and kids are just minor beings, right?

Rosa slams out of the room. Mick yells at her to come right back. Nat hits Jordan and he bursts into tears.

Mick throws a tea towel onto the table.

Still glad you came? he says to Lacey.

After supper, the kids go to bed and we sit and watch the news. Lennie isn't on it any more. Now it's just about the government and war and tax. Mick seems to have run out of talking. He half does the crossword, half throws a tennis ball for Fletch. Each time he chucks it, the dog bounces off to fetch it, drops it at his feet, then sinks down, chin on paws, eyes on Mick's face. If Mick doesn't throw it again within five seconds, he barks.

That dog doesn't give up, does he? Lacey remarks at one point and I think Mick laughs.

When Lacey yawns and excuses himself, I go upstairs with him to show him where to go and give him towels and stuff. The landing is dark and messy, with Mick's papers strewn on the floor and washing hanging on the airer. The sound of breathing comes from Jordan's room.

He doesn't exactly snore, I tell Lacey, but he's a bit of a heavy breather. I hope he doesn't keep you awake.

Lacey smiles.

I can sleep through anything, he says.

Lucky you.

I know. It's a skill I was born with.

I laugh and so does he.

We stand on the landing together in the half-darkness and I hand him a big towel and a small one, both fat and crunchy from the outside washing line.

There's hot water, I tell him, if you want a bath.

Thanks, he says, but I'm OK. All I want to do is sleep.

He looks at me. We stand there a moment, with only the mess and the darkness between us.

It's very good of you, he says.

Don't be silly, I say.

Well, it is.

He hesitates.

What? I say.

Mick told me, he says. About Al — what he did.

I feel the heat rush to my face.

He did?

You shouldn't worry about it, you know.

I'm not — I mean, I'm not worried about that. It's just, I'm worried about him.

He doesn't know what he's doing, Lacey says, not just now.

I say nothing.

He's barely able to think straight.

OK, I say. You're right, I know.

I smile.

What?

Mick wasn't supposed to tell you —

Oh? I'm sorry.

It's OK.

We stand there a moment on the landing and then we say goodnight.

Rosa asked me something, I say suddenly.

Oh?

Yes. She asked me if you had kids.

He looks at me.

And I didn't know the answer. We hardly know anything about you.

He looks at me and my heart thumps.

Or — your life, I say.

My life?

Yes, I say in a whisper.

There's nothing to know, he says.

Oh?

I mean, I don't. No kids, no wife —

Nobody?

Just a girlfriend.

I blink.

Natasha, he says.

Ah, I say. In London?

In London, yes.

Oh, I say.

Tess, he says softly, look —

Yes?

I'd like to talk to you — about all of this — about Alex. Are you around? Maybe tomorrow? Or the day after?

I almost laugh.

I'm around, I say, all the time. You know I am.

He smiles.

I'll find you then?

Yes, I tell him. Find me.

Chapter 8

BUT IT'S NOT JUST LACEY WHO WANTS TO TALK. MAWHIN-
ney wants to interview me again. Alone, he says, without
Mick.

An incident room has been set up in the back of the
Dolphin Diner on the pier, in the storerooms, where cater-
ing boxes of ketchup and salad cream, and bumper-sized
tins of peeled plum tomatoes and baked beans, are piled to
the ceiling. Orange plastic stacking chairs and Formica ta-
bles have been borrowed from the school and the murder
squad have brought in filing cabinets and phones and a
couple of computers. Each window contains a smooth grey
square of sea. When the weather's bad, the walls moan and
shudder and waves heave and smash against the windows.

Mick's already been in there. He says that even with the

big doors shut, you can still smell the frying and hear the clatter of cups and hiss of steam from the Ramirez brothers in the Dolphin Diner. Normally the brothers would be thinking of shutting down now for the winter, but not this year. It's their busiest October ever. They've never taken so much out of season.

Taped to the wall of the incident room is a map of the town blown up big, with yellow Post-it notes all over it and the car park and pier area outlined in pink DayGlo marker. Other significant spots such as Alex and Lennie's cottage and the area around the school are also marked in colours.

Looking at this map, I can't believe how the distance between all those familiar places is skewed and unlikely. The detailed hugeness of it turns our neat and cosy town into this great big alarming place full of alleyways and twisty streets and endless nooks and crannies. Places where a murder could happen. Places where a murderer could quite easily slink away and hide.

Mawhinney asks me to go in and see him at two, but at five past he's still not there.

It's lunch, says a man sitting at a desk eating a burger. He said he had some stuff to do.

When I tell him Mawhinney was expecting me, he shrugs.

I can call him on his mobile if you like?

He picks up a biro and uses it to stir his coffee.

No, I say, it's OK. I'll go for a walk, shall I?

Ten minutes, says the man. Give him at least ten.

*   *   *

I have Liv in her sling, so I decide to go down on the beach, something I can't easily do with the buggy. The wide concrete steps are gritty with sand, the public toilets are shut for the winter. So is the coastguard's red and yellow hut, padlocked up.

The tide is right in and brown water crashes against the groynes and against the pairs of legs of the pier which stretch a long way out to sea. Rosa always says it looks like a big long creature, crawling slowly away from the shore.

I shut my eyes for a second, feel sun squeezing through the clouds and onto my face. The wind blows my hair and ruffles Livvy's too, but she's deep asleep, head wedged against the strap of the sling. A seagull swoops down over us and for a second its shadow wobbles on the sand. Then away. When the sun goes in, all the shingle turns dark blue.

Far off there's a young man with fair hair walking along the beach with a carrier bag. If I look the other way, I can just see the car park, but I won't look, not today. Sometimes, in a bad winter, that part of the prom is sandbagged up and the beach huts beyond the pier are dragged into the car park and stood there on bricks, since on a rough night the sea can come crashing over the low wall. If that had been the case this year, then Lennie couldn't have parked there.

I walk a little bit further along, away from the pier, but the sling is killing my shoulders and anyway when I turn around I see someone I think is Mawhinney going in, so I go back.

* * *

He says he's sorry, that he got waylaid. He seems more tired than when I last saw him. His clothes smell of smoke, his jacket's creased, his tie's pulled undone.

How's that baby of yours, then? he asks me, peering at Liv's dark head in the sling. Got the feeding sorted yet?

Not really, I say.

Our first was the worst, he says. The second was a dream after that.

Better that way round, I tell him.

But we stopped there, he says. And you've got four? I don't know how you do it, how you manage.

We don't always, I tell him, though I know it's not true, not really. And also that Mick would never tell anyone that. Mick would never even feel it. He may not have wanted Livvy, not really, but once the deed is done, he's loyal. That's Mick for you.

OK, Mawhinney says and he pulls out a bunch of files from behind him then puts them down again. What I wanted to ask you is, do you know a boy named Darren Sims?

Yes, I tell him, surprised. Of course. Everyone knows Darren. Why?

Mawhinney looks at me and hesitates.

Works at the farm shop in Blythford?

That's right, I say. Now and then he does, anyway. I think he just helps out. Why?

He's been in already, of course, to talk to us — all those young blokes have — funny lad is he?

He has a few problems, I tell Mawhinney carefully. Educationally, I mean. But he's OK. He means well.

Yes, Mawhinney says slowly. That's about what I thought.

Why do you want to know about him? I ask.

Mawhinney hesitates.

Despite the dumpy warmth of Livvy against me, I shiver. Outside you can hear the sea slamming at the creeping legs of the pier. I wait for him to answer. Instead he goes off on another tack.

You and Mrs Daniels — Lennie — were good friends? he says. Close friends, you know, intimate?

Yes, I tell him, slightly impatient. Yes, you know we were.

Mawhinney spreads his fingers out on the table. He takes a breath and looks at them as if they were something interesting and new.

The thing is, he says, and this is very difficult, you must forgive me, I know how this must sound — would she have told you if she was involved with Darren in any way?

I stare at him.

What? Lennie?

He nods.

With Darren? What do you mean involved?

He looks me in the eye this time. Well — I mean sexually.

I can't help it — I laugh.

I'm sorry, I tell him, shaking my head. I mean, no way.

Mawhinney gives me a cool look.

You're surprised by the idea?

Yes of course. Totally. Well, it's not true — she wasn't.

You can't believe that would have been the case?

No, I say again. No way.

I run my fingers over the top of Liv's head and Mawhinney folds his big arms and tilts his chair back. He waits a second or two before saying, Well, Darren has implied to us that it was.

I laugh again. Liv stirs against me, makes a snaffly sound with her lips.

Implied?

He's said as much.

Well then, I say, he's having you on. He's making it up.

Pretty sick thing to do, Mawhinney comments.

I shrug.

He has problems. I mean, I'm not standing up for him or anything. I'm just saying he has.

Mawhinney seems to think about this.

You think he'd say such a thing to get attention?

Quite possibly, I say.

Even though it made him — possibly — a murder suspect?

I shrug.

I thought people confessed all the time to things they'd never done — disturbed people, I mean — I thought the police were used to that?

You think he's disturbed? Mawhinney says quickly.

No, I begin, and then another thought creeps in.

You're not thinking Darren did it, I say. You don't think he killed her?

Mawhinney smiles.

I'll be honest with you, he says. It's really impossible to know anything at this stage. Time is passing.

Darren wouldn't hurt anyone, I tell him, I just know he wouldn't.

Mawhinney says nothing. He has the face of someone who's heard it all before.

As we go through the next room I try to glance again at the map, but Mawhinney seems eager to move me on. The Post-it notes have what look like phone numbers on them. I wonder if these are leads the police are chasing — or whether that's just the way it is on TV.

I'd be most grateful, he says, if you'd keep this conversation just between ourselves.

What about Lacey? I say and feel my colour rise as I say it.

What about him?

Does he know, about Darren?

Mawhinney holds the door open and I catch a whiff of deodorant as his arm goes up.

Oh, he says, Lacey knows.

He reaches in his trouser pocket and tears the foil down on a packet of Trebor Mints and offers me one. I shake my head.

Darren didn't even know Lennie, I say. Or she didn't know him. Not any more than I do anyway. They may well have spoken at the farm shop but that's it.

Mawhinney considers this.

Trouble is, he says, you think you know someone — you could swear you knew what they were capable of — and then they go and surprise you. Human nature.

He smiles at me.

Happens all the time in this business.

*   *   *

Darren is one of a small gang of lads — Dave Munro, Roger Farmiloe and Brian Whittle, too — who spend a lot of the day in The Red Lion doing nothing much except watch TV.

The day after Lennie dies, Darren very nearly makes the six o'clock local TV news. But in the end they plump for his mate Brian, who's employed by Waveney District Council to sweep the area between North Parade and the pier and therefore has a closer connection to the scene of the crime.

Meanwhile reporters have spoken to just about everyone in town: hotel people, shopkeepers, chambermaids, the staff at the brewery, the woman who cleans the toilets at The Anchor.

Ellen Hasborough, who runs the Whole Loaf Organic Deli on the corner of East Street and Pinkney's Lane, tells the local radio station that, Our rustic idyll is shattered. People used to come from miles around for a peaceful day here, for our famous coastal-path walks. I can't see it happening any more.

And a local councillor is reported as saying, They are lovely people here and it's a shocking business. The whole community is taking it very badly.

With no funeral in sight, the town creates its own small marks of respect. The flag which normally flies from the mast in the middle of St James's Green is lowered for a week and the bakers and the fish shop draw down their shades even though business goes on as usual behind them. Even the Ramirez brothers go so far as to place an old-fashioned black-edged notice in the window of the Dolphin Diner next to the dusty fisherman's netting and dried starfishes, expressing their Deepest Sympathy for the family of Lennie Daniels who was so close to our hearts. Which, as Mick notes, is rich, considering that for two years running Lennie begged them to donate a fish and chip supper for the school summer raffle, only to be met both times with a flat and charmless refusal.

Next day, Saturday, Lacey finds me on the promenade.

A thunderstorm during the night has left the air soft and silky, the crackle washed out of it. The tide's far out, the groynes exposed, the brown beach laced with hundreds of glistening creeks.

The drama class Rosa and Jordan go to on Saturday mornings has been cancelled, so we're on the beach instead, chucking a Frisbee on the driest band of shingle. Fletcher is straining on his lead, desperate to go down and join them, but he's not allowed. There are places where dogs have to be on a lead, even out of season.

It's chilly but there's no wind. One or two brave, elderly people have opened up their beach huts and put kettles on and started edging down to the sea, towels wrapped around their waists.

Suddenly he's behind me.

They're not really going in are they?

Oh, I say, blushing furiously.

Sorry, he says, I could see you were in a dream.

Well, I say. Hi.

It's freezing, he says. Do they really swim in this?

I shrug.

It's warm enough, once you get in.

Lacey shivers.

I was looking for you, he says as Fletcher wags and wiggles.

I try to turn Liv's buggy round so it doesn't face into the wind.

Oh? I say. Really?

It sounds ruder than I meant it to. I glance towards the kiosk. Estelle is watching us intently, cloth in hand.

Lacey looks at me.

Want some coffee? he says.

OK. Please.

I watch him get it — his tall straight back as he stands there talking to Estelle. How Estelle smiles and leans her elbows on the counter, then touches her hair.

So, he says, when he returns with two mugs.

So, I ask him, you got yourself a room?

He smiles at me.

Yes, he says, I got one. Thank you.

He's laughing.

What? What's funny?

You are. He rips open a sachet of brown sugar and crumbs spill on the white table. You make me laugh. The way you talk, all your funny questions.

It's you, I say. Then I blush again.

And you're always blushing, he says.

I ignore this.

I only asked you if you got a room —

I know, he says, and he sits back in his chair, relaxed. I didn't mean that.

What, then?

He thinks for a moment.

Only that it's possible to talk to you for ages and find out nothing.

I laugh.

What exactly would you want to find out?

I don't know, he says. You tell me.

You see! I cry. That's what you do all the time — turn everything back into a question.

Lacey smiles. At my feet, Fletcher wimpers, strains at the lead and then pants.

Poor dog, says Lacey. Can't he join them?

No, I say, we'd never get him back.

I watch as Lacey rubs Fletcher's head, pulls at the silky scrags behind his ears.

Does he want a drink?

I shrug.

Lacey picks up Jordan's Mickey Mouse bucket.

I'll get him one, shall I?

If you want, I say. The tap's over there.

He goes over to the low concrete wall and fills the bucket and carries it back. He carries it the way Jordan would — concentrating, taking care not to spill any.

He sets it down in front of Fletcher and the dog laps enthusiastically.

There, you see, Lacey says, he was. Poor dog was thirsty.

The wind blows and Estelle's tub containing beach bats and fishing nets falls over and rolls clattering over the prom. Estelle comes out and gathers it up and takes it back. The old people are coming out of the sea now, tiptoeing up over the shingle, towels over their shoulders.

The Frisbee flies up and clatters across the concrete near us. Lacey straightaway picks it up and tries to throw it back. But he can't do it because the wind is against him and it lands back on the prom. Both kids shriek at him.

Like this! Jordan shouts, showing Lacey the flick of the wrist. Fletcher is now vigorously chewing the side of Jordan's bucket. I take it from him.

You said you wanted to talk about Alex, I remind him.

He looks surprised.

Yes, he says, yes. If you don't mind. There's something I need to ask you, actually.

You mean to do with the investigation?

I can't really claim that it is, he says. Or at least, it might be, but, well, I'm not sure.

Well, I say, go ahead.

You'll blush if I ask it.

Really?

I laugh and my heart races.

Yes, he says, I think you will.

I wait and he looks at me.

You and Alex, he says, you used to be involved?

Well, yes, I say steadily. We went out. Years ago. Before Lennie and before Mick. It's not a secret — everyone knows that.

Lacey thinks about this.

I've known him since I was a teenager, I say. I'm very fond of him. Mick's known him almost as long.

Lacey's silent. I wait.

OK, he says, OK, but — I'm sorry to ask but — is there still an excitement between you and Alex?

I put my hand to my face.

What? You mean now?

Yes. Now.

Lacey's eyes are on my face.

No, I say quickly as the blood rushes to my cheeks. Well, no, I don't think so.

I make myself busy by stuffing the bucket into the buggy's rain hood.

You're not sure? Lacey says.

I mean, as I said, there used to be. A long time ago. We — liked each other. But it's over, from my point of view.

And from his?

I try to look Lacey in the eye.

Why on earth are you asking me this? I mean, has he said something?

Not a word, Lacey says in a strange, solemn voice. I promise you. Nothing.

Well then, I say, it's a bit personal, isn't it?

I'd still like an answer, he says gently.

Well, I — excitement's a funny word for it, I tell him at last.

What word would you use, then?

I pause a moment. I feel suddenly drained, exhausted.

Look — is this really relevant to anything? I ask him.

I don't know, he says. Is it?

Minutes pass and we both do nothing. Just sit in silence and watch the kids and the sea.

Sorry, he says after a moment or two. I shouldn't have asked you that.

I keep a blank face.

I don't care, I say. Ask me anything you want. I'll tell you anything. I don't care about anything much just now.

He pauses a moment.

This must be a nightmare — for you, he says at last.

In a nightmare, you wake up.

I'm sorry, he says again.

Is that it? I ask him.

What?

Is that all you're trained to say? Sorry? Because really I'd have thought they'd have given you something better.

Better for what?

For — I don't know — for fobbing people off with.

He says nothing.

Sorry, I say after another moment, I didn't mean that. I'm just so fucking sick of it all.

Yes, he says.

I hate how it's become the way we live. Every day we wake up and it starts over — all of this.

You're still in shock, he tells me.

I think about this.

I don't know, I say. Am I? I'm surprised at how OK I feel, really. Like I'm in a dream and most of me is somewhere else.

Lacey's looking at me.

Everyone responds differently, he says.

But, I insist to him, it can't last — you have to come out of it eventually, don't you?

I don't know, he says quietly. I've never experienced what you're going through.

Also, I tell him, I feel different —

Different in what way?

I don't know — bad, irresponsible —

Really?

Yes. Like I could fuck things up and not care at all.

What sort of things?

I don't know. Just things. It's as if I genuinely don't care at all — or there's nothing at stake. Not even the kids sometimes. It scares me.

Why?

Because it's not normal. It's not how I usually am.

You're too hard on yourself, he says. None of you are to blame for what happened.

I know that, I say.

Well then, I say after a pause. Maybe I'm just very angry.

Tess, he says gently, you have every right to be.

Why would anyone do it? I ask him.

He looks at me carefully.

Why would anyone want to take her heart?

Do you know what a trophy-taker is? he asks me.

No, I say. And then it dawns.

A body part, he says. Any part. It's usually something smaller, something sexual maybe. A heart is rare.

Why?

He takes a breath.

Well — it's very hard to take out.

I look quickly away at the sea where the horizon dissolves and water and sky blur.

Sorry, he says, but you did ask.

Tears spring to my eyes.

She's dead, I tell him, I know that. I know she's not coming back. But you see, to me — this place is still so full of her.

Lacey says nothing.

You think I'm silly, I tell him and I pick up a paper napkin and hold it to my eyes, or mad. Crazy.

No, he says. No I don't.

He passes me another napkin. His fingers close to mine.

I don't think you're any of those things, he says.

Then what?

He doesn't answer.

I fold the damp napkin, over and over, smaller and smaller.

In the end, I tell him, it's this. Your life — anyone's life — it just doesn't belong to you, does it?

He is silent for a very long time and then he says, No. It doesn't. But you still have to act as if it does.

Alex says that all he wants is for people to leave him alone now.

He says he's sick of all the offers of help — sick and tired of people cooking him food and leaving toys and notes and stuff in the porch. He doesn't want any babysitting, or a free takeaway from Mei Yuen's, or a bag of plums or a bacon quiche or an unripe marrow. He doesn't want his windows cleaned for nothing, or extra fish thrown in when he orders from the fish shop. He especially doesn't want the king-sized crocheted blanket, a monstrous acrylic thing in cheap scarlets and blues and pinks, made by the ladies of the Reydon Society.

He says his GP's given him some Prozac. And that's it, that's nice, that's all he really wants for now. Just that and maybe the chance to bury Lennie. Ideally with her heart — but if that's not possible, then what's left of her, laid to rest, without it.

But none of it may be possible, not for a while anyway. Lennie's body is still being looked at and Alex has been warned that a second, independent autopsy may be required. It could be some time before the coroner will release the body to the family for a funeral.

Meanwhile, Bob's worrying about how long this is all taking. It's impossible, apparently, for anyone to say. He's frail, he ought not to travel unnecessarily, but it could be weeks and he's wondering if he should fly back and then return when Alex has more information. And Bob has dogs at home. He's concerned about his dogs. Two chocolate Labs, one of whom is elderly and needs regular injections. A neighbour is taking care of them right now.

But I can't rely on their kindness forever, he says.

He tells me how Lennie phoned him just about every week and how he was thinking of getting e-mail so they could stay in touch that way as well. Keeping up with the times. Except maybe not, maybe he could never have done it, because these days his hands don't work so well.

Look at them — he spreads his ropy, mottled fingers in front of him. See? I have the shakes nearly all the time now.

He frowns at them.

I don't think they look too bad, I tell him.

He ignores me.

She was very popular with the boys, you know, he says. As a teenager. A good-looking girl, like her mother. Though she could be wicked, you know, really wicked — oh my goodness — playing them off against each other —

He laughs. So do I.

I can just see it, I say.

Can you? he says, narrowing his eyes. I pitied some of those poor guys, oh my God, oh dear, I really did —

He stops and recovers himself.

And what about you? he says. Bet you had a lot of guys after you? You're a good-looking girl as well. Now don't mess with me, I bet you did.

Some, I tell him, but not a lot.

He tries to look astonished.

But — a girl like you?

You're exhausted, I tell him.

You know, he says, I can't see you well. You do look very far away to me.

You're just exhausted, Bob.

Yes but I can't rest though, he says quietly. I'd like to sleep, I really would. But I won't. Not now. That's the tragedy.

I push a fresh cup of coffee towards him and his fingers close around it, eager as baby's fingers. He does this, even though we both know he'll leave it to go cold like the last one.

I shouldn't really have coffee, he confesses.

How about a brandy then? I say.

He begins to weep.

OK, he says and I pour him a generous one and he downs it in two swift gulps. Then he tells me he's not allowed that either.

But what the hell, he says. You know, the way I figure it, who's left to mind?

Chapter 9

TWO O'CLOCK IN THE AFTERNOON, A DARK DAY. THE KIDS at school for at least another hour and Liv down for her nap, arms flung up beneath her blue bunny blanket.

Mick wraps his arms around me.

What? he says. What is it?

I try to wriggle out.

What's what?

You seem far away.

I don't think so.

Something's getting to you.

I look at him.

I mean, something else, he says.

I'm fine, I tell him. Hearing the coldness creep into my voice.

He releases me, drops his arms down to his side.

You want me to leave you alone?

I turn and look at him.

I didn't say that, no.

Then — what, Tess? Tell me —

I sigh.

Oh Mick, I say, I don't know. I don't mind — I don't care what you do. What do you mean, leave me alone? I'm not asking for anything. What you're doing is fine.

He smiles, but I can read the smile. Unreasonable, it says.

What you do is always fine, I tell him.

I love you, he says. Do you know that?

Thank you.

What do you mean, thank you?

Just — I'm glad.

It's not something you say thank you for.

What, then?

He kisses my hands, both at once, then separately, finger by finger.

You're in another world these days, he says.

Well, I say, we all are. Aren't we?

He stops the kissing.

Maybe, he says. But I'm trying not to be. And the difference is, I feel you want to be.

I remember a time when sex was a glue, a healer — it would smooth, ease, mend, bring us closer together. As well as for pleasure — we could rely on it for that, nearly always anyway. Not any more. Now it's a thing that comes between us, pushing us further away.

Upstairs, the bed is still unmade, still covered in child clutter. Livvy's bright-coloured teething monkey and a pile of Rosa's navy school socks. On the carpet, Jordan's forgotten homework sheet — signed by us but never delivered to school — a pack of Disprin, a pair of my knickers.

Mick sweeps the stuff off and pulls the duvet back and I lie on the sheet which is cool as water. I start to undo my jeans.

No, he says, let me —

He does it slowly and carefully, laying each bit of clothing aside like someone who knows they'll have to pick it up later.

I laugh.

What?

You don't have to fold them, I say.

He smiles grimly, determined to be amused, yet obviously bothered that the mood's disturbed. He senses it's going to be tough, that I won't play.

But, I think, I want to do this.

He kisses my face, my neck, my hair. Then he takes his own clothes off more quickly. I put my face close to his body, dutifully take in the familiar chill of his skin, the folds, the curves, the hair.

Come on, he says and pulls the duvet over us, pulls me onto him, gathers my hair so it doesn't dangle in his face.

It ought to be possible, I tell myself as his fingers move over my bottom, my thighs. I try to get them into my head —

those weird and dirty thoughts, hot and shameful, to get me going. It usually works for me. But it's impossible and my mind is pulled up and away and I float free. Instead I see Lennie, biting her lip as she tries to back her car into a tight space on an afternoon after school a long time ago. I see the pier, battered by wind and storms, and all those ketchup cans piled up behind Mawhinney. And the slice of grey, choppy sea through the window behind.

And then, suddenly, I see Darren Sims. I remember his denim jacket lying on a clay-spattered stool in Lennie's studio. I check the memory — it feels real — and I tense up at this surprising thought.

Mick wets his fingers and puts them inside me.

He kisses my nipples, touches me, delves around. I try to feel it. I try to push the thoughts away, but they come creeping back, unstoppable as smoke.

My conversation with Mawhinney comes into my head.

Mick pushes me over onto my back.

Hey, he says as, lazy-eyed, he licks his fingers and strokes between my legs again. What are you thinking?

Nothing, I tell him. I'm trying to concentrate.

On what?

On this. The sex.

He sits up. He's giving up.

I push him over. His penis is standing right up. I bend my head and grasp its stem like a flower and kiss the end of it. It smells of spit and cheese and the hotness of men before sex. He makes a little noise of encouragement. Before he can start asking to come inside me, I make my fingers into a circle and then hold him there.

He lies back and closes his eyes. He has a lovely face when his eyes are closed — young and smoothed-out and trusting.

Oh, he says, oh, o-oh.

Moving my hand up and down, I feel like a sober person watching a drunk one.

You like this? I ask him in the low, barely-there voice I use to make him come. It pleases you?

He moans.

I stroke the length of him and then bring my hand tight around him again and move it up and down.

He groans.

I think of how many times we must have done this — and then I realise that I can't remember any of them. I can't remember how love felt in the days before Lennie died.

Each time I tighten my hand, he moans. I try kissing the tip of him again, slipping it in my mouth, and it's clear from the sounds that he likes it but eventually it hurts my neck so I lift my head up again.

Through the window is the silvery, waving eucalyptus tree that could do with a trim, and beyond it, sky. Afternoon sun is squeezing itself out from between grey clouds. Later it will rain.

Hey. Not too hard, Mick whispers, eyes still closed but reaching out with his hand to mine. Get some oil.

Under the bed is a small brown glass bottle of oil. I

reach down and unscrew the cap and tip some into my hand and slide my fingers over him. He sighs. I slip my hand up and down, up and down, until he begins to pant and lift his pelvis up off the bed and then I know it's about to be over, and then it is.

When he comes, there is such a big, arcing spray of gunk that some of it goes on his face.

I should make you lick it off, he says and I try to look as if, on another day, I might've.

I wait till Mick has gone to fetch the kids from school and I'm alone in the house. And then I dial the number of The Angel where Lacey's staying.

OK, I tell him when they put me through. Maybe it's this. I don't want to lie to you about Al. He's my friend — he's always been my friend — but it's more complicated than that as well —

Yes, says Lacey. He waits. I can hear his attention, his concentration. I go on.

He loves me, I say. And — well — I love him too. I told you. But he's let it get — bigger —

Yes, Lacey says again. I've no idea what he's thinking.

Look, I tell him, I'm trying to be honest here.

He waits.

And, I say, it's not just that. He's sometimes told me things. Stuff I wished he wouldn't — about him and Lennie.

What sort of things? Lacey says.

Just stuff.

What stuff?

About their relationship. I mean, I asked him not to, but he still did —

Did what?

Go on about it — how they weren't always happy to-gether.

Really? Lacey says, though he doesn't sound especially surprised.

Lennie never said that, I tell him, never. Only Al.

And you didn't think he should have told you?

No, I say. But —

But what?

Well, I still spent time with him, didn't I?

Lacey's quiet.

You think you let him? Lacey asks.

My heart thumps.

I wasn't a good friend to Lennie, I tell him then.

But Tess, he says slowly, you mean, you and Alex — you've —

No! I tell him, horrified. No, never. I would never do that. Not to Lennie, not to Mick. But I've sometimes been lonely. And he's been there for me. He knows me. And I find his attention and his company —

Lacey waits.

Tempting, I say. Flattering. Satisfying.

I can understand that, Lacey says.

Can you?

Everyone gets lonely, he says.

I glance at my watch. Mick will be back soon.

I'm not sure I should have told you any of this, I say.

I'm glad you did.

Well — it's not all —

Oh?

No, there's something else. It's to do with that night — when she died. I was there, you see.

Now Lacey's voice changes.

What? he says. What do you mean?

I have a place I go to, I tell him, a beach hut — one of the huts on the front, the other end, towards Gun Hill. It's mine. I go there at night sometimes. I was there that night, the night it happened —

Really? he says, and it sounds like I have finally surprised him. On your own? So late at night?

Yes. No.

I feel tears coming and take a breath to stop them.

Not on my own. Not this time. Usually I do — go there alone. It's always felt so safe. I get up in the night and I just go there — the whole point is to be alone. Otherwise, in the life I have, I never get to be in peace or in silence, not ever. You can't understand that, can you?

Lacey is silent.

But that night?

Alex came. He insisted. He knows I go there and he came. Mick doesn't know.

He doesn't?

No. Al's done it before. Come there. To talk about her —

about their problems. Anyway we drank some wine. They'd had a terrible fight that evening, a really big one, and he was thinking of moving out.

Lacey says, You didn't tell Mawhinney any of this?

No, I say.

Why not?

I didn't think —

Didn't think what?

I suppose I just didn't think.

And that's all?

Well, I tell him, only that we were talking about all of this and suddenly I had this feeling — such a strong feeling — that he should go home to her. I was very frightened. I knew something was going to happen —

What do you mean, something? Lacey asks me quickly. How could you know?

Sometimes I just — feel things.

There's a silence at the other end of the phone.

You could never have known, Lacey says finally. Don't punish yourself, Tess.

But —

You're rationalising after the event. It's a common enough thing to do.

I decide to let this go.

I told him, I say. I told him to go straight home and be with Lennie —

And he did?

He did, I tell Lacey. He waited all night. And then he called me.

* * *

After school Jordan and I walk Fletcher across the Common towards Blackshore. On our left, the golf course, on the right, dull-faced cattle chomping lippily on gorse.

You know what it means when the cows lie down? Jordan asks me. That it's going to rain!

Certainly, the air is damp and clotted, the sky tight with swollen clouds moving too fast across it.

Once we've passed the golf course we let Fletcher off. He's a dog of habit and he knows exactly what to do. He sits and waits to be unclipped and then he soars.

Good dog! Jordan shouts and Fletcher darts away, ears flat, belly low to the ground. He isn't allowed into the cow field but we let him scoot and dodge over the long-grassed Common which stretches as far as the coastal path on one side and to the fishing shacks and chandlers of Blackshore on the other.

It's wonderful to see Fletcher run — same as I think it might be to fly a kestrel or hawk. It makes me feel smaller, safer, a speck on the ground.

We continue on up the lane, towards the water tower. In the distance, a tractor putters and stops, then putters again. Jordan is asking me whether, if a child stole some money from his parents when he was a child, and then the parents found out, they could sue him.

But they wouldn't want to, I tell him. Mums and dads never want to take their kids to court —

Yes, he says, dancing backwards impatiently along the asphalt road in front of me. But that's not what I mean — I mean if the parents found out when the child was a grown-up — would they punish him then?

I laugh.

But sweetheart, he'd still be their child. When your child grows up you go on loving them just the same, however old or grown up they are —

But Jordan isn't satisfied.

Wouldn't they at least be cross? he wants to know.

Well, maybe, I say. But when a child does something bad like take money, usually his mum or dad just want to find out what's wrong and why he did it. That's more important than punishing him, you see.

Jordan thinks about this.

The cows are following us along the line of the hedge. Fletcher's nowhere in sight.

But has it ever happened, he insists, that a mum or dad takes their child to court when they're grown up?

He snaps off a long stalk of cow parsley and waves it like a sword. Oh look, Mummy! he says, because Fletcher has found another dog. Back on the road, next to the damp verge, he is sniffing the rear end of a lean, shabby, black and tan animal. Both dogs very still, alert, erect, concentrating.

I know whose dog that is, I tell Jordan — and I look around for Darren Sims. Except I can't see him. Seconds later, he climbs out of the ditch.

Hiya, he says.

Hi, I say, hoping we can move on quickly. I don't really want to get stuck with Darren.

You didn't see me there, did you?

No, I tell him.

Did you come out of the ditch? Jordan asks, staring at him in frank and open amazement.

Yeah, he says. You see down there? — he indicates down behind the hawthorn tree that grows on a steep slope beyond the ditch. Jordan nods and stares.

Well, I found something.

What? says Jordan. What?

Want to come and have a look?

Yes, says Jordan immediately, but I pull him to me.

Not today, Darren, I say. We have to get back.

Oh, Mummy, says Jordan.

Another time maybe, I say. Or you could just tell us what you found?

Darren grins at me. His neck is spotty and his Adam's apple sticks out too much.

I'm keeping it to myself, he says, still smiling. No one else will find it, that's for sure.

Jordan starts to move towards the ditch, but I grab his sweatshirt. The sky is darkening.

Another day, OK? I say and take a step back towards home. Darren's dog comes swaying and sauntering up, looking depressed. Fletcher has already disappeared, back into the furthest smells of the Common.

Darren doesn't move.

That dog of yours, he says. Coming along nicely isn't he? How old is he now, then?

Two and a half, says Jordan proudly.

Two and a half? says Darren. Really? I'd have had him down as younger. Runs around a lot, doesn't he?

When he was a puppy, Jordan says, he fitted in my mum's handbag.

Inexplicably Darren's face falls.

He doesn't bite, does he? he says.

No-o, says Jordan, kicking grit on the road, losing interest.

Darren looks at me.

Them dogs the police had, he says. Did you get a look at them? They weren't German Sheppers, I don't know what they were, even me nan didn't know — did you see the teeth on them?

Which dogs, I say, when?

All last week, Darren says. Days and days. Dogs and dogs, sniffin' all around the pier and whatnot.

Maybe they were bloodhounds, Jordan offers.

Something occurs to me and I bite my lip.

Darren, I say carefully, you do know, don't you? About Lennie? Mrs Daniels — what happened?

He looks hurt.

Of course, he says slowly. Of course I do. It's all my mum and my nan want to talk about. All that business.

Well then, I say, police often bring in dogs. They're just going over that area in detail I would imagine, it's what they have to do.

Doing their job, says Darren.

Exactly.

She was going to give me a job you know, he says then.

I look at him.

Who was?

Her. Mrs Daniels.

Really?

Darren looks pleased with himself.

Yeah, she was. Sweeping and that. And learning to make them things of hers.

She said that?

Yeah. She promised. Had me round and gave me a Coke. She promised. Won't happen now, though.

No, I tell him, it won't.

A shame, isn't it? he says. It would have been good.

It would, I agree.

And he says goodbye and we watch his long body and the skulkier one of the dog move slowly up the hill towards the golf course.

Jordan skips along beside me in silence.

I wonder what Darren found, he says.

Yes. I wonder.

Shall we go back and have a look?

No. Not now.

Mummy, what sort of dog is Darren's dog?

Mongrel, I suppose, I say.

No! says Jordan. Mixed breed. You don't say mongrel.

Oh, I agree. Right.

Yeah, says Jordan, it's like Mixed Race. And Special Needs.

He turns to look at me.

Is Darren Special Needs?

*　　　*　　　*

Alex stops by the clinic just as I'm locking up and putting the rubbish out in Dene Walk. Suddenly he's there in front of me, next to the scrubby buddleia that springs out from the cracked cement of the wall.

What is it? I say. What's happening? Are you OK?

They're having a fire practice, he says. At The Angel. Loads of old people lined up in the car park.

Oh, I say.

Laugh, then, he says.

Why?

Because it's funny. You should have seen them.

What is it? I ask him.

What do you mean what is it?

Why're you in such a weird mood? I say.

I'm not, he says, I'm great. Why? Do I always have to be down and suicidal?

No, I say, but I don't like the look in his eyes, a glitteriness that means trouble.

I mean it, he says when he sees me looking at him, I thought I'd just drop by and say hello.

I say nothing, squash the garbage bag down into the dustbin and try to get the lid to shut. A smell of decay mixes with the whiff of setting lotion and cigarette smoke from the hairdresser's across the alleyway. Suzanne Hair Fashions is open late on Wednesdays. Their new beautician smokes all the time. She's probably out in the yard right now, puffing away.

I shiver because I've taken off my whites but not put my cardigan back on.

I've got to lock up, I tell him. Fine, he says and follows me in. He sits down on the edge of the reception desk, on a bunch of papers — a whole load of cheques and order forms that Nicky who comes in on Tuesdays has left for me to sign. I pull the papers out from underneath him. He doesn't help me. Then I go and get my cardigan off the hanger.

What is it, Al? I say again. Please tell me.

He laughs. I told you, nothing's wrong, I'm great. I just had this hankering to see you alone, that's all. Anything wrong with that?

I sigh. I'm tired and I want to get home.

I can't play games, I say, switching the answerphone on and starting to shut down the computer. I'm tired.

I don't know what you mean, he says. What games?

How are the boys anyway? I ask, ignoring him. Are they OK?

I believe so, he says. They're round at your place actually.

Oh?

Mick said he'd feed them.

And does he know where you are right now?

Alex laughs.

No, he doesn't actually.

As I go into the next room to get my bag, he says, I loved her, you know.

What? I call out. Even though I heard him perfectly. I pick my bag up off the floor and stand there, waiting.

I loved her, he says. It may not always have looked that way, but I did.

I know you did, I tell him more gently as I come back in. I move the appointment book out of the way, stack sets of notes on top of the cabinet for filing. I put a hand on his wrist.

You don't have to tell me that, Al, I say.

But he's not listening.

They think I killed her, he says.

I stare at him.

No they don't. Don't be so ridiculous —

Oh yes, he says, very softly this time. Oh Tess, I mean it, they do.

No —

I mean it. Would I lie about something like that?

They? Who's they?

Lacey. Lacey does.

But, I say, suddenly slow and stupid, I thought you liked Lacey?

He thinks I did it. He thinks I cut up my wife. He thinks I took her heart out and went and hid it somewhere just for fun.

I sit down. He looks at me.

You've got it wrong, I tell him. There's no way Lacey would think that.

Whatever, Alex says, suddenly sour. You should know.

What do you mean?

He doesn't reply.

What's that supposed to mean? I say again.

He says nothing.

I just — don't — believe, I tell him, that he would think that.

I can see it all over his face, says Alex. All the time, whenever he talks to me.

Oh, I say, relaxing a little. So he's never actually said anything?

Alex folds his arms and closes his eyes.

He doesn't have to.

Oh for God's sake, you're being ridiculous, I tell him. I'm sorry but you are.

Don't you think you look ridiculous, he says, going round with him all the time.

I pull my cardigan on.

Everyone knows it, he says. You've been seen.

Oh don't be so stupid, I tell him.

I said you've been seen.

So, yes, I say, OK. I know him. We all do — he's been here in our lives for days. It's his job — to look after you and the boys.

Ah, says Alex, but the word is, he only sticks around because of you.

My heart jumps.

Well, I say, the word's wrong. In fact all he wants to do is talk to me about you.

That's what he says?

Alex smiles. I ignore him.

Who the hell's saying this anyway? I ask him. Who's this everyone?

Who do you think? he says. The whole fucking town.

I suddenly feel sorry for him — for his tired face, his red eyes. I go over and touch his arm.

Al, I say, don't do this. Please. You don't mean it. I know you don't. Please, Alex.

He shrinks from my touch, flexes his hands and stares at them.

You look terrible, I say. What is it? Aren't you sleeping?

I love you, he says then.

No, I say steadily. You don't.

I can't stop thinking about you. All the time, when I should be thinking about this.

Oh Al, you know that's not true.

It is. I do. I love you. If she hadn't — if she wasn't gone — I'd still feel it and I might still tell you.

No you wouldn't. It's just all of this. You're confused. You said you loved her just now.

Not in this way.

He puts out his hand but I pull away from him.

Don't tell me. Please. I don't want to hear about it.

He makes a funny sound then, half of pain, half of excitement, and he pushes up the sleeve of my cardigan and lays his fingers on my bare arm.

I never wanted to hurt you, he whispers.

But you haven't, I reply. I don't know what you mean, Al. You haven't hurt anyone.

Chapter 10

EVERYONE'S BEHAVIOUR HAS ALTERED FOR THE WORSE.

At school, Jordan has been lashing out at other kids, even the bigger ones. He punched and kicked Debbie Suffling who, though tall and strong-looking, actually suffers from a blood condition that means she must not be hit.

Julie Edmunds, his teacher, sent Jordan straight to the head's office where he sat stony-eyed and sullen and refusing to say sorry. That's what Julie tells us when we go in to see her — that it's not the incident itself but his total lack of remorse about it that she takes most seriously.

I'm sure he's sorry, Mick tells her. He's just too proud to say it.

We don't encourage that sort of pride in this school,

Julie says. We try to encourage children to respect others and put the truth first.

And she eyes Liv's buggy and I know what she's thinking: what's she doing with another baby at her age when she can't even control the ones she's already got?

But it's not just Jordan. Rosa, who's loud and difficult at home but normally an angel at school — so good and conscientious that she will literally sweat if she doesn't get her homework done on time — has lost her pen, her PE kit and half of her books, and been in trouble more than once for talking in assembly.

Our Rosa? Mick says. Talking in assembly?

Not only that, but her shoelaces are fraying, her shirt's perpetually splattered with ink, her fingers are grubby and her arms covered in strange itchy spots which she picks till they bleed.

Who's throwing ink at you, Rose? I ask her. Someone's flicking it at you, aren't they?

It's my cartridge, she says flatly. It leaks.

All over your back?

She makes an ugly face at me.

And the spots — I wonder if they're flea bites. We must get Maria a flea collar, I say.

It's not Maria, Rosa almost shouts. Maria's fine. You leave my kitten out of this!

Well, what's biting you, Rosa?

I don't know, she says. Mosquitoes, maybe?

In November?

Leave me alone, she says. I'm fine, OK?

What is it? I ask her when she bursts into sudden tears. What's the matter, darling?

But she won't talk to me, just stomps upstairs. Half an hour later I find her asleep on her bed with the kitten purring on her chest.

And then there's Nat. I'll ask him to do a simple thing like empty the dishwasher or tidy his room or eat an egg on toast or remove his school blazer from where he just lets it drop in the hall and he'll immediately attack me.

Why do you insist on making my life hell? he screams.

I'm surprised at how much I want to hit him — I, who've never laid a finger on my kids. How can Nat — once the sunniest, easiest boy (far easier in many ways than the other two) — have turned into this monster? He sits in his room with the curtains shut and something electronic in his hand. He slouches around the house complaining. And then there's the food thing.

OK, I say as he pushes his plate away, why aren't you eating? It had better be good.

You — know — I — hate — scrambled — eggs.

I don't know that at all.

I told you. Last time. I hate the skin on them.

What skin? There isn't a skin —

There is, look. And he pokes with the edge of his fork.

Eat them, boy, Mick advises softly from behind his paper.

Oh God! Nat wails, letting his head sink into his hands. I'll throw up, I'll be sick.

Don't you dare be sick! I warn him.

All this organic crap, he mutters.

It's not organic, I shriek at him. These eggs are not organic! Whatever they bloody well are, Nat says, I don't like them.

Swear again, says Mick, and you'll get no pocket money this weekend.

But, I say, my anger mounting, you don't like anything. You don't like porridge, or baked beans, or toast, or fried, poached or boiled eggs or anything except fucking processed cereal with sugar on it.

She's swearing, Nat tells his father. You don't say anything to her.

Mick ignores him.

I push Nat roughly out of the way so I can wipe the table.

Ow, he says.

What? I say.

That hurt.

I didn't touch you.

That's a lie. You did.

I look at him. My heart pounds. I would like to hurt him.

I can't eat, he says flatly.

Why not? I ask him in a calmer voice. Why can't you eat?

I have a full feeling.

And you didn't have this full feeling when you ate a whole pack of citrus Polos yesterday?

Nope, he grins. That's because Polos are nice.

And eggs aren't?

No.

He is smiling at me.

It's not funny, I say.

I'm not laughing, he says. And laughs.

Leave him, Mick says. He'll eat later. Won't you, Nat?

Nat says nothing. He doesn't say yes.

No, I say, I won't leave him and he won't eat later, he'll eat now and he'll eat what I've cooked for him even if I have to feed him like a baby.

Nat shoves the plate away again, defiant, waiting. I feel a tear, a ripping inside me. I step forward and slap him hard on the face. Hard as I can. A flat noise — a satisfying gasp from him.

He stares at me for a dazed moment then begins to cry. Good.

Trembling, I chuck the whole plate of eggs in the sink. Then, not wanting to waste it, I scoop up what I can and put it in Fletcher's bowl. The dog, alert to the sound of food, rushes up and eats it in two swift gollops.

I wish I was dead, Nat says.

Don't you ever say that.

I do. I want to be dead. It would be a relief. I really really hate you.

Go to your room, says Mick quietly.

He gets up but I don't let him go. I grab him by the shoulders.

Never say that, I yell, shaking him hard, do you hear me? Never, ever fucking well say you want to be dead!

With each word I shake him harder. He is sobbing but he does not resist. The whole thing takes only a few seconds but it feels like much longer. There is time for me to understand that he no longer feels like my child, my flesh. There's time to understand what I could do.

He's crying but he's far too shocked to hit back. If he was not so shocked, he might, he would. He's getting so big he could hurt me, I know that.

Go, I tell him. And when he doesn't move, I scream the word again.

Two pale strings of snot hang and wobble from his nose. He runs from the room. He is humiliated. So am I. I sit and I shake. I won't look at Mick. I don't have to look at him to know he isn't on my side.

Lennie's Pay & Display machine, the one where it happened, has been removed by the police. But there's another, closer to the pier itself, which is where they've put all the bouquets. Except that now most of these are dead and brown and battered by the wind — each bloom reduced to a colourless mush, each stem and frond black and dead.

Someone should remove them, I say to Mick as we stand there and look at them.

He says nothing. I glance at him, his profile, stern and tight and shut off from me in the wind. Unguessable.

How will we go on living here? I ask him.

He takes my hand. His jacket is zipped to his chin, against the wind. There's a strong breeze today. Everything that can move is moving. The sign with the boating-lake opening times on it, the grey tarpaulins pulled over the big boats, the conifers next to the phone box on Pier Avenue.

Bad things have happened nearly everywhere, he says. All the time — think about it, they must have. It's just that you don't know about them.

I say nothing.

He squeezes my hand, then puts an arm around me, pulls me to him.

Other things will happen, he says.

Will they? What things?

All sorts of things, he says. You'll see. Good things.

In her buggy, Liv is concentrating so hard on her transparent teether that her toes are curling and uncurling with the effort of it.

Don't get like this, Tess, Mick says suddenly.

I look at him, surprised by his tone of voice.

What do you mean? Like what?

He sighs.

Like this. Don't go all helpless on me —

Christ, I say, I was only being honest.

That's what you call it?

Yes. It is what I call it.

Do you think I don't feel as you do? How do you think I'm coping? We have to move on from this. We all have to. Think about the kids.

I do, I tell him as the tears creep up on me, I do think of the kids.

So, OK, he says, be serious. What are you saying? That we should leave this place? Just pack up and leave, just like that?

Not just like that —

Well, then.

I don't know, I tell him, but it's a possibility. Isn't it?

He looks away from me, his face grim.

Not for me, he says, no, it isn't.

But why not? You haven't even got a job — you've got least of all to lose, I point out.

Thanks, he says. Thanks for rubbing that one in.

I didn't mean that. I meant you're free.

Yeah? No freer than you.

I don't feel free, I say.

Livvy flings her arms up in the air and makes a noise of total happiness.

She's lost a sock, Mick says.

I glance back along the way we've come but I can't see it anywhere. It must have dropped off somewhere along North Parade.

OK, so you don't feel free. But you feel free enough to leave? Mick says.

I think about this.

If it's the right thing, then yes, I do.

Vic Munro, Dave Munro's father, comes out of the Dolphin Diner. He walks over, lighting a cigarette, hands cupped against the wind.

Terrible things happen everywhere, Mick says before he reaches us. Running from here won't solve anything. It's not the place, Tess —

What is it, then?

All right? says Vic. Mick says something back. Vic's nails are thick and yellow-grey. I look past him, past his stained down jacket and long oily hair, out at the grey and swollen chop of water that stretches beyond Covehithe. A small boat bobs out there, some way off.

They got anything yet? Vic asks us.

People still talk about Lennie's death as if it's the only subject.

Mick shrugs.

You know as much as I do.

They did house to house, or door to door, whatever, on the first day, says Vic. Everyone I know has been seen.

Mick nods.

But they won't get him now, Vic says. Not if he's gone this long they won't.

He gives a mirthless little laugh and sucks so hard on his cigarette that his cheeks cave in. His skin is a mass of tiny wrinkles, the sort of skin that would make Rosa stare in amazement. Vic was a fisherman once long ago — he even worked on the lifeboats. But then he had some kind of nervous breakdown and now he doesn't do much of anything at all except bet on the dogs or the horses and sit all day in the Dolphin Diner and drink tea with the Ramirez brothers.

He once tried to set himself up as a painter and decorator, but did such a terrible job of Barbara Anscombe's hallway that the two of them are still locked in a legal dispute over it.

Where you off to then? Vic asks, turning to me this time.

School, I say. To see our son's teacher.

Again, says Mick.

Vic grins, He's been a bad boy then?

He stubs his cigarette out on the white metal railing.

Dave was always being hauled up, you know, he says. Whole of his time in that place. I was in and out of there like a bloody jack-in-the-box. I expect they were glad to see the back of him, the bugger. Him and Darren Sims, the pair of them.

Oh I'm sure they weren't that bad, says Mick.

Oh, they were, Vic says cheerily.

Just then I catch sight of a figure on the beach — tall and straight and walking ever so slowly along the wet part of the sand where the tide licks it.

Lacey.

Quickly I look the other way, out to sea. The brown sailing dinghy has moved a long way, almost out of view towards Covehithe.

We should go, I tell Mick as I glance once more at the figure on the beach.

We say goodbye to Vic and move off up Hotson Road towards the school. I hold Mick's arm as he pushes the buggy.

You think Lennie would want us to run away? Mick says.

I don't know, I reply. I've no idea what Lennie would want.

We've been happy here.

Yes, I agree. We have.

Bob is picking at the sandwich I've made him and telling me about Alex.

He says he wants to make it himself. The coffin. That's what he's saying now.

Oh, I say. Someone else told me that as well. A patient of mine.

Well, says Bob, how the hell would a patient know?

I shrug.

It's a small place. Things get around.

Bob sighs.

Anyway, he says, I'm surprised he hasn't told you anything about it.

He doesn't tell me everything.

Bob sighs again.

Well you know, I tell him, maybe it's a good idea. I mean if he wants to. It's what he does for a living after all — he knows about wood. It does make a kind of sense.

You think so? Bob says.

Yes, I think, I do.

In fact, if I shut my eyes I can almost see him doing it. Choosing the wood and bringing it back to his barn, handling it, touching it. Sawing and mitring and glueing and machining.

Bob sighs again and looks at his sandwich. He hasn't eaten a mouthful.

He has all the necessary tools, I guess. He said something about wanting to use American red oak. I don't know that wood — do you?

He looks at me and his mouth turns down and his eyes fill up.

Oh Bob, I say, you're not keen on this idea are you?

He doesn't answer, only feels around in his jacket pocket for his pills and then, when he finds them, takes them out and stares at them.

Did I take one of these things already this morning?

You took one at eleven.

He continues to stare at the pills. His lips are shut in a tight straight line.

It's just, I was going to go along and look into it myself, you know. I never paid much towards the wedding — she had to go ahead and do it all so quickly and Maya was really so ill by then and —

I reach out and put my hand on his wrist.

I ought not to feel this way, he says.

Don't be silly, I tell him.

She's still my child, he says.

When Bob's gone off to have a rest, Rosa — who is supposed to be off school poorly — bounces in.

Hey, you look better, I tell her.

She seems to think about this.

I'm not better, she says slowly and carefully, I'm just trying to be nice that's all.

But your tummy's OK?

Kind of. It's gone into my head now.

I look hard at her, wish I could understand the ups and downs of her. She turns away from me.

What's the matter with Bob? she says.

Things are very hard for him right now, I tell her and she frowns.

If my child had been killed by a bad man, I'd hunt him down and shoot him or something. I'd want revenge.

Well, I pick Livvy's rattle up off the floor where she has

flung it, life isn't like that, Rosa. Not real life. You can't just go round killing people.

I know, I know.

Rosa sighs and blows out a puff of air so her fringe goes up. She watches the effect in the big mirror on the other side of the room and, seeming to like it, does it again. Fletcher is lying dead-dog style on the floor. He likes the cool of the lino, even in winter.

Rosa places one bare foot on him.

Hey, I say. Careful.

Rosa ignores me.

Don't put your weight on him —

He likes it, she insists, still watching herself in the mirror, He's my own personal fur rug.

She stands for a moment and sings to herself.

So, she says, is he unhappy about the coffin?

I look up, surprised.

What do you know about that?

Well, Con told me. How Alex is being really mean about it and all that.

He said that?

Mmm, Rosa sits down next to Fletcher who opens his eyes and lifts his head towards her.

Why? What did he say? In what way mean?

Well — Rosa rubs Fletcher's tummy with small brisk hands — he says they're each allowed to do a design, Con and Max, right?

I come over and sit by Rosa.

What? I say. What do you mean, a design?

You know! she says impatiently. They can each design a picture or some writing or something — it doesn't have to be a picture — to be carved on the side of it —

You mean actually on it? On the coffin?

Yeah. Only Con doesn't want to do either, not a drawing or some writing — he doesn't like drawing because he's no good at it, so he wants to stick some stickers and pictures on. Or something that he's got anyway. And he won't let him.

What, Alex won't let him?

No and I think it's really unfair.

I think it's unfair too. In fact, I think everything's unfair. I don't know what's wrong with me. I'm not the person I used to be. I can't focus on anything. Mick finds me standing at night in the garden in a black cold wind without a jumper on.

What are you doing? he calls from the porch. You'll freeze to death. Aren't you cold?

No, I say, enjoying the feel of my skin turning itself inside out, I'm not. I'm not anything.

What I am is numb, deliciously cut off and numb and unsettled. Mick would never understand — it's beyond anything he believes in. All the things that used to please me, that were a part of my good, blameless, ordinary life, are gone. I'm so impatient. Each normal thing — each school run, each family meal — has lost its sweetness and its shine and is just something to be got through. Until I can get away and be alone with these feelings.

And this isn't about Lennie, it wouldn't be right to claim that. This isn't shock or delayed grief or anything with a reasonable name. It's just, I feel I have the power to predict which way things might go. And the knowledge that just now only one thing keeps me going. The possibility, always there, that I might see him.

But I am rushing down Bank Alley having cut through Tibby's Green, late for my first appointment, my mind so filled up with him that when he materialises right bang there in front of me, I am for a second or two stunned.

Oh, he says. Hello, Tess.

I'm hot and tired and I haven't put on make-up or brushed my hair.

Oh, I say. Hello.

Hello, he says again.

You're still here then?

Yes.

His hands are in his pockets and he tilts his head back a little as he looks at me.

No baby?

It takes me a moment to realise what he's talking about.

At home, I tell him. She's with Mick. I left her. I'm — going to work.

He stands there absolutely still, frowning slightly.

So what's going on? he says. Where've you been?

Where have I been? I say, surprised.

Yes. After you phoned me, you disappeared. I've been looking all over for you.

But I've been — here, I tell him, flushing.

Where?

Here. At home, at the clinic — everywhere.

He smiles.

Outside the butcher's, there is sawdust on the pavement. In the window fake grass, brightest green — a foil for the pink and red of the meat.

Are you OK? he asks me.

Yes, I tell him. I push my hair out of my face and my heart swerves. No, not really, I'm late.

And I turn and do something I didn't think I could do. I run up the High Street, past Butlers, past Parsons' Tea Rooms and Sheila Fashions. Past Mei Yuen's and the dry-cleaner's and up to the spot where I can see the safe wooden sign for Empson's Books rocking gently in the wind.

By the time I reach the clinic, I'm already missing him. But I had no choice. I suddenly knew that if I let myself stand there on that pavement with him a moment longer, things might not remain the same. Your whole life can be changed in a single moment if you let it.

I park the car on North Road just next to the boating lake, about fifty or maybe a hundred metres from the place where Lennie died. The lake is closed for the winter, a large heavy chain and padlock draped across its wrought-iron gates. Some paddle boats are pulled up on the side of the grey, wind-rippled square of water, under the tarpaulins — the rest have probably gone to be spruced up and repaired for next year.

In front of me is the cream concrete face of the Dolphin Diner and, beyond, the long wind-lashed expanse of the pier. It has a fitness centre on it now, except that no one goes to it as far as I can tell. And next to that, the arcade with its money machines.

I sit in the car and look at the pier and think of Mawhinney and all those others slaving away to catch someone who Vic Munro thinks will never be caught.

I look at the pier for a long time, till my hands no longer know where they are or whether they're still on the steering wheel or on my lap, till I no longer remember where I am or what I'm doing or why.

I wonder if I'll see Mawhinney come out, but I don't. I see no one. I wait for a long time, till the windscreen is specked with rain, and still no one emerges from that pale concrete building.

After that, I leave the car where it is and walk along the front as far as my hut. The Polecat. It is almost dark, the sky greenish with dark, but I know the walk so well I don't need light.

It's spotting harder now with rain and because I haven't been here since that night — haven't been able to bring my-self to come — I can feel the nervy pulse of my blood in my tongue, my throat, in the hotness of the hair behind my ears.

The sea is crashing down. You can tell by the sound of it that the waves are pretty huge.

At the end of the concrete ramp, a couple of kids are

forlornly skateboarding, but otherwise no one's around, just the waves making a tearing sound as they hit the groynes. Soon their darkness will join up and melt into the dark of the sky. I love that moment when you can't see what's what any more and sea and sky are one.

The key to The Polecat is in my pocket. It's a normal key, small and steel, the type that would open a shed or cupboard. I put my foot on the second wooden step of the hut and shove the key into the lock and at first it won't turn but then I push a little harder and it does, it gives.

The door falls open. I stand there in my hut and breathe in hard, enjoy its familiar smell of slightly damp curtains, wood preservative and the faintest, blueish whiff of gas.

Later, back home, I climb the stairs and I look at Livvy, asleep in her cot. I stand there and wonder what I'm doing. Panic builds in me. I don't recognise the person I've become. I stand there and I hold my fingers up to my eyes, ready to wipe the tears before they even come.

The hanging of the Annual Art Circle Exhibition at the old school gym is something that Lennie usually organises. It's not really about the art — tepid purplish watercolours of the area, the ferry, the fat silhouette of Blythburgh church, the creek at dawn — but about the spirit of community. There are some dedicated amateur painters in our town. All the paintings and drawings are for sale, with a percentage of the proceeds going to charity. Harriman's always donates the wine for the private view.

Everyone has agreed that this year the exhibition will be dedicated to her memory. Some people considered that it should actually be cancelled, but Polly and Maggie insisted that Lennie would have wanted them to go ahead. They say they intend to make it the best yet. They're roping in everyone they can find to help with the hanging.

I call Mick and tell him I'm dropping Liv back after work so I can go and help.

At the gym? he says. But I thought you were going to get out of it?

I was, I tell him, but I've thought about it and it wouldn't be right.

I put down the phone and breathe in the silence.

I don't go there. I hurry instead down Stradbroke Road, where a man is smoking a cigarette with one hand and sweeping crab apples into the gutter with the other. Further on, by the lighthouse, some oldish women are standing on the corner with their PVC shoppers. One of them, Mrs McGowan, is a patient. She waves and I wave back.

I turn quickly onto St James's Green. It's dusk and a brisk wind ruffles the surface of the sea. Alan the greengrocer is just closing, pulling in his awning, dragging in the crates and buckets, folding the cloth that looks like bright green grass. A brightly coloured poster in his window announces that he stocks fireworks. It will probably stay there till Christmas — everything does in this town. As I pass, Alan looks up and raises a hand to me. I do the same and hurry on.

Chapter 11

IN THE HOTEL RECEPTION, A GIRL WITH FIERCELY PULLED-back hair is chatting on the phone, pretending she hasn't seen me waiting there. I ask her if Lacey is in. She shrugs.

No idea, she says. I haven't seen him go out.

So he's in?

Unless I wasn't looking at the time.

I ask her if she'd mind calling him. She asks rudely for my name and I tell her.

He says to go on up, says the girl, with no expression at all on her face. Straightaway picking up the other phone to carry on talking. I start up the wide, hushed staircase then have to come back because I don't know his room number.

Four, the girl snaps.

Up on the first floor, a chambermaid is hoovering the

landing. I think I recognise her. She may have babysat for one of us. She moves the hoover out of the way as I knock on his door.

He doesn't have a jacket on. Just a kind of dark shirt with a blueish T-shirt under. He hasn't shaved either.

Hello, he says.

Hello.

I can't look at him. I hold on to my handbag and touch the buttons on my coat and look at the room.

What a surprise, he says.

He offers me the only chair, pulling it out from the girlish, glass-topped dressing table. I sit. Next to me are small careful piles of his loose change.

This is awful of me, I say.

He looks at me with relaxed interest.

Why?

I mean, just barging in like this.

Barge in any time, he says with a bit of a smile.

Yes, I say, but unannounced.

They rang me, he says, from reception.

Oh look, I tell him, you know what I mean.

He has nothing to say to that. He asks me if I want a drink.

I look at my watch. Though I know what time it is.

OK, I say.

He opens the minibar.

Gin, whisky or vodka?

Vodka.

He pours it carefully, hands me a glass.

I take a sip. The taste is blue, metallic.

Do you want something in it?

He passes me a tonic.

Thanks. I pull back the tab and tip it in, watching the quick fizz.

I can smell cooking and bar smells from downstairs. He holds up his drink and looks at me. Far away a phone rings. He keeps looking as if he's about to laugh.

Well — cheers, he says.

I smile. And dare to look around. The place is very neat. You wouldn't think a person was even staying in it. As well as the change piled on the table, there's a wad of folded notes. A large notebook, a couple of pens. A laptop computer. A jacket, his one, flung on a chair. And a towel. A pair of boots pushed carefully under the TV. And a faint, enticing smell in the air — a smell of him.

He moves a newspaper and sits there on the neat, oatmeal corner of the bed and looks at me. He doesn't seem to feel any need to speak. The silence spills over between us and terrifies me.

You like your room? I ask him.

It's OK, he says. Apart from the noise of the bloody barrels.

What?

First thing in the morning. They start trundling them around, or unloading them or something. You should hear it. Before six it starts, the noise is incredible —

It's the brewery, I point out.

Yes, he says, looking at me.

I sip my drink, feel it pounce into my heart.

Tell me about Natasha, I say then, surprising myself.

He looks up quickly.

Natasha?

Yes, I say. Tell me what she's like.

I feel my cheeks get hot.

You're blushing, Tess, he says.

I laugh. For once I don't care.

I always blush, I tell him, with you. You know that. You should be used to it by now.

He bites his lip.

I can't get used to anything about you, he says quietly.

No? I hold my breath.

No.

Well, I say softly, I don't know. Is that good?

I don't know either, he says to me. It might be. It might not.

For a moment we're both silent. He puts down his drink.

There's not much to say about Natasha, he says. I mean, I don't know what you want to know. We go right back, I've known her years.

What does she do?

He looks at me.

She's a solicitor.

In London?

In London, yes. She does other things as well. She works with children, as a volunteer. Counselling and stuff.

She does a lot, I say.

Yes, he agrees. She does.

She sounds nice.

She is, yes.

He looks at me, waiting. We both wait and say nothing. I wonder what she looks like. How old she is. Whether he's spoken to her today. What he said.

So, I ask him, do you like it here?

This town?

I nod.

Not much, he says.

Really? Why not?

He shrugs.

It puts me on edge, he says. Too much water, too much sky.

But I love that! I tell him straightaway before I can stop myself.

Well, I know you do, he says, obviously. That's why you moved here. But I'm a city boy. I like buildings, people, mess, dirt.

I used to like that, too, I tell him.

But not any more?

No. I don't think so, no.

He smiles at me.

And Natasha? I say.

What about Natasha?

Does she like that, too?

His face when he looks at me is unchanged.

She does, I suppose, yes.

I look down at my drink.

I don't live with Natasha, he says.

Oh, I say. You don't?

No.

The windowpane has turned black and outside in the street there are noises now — evening noises that I suppose I must be used to because I hear them all the time. Except not normally from up here.

I hear the heavy, clanking sound of the security grille of the Amber Shop. A lorry backing up. A child's shrill complaint, wanting something. A lone bicycle bell. Ding ding.

I don't think of my own children. I've never been so far from them. For now, they're little specks, they're nothing, they don't exist. If I ever wanted to shock myself, this would be the moment and this would be the way.

Tell me something, he says as he leans over to pour me the rest of the vodka. Why did you run away from me?

I make an effort to sit up on the chair, cross my legs the other way.

What? I say.

The other day. In the street. You ran away.

Did I?

Yes. You know you did.

I put down my glass and knit my fingers together and sigh.

I did, I agree, yes, I'm sorry.

No need to be sorry.

Well, I am.

Why?

Because it was rude —

No. Why did you do it?

I think about this.

Oh, well, I was scared, I tell him at last.

He looks at me closely, as if it can't be true.

Really?

Yes. I think so.

What, scared of me?

No, I say, struggling to get it right, not of you, just —
well — I didn't know what was going to happen.

In what way happen?

I glance up and my heart bumps. I can't say it.

I can't say it, I whisper.

He is sitting on the edge of the bed and he reaches out
and touches my hand, the one that is on the table, the one
without the glass. Just touches it. The touch — warm, terrifying — makes me breathless. I don't look at him. My heart
flips over.

And do you know now? he says.

Know what?

Do you know — what's going to happen?

No, I say. Leaving my hand there, looking at it.

No? You don't know?

I take a breath and look at the window again. Shut my
eyes. I daren't even think about it, I say.

The moments pass. Nothing happens. I take my hand
back and put it in my lap. Safe.

Why did you do that? I ask him.

Oh Tess, he says, don't ask me that —

He leans forward from where he sits on the bed, but he doesn't touch me.

Tess, he says.

Yes?

You came to see me, he says.

I shouldn't have. I'm sorry. I didn't think, I just did it without even thinking —

But I love that! he says. The way you just do things — so frank. I mean it. That's what I liked about you from the start.

I'm not frank, I tell him, looking at him now. I'm not being frank with Mick. I'm only frank when it suits me to be.

You're lovely, Lacey says quietly.

I close my eyes.

I shouldn't be sitting here, I tell him.

It's easy to say that.

Is it?

You're lovely, he says again.

Well, I tell him, it's easy to say that too —

Not for me.

It's wonderful that you think it — I mean, it's exactly what I want you to think — but I also think I'm misleading you.

Oh? he says.

I mean, I don't really want anything to — happen.

You don't?

He is looking at my face all the time.

I'm sorry, I tell him, I really shouldn't have come. You see, it's — I'm waiting.

Waiting?

To get used to you. For this to wear off.

For what to wear off?

This thing — this —

He smiles, waits.

This pull, I say.

He sits back and gives me a long look.

Do you feel it, too? I ask him.

Yes, he says, I feel it.

I just want to be your friend, I tell him and he smiles
again even more.

Me too, he says.

This feeling. It will pass. I know it will. In the end you'll
just seem ordinary to me.

Oh, he says, sounding disappointed. Will I?

Yes, eventually.

He seems to consider this.

But, hey, look, what if I don't?

No, I tell him firmly, that's why I'm here, if you want to
know. To make it happen —

It?

Make me used to you —

But, he says, not laughing now, how do you know,
Tess, that it works like that?

I just know.

You know a lot of things.

Yes, I agree, I do. I told you I did. But please don't
touch me.

He lies back on the bed with his drink. He does exactly
as I ask, I'll give him that. He doesn't touch me or come

near. But he might as well not bother to do this distance-keeping. Because the truth is he has found a place in me that no one else has ever discovered — not Alex, not Mick — and he's there right now and it makes me go absolutely still and calm, hypnotised.

I don't tell him this.

Talk to me, he says. He is a little drunk. So am I. The room has become both larger and smaller, our place in it more tilted and strange. Amazing how drink stops you minding about things.

I ask him if he likes his work. He hesitates.

I keep on telling myself I'll stop, he says, that this will be the last one. Then something else comes up — and I worry about why I'm doing it.

What do you mean worry?

Well, each new case, the details of it, the people, it takes a piece of you. You get sucked into people's lives —

Is that bad?

Not bad exactly, but taxing. Difficult.

He looks at me and smiles, such a warm smile.

I told you before — you get too involved. It can be sort of — hard to resist.

Because you're good at it?

No, he says, because it's too interesting, too exciting. Whether you want it to or not it gives you a buzz.

He looks at me.

Yes, even something like this, he says. Does that shock you?

No, I reply, wondering whether I mean it.

It should, you know — it's not a good thing. You get habituated. That's not healthy.

I shrug and the room tips a little.

Lots of things aren't healthy, I tell him.

Your job is, he says. The job you do is healthy.

I try to think about my job, but in my head it dwindles and slips away from me.

It's all I can do. I've never thought about it like that.

Yes, but do you like it? Does it give you a buzz?

I laugh.

I can cure babies of colic and make them sleep all night. I can make old people walk more comfortably. I can take pain away.

He stares at me.

That's wonderful. It's just what I would expect you to be able to do.

Would you? I ask him.

Yes, he says. You're an angel. I thought that from the start. There's something boundlessly good and true about you.

I laugh.

Boundlessly good and true? I like that!

No, he says and his face is suddenly serious, there is. I mean it. I wouldn't say it otherwise.

In the end I begin to cry.

What? he says. What is it?

Nothing, I tell him. Just — I may be drunk.

He gets up and moves over to me. It only seems to take a second, too little time to stop him.

It's your fault, I tell him.

What is?

All of it.

His hands are on me, on my shoulders, but I pull back.

Tell me, he says. What's made you cry?

I ought to go, I tell him and I put down my glass and reach for my coat. He looks at me.

You know something? he says.

What?

No. Forget it. I was going to say a bad thing.

Don't, I tell him, suddenly wanting more than anything for him to say it.

OK, I won't. But look, tell me something. Is it working?

Is what working?

This thing of ours — is it wearing off?

I glance at his face.

I don't know, I say as I pull on my coat. It may take a little while.

He says nothing. He just lies back on the bed and smiles.

Will I see you again? he says, and when I don't answer he doesn't look at all surprised, just goes on smiling.

I can't lie to Mick. I tell him half of the truth. A version anyway. That I ran into Lacey and had a drink with him. That's where I've been. Yes, really. All of this time.

A drink?

Well, two.

He stares at me blankly from the sofa where Livvy is lying, cranky and fidgety, across his lap.

But what about the exhibition?

Oh, I say as casually as I can, they had enough people. More than enough. They were fine.

He stays looking at me and saying nothing.

What? I say.

More than two drinks, he says.

No, I chuck my coat at the chair but I miss and it slithers off onto the floor. I pick it up again. It's just — I'm not used to it.

It's true. I haven't drunk properly since Liv was born.

He says nothing. He looks at the TV, then back at me.

This baby's very hungry, he says at last.

I know, I tell him because my breasts are bursting.

You think you should feed her when you've been drinking?

I shut my eyes.

I have to — now. But OK maybe we should start trying her on formula.

He makes a face of surprise.

I thought you wanted to carry on as long as possible?

I do.

Well, then.

He stands up, hands her to me. Livvy's eyes gleam at the sight of my face.

My head aches. As she gasps and closes her mouth over my nipple, fixing me with her hot black eyes, Mick goes to the kitchen and returns with a glass of water. Passes it to me. In silence.

Thanks.

I put my finger into Livvy's small, proffered fist. She re-leases the nipple a second to register pleasure, takes a quick breath, latches on again. How could I be late for this child?

Mick sits down in the armchair, watches the TV, then watches me. Eventually he flicks the TV off.

So. What did you talk about? he says. I feel a rush of sympathy for him.

What? With Lacey?

Of course with Lacey.

Not a lot.

Come on, Tess —

Oh, you know, all sorts of things, I tell him vaguely.

It's nearly the truth. When I think back, there are no words I can grasp.

Stuff about his work, I tell Mick.

Fair enough, he says, and what are you doing now?

I'll feed Liv and maybe watch the telly a bit, I say. And then go to bed.

Fine, he says and gets up.

Where are you going?

Bed. I'm skipping the TV part. I've done that. Turn off the kitchen light before you come upstairs, he says.

I change Liv and put a clean sleepsuit on her and lay her gently in her cot. I wind up her mobile, the one that takes a full seven minutes to run down.

Normally this would send her off, but tonight she barely

needs it, she's ready to sleep. Maybe it's because she had a chance to get properly hungry, because I wasn't on tap for once.

Anyway her eyes flutter open briefly and then shut again. Her thumb is jammed in her mouth, the cuff of her sleepsuit pulled up over it, her fat cheek moving furiously as she sucks. If we're lucky, she might not wake now for a whole six hours.

In the bedroom, Mick looks asleep, the duvet pulled up right over his head and only the top of his black hair poking out.

I take off all my clothes then go to the drawer on the landing and pull out the boned and buttoned and strappy thing in violet lace that Mick bought for me before I got pregnant with Liv, in the days when I still had a body and knew what to do with it. A piece of underwear, I don't remember what you call them — half alive it seems now as I turn it over and around in the thick, drunk half-light and try to remember how it goes on.

Hooks and eyes, maybe twenty pairs of them. You do them up in front of you and then when they're done, you twist the whole thing round. I hold my breath, feel the lace rub on my skin. Then push my two breasts, tired and empty of milk now, into the funny, strapless cups.

I try not to look in the mirror. Instead I go back in the bedroom and sit on Mick. He makes a small sleeping noise and then he half wakes up.

What? he says. Tess, for fuck's sake, what're you doing?

I turn off the light, kiss him as if I mean it.

Sex.

What?

I thought we could do it.

I think at first that he's going to resist but then I feel it —
him moving under me — and I think how I'd forgotten how
easy it all is. So easy if you just don't think about it first. He
touches the tops of my breasts, the place where the flesh is
crammed in and jiggly. Then he slows and hesitates.

No, he says.

What?

You're drunk.

I'm not.

I know you are.

Not any more.

OK. Then come here, come and kiss me first.

I tell him I don't want that, I just want to do it.

He lets his hands fall back on the bed.

I want you to be aroused, he says.

I am — I am aroused.

He sighs and puts a hand between my legs.

Wet me, I tell him. Go on — do it. Spit on your fingers.

But he doesn't. Instead he kisses me — a small, snappy
kiss on the inside of my arm. It's not enough.

I bend my mouth to his ear, smell the warm sleep and
skin smell of it.

Hit me, I suggest in a whisper. Hit me if you want.

He touches my mouth.

No, he says, in a voice thick with the beginnings of desire, I don't want.

I want you to do things, I tell him.

Come here, he says. Let me get you wet properly.

No.

I want you to enjoy it too, he says again, moving his fingers over my thighs, trying to put his tongue on any part of me he can reach.

Fed up of trying, I sit and put my hands on his bare chest and I wriggle on him and try to stuff him into me. But it won't go, it just bends, only half stiff. He pulls me off at last and sits up.

Ow. Stop it. What are you doing?

I don't know, I tell him truthfully. I notice in a distant kind of way that my eyes are closed.

I don't know either.

He sounds hurt. As he speaks I feel his hardness sliding away. He gives a long sigh and reaches for his watch and tips the face to read it.

I don't know what's the matter with you, he says. I can't begin to work out what the matter is. Don't you want me any more? Is there something else you want?

I lie down in silence, arms folded on my chest like a stone person on a tomb.

Is there?

I close my eyes. The world tilts. I'm spilling out of it.

Is there something or someone else? he asks me again, and as he says the words, I try to listen, try to ask myself the same question, Is there?

Speak to me, Tess, he says as sleep comes up and punches me in the face.

In the morning, the garment is somehow off me, down by the side of the bed. Downstairs I can hear the sound of the TV and, above it, the children shouting. My head hurts and my throat is sore. Mick brings me coffee.

Last night, he says, a weird thing happened.

I know, I say.

He doesn't seem angry any more. He sits there on the edge of the bed in his old saggy jeans.

No, he says, not that. I mean while you were out.

I'm sorry, I tell him.

He ignores me.

Well, at about six or six thirty, the dog went crazy — barking furiously as if there was someone there — and when I went down, there was no one. But the back door was open —

I sit up.

My God, Mick, I say, but who'd have opened it? Were the kids downstairs?

Well, he says, it could have been anything — the wind, or maybe it wasn't properly shut in the first place —

It shouldn't open on its own like that.

No, he agrees, but listen. That's not all. Fletcher was really going berserk, you know, running in and out and growling and growling —

Someone was there?

No. But I could hear the sound of talking. Just a very

low, quiet voice, barely audible — and then I realised Jordan was in the room and he looked like he'd been crying and I asked him what was the matter and who had opened the door and he wouldn't tell me.

My heart goes cold.

It wasn't Bob? You're sure Bob hadn't just popped round and forgotten to close it or something?

No. It wasn't Bob. In fact Jordan said it was Rosa who'd opened it. So I called her down and I could tell by her face that she knew what was going on, so I assumed he was telling the truth. And then I got quite cross — and guess what she told me?

I stare at him and shake my head.

She said that Lennie had done it.

I take a sharp breath.

What?

She said that she and Jordan keep on seeing her.

Panic squeezes my heart.

I don't —

Mick looks calmly at me, watching my face.

Just that. That's what she said.

But — I put my coffee cup down — seeing Lennie? What do they mean, seeing? Mick —?

She said they keep on seeing Lennie and she keeps on telling them things.

Oh God no, I say. What sort of things?

He laughs suddenly.

Tess, he says, look at you. You look petrified. You don't believe it, do you?

But —

Come on, he says, it's one of Rosa's funny stories. Except it's not funny — she's scaring Jordan. I told her so. I'm not having it. It took a while to calm him down.

Jordan's seen her too?

Mick sighs.

He says he has. Christ, please don't get in a state about it, Tess. Or I wouldn't have told you. It's a game, clearly.

I say nothing.

It's perfectly natural. It's a child's game, a way of dealing with a terrible situation. The only slightly worrying thing is the door.

But — I thought it was Rosa?

No, I told you, Jordan said it was her, but she denied it. She swore she'd been nowhere near it. And for some reason I believe her.

But someone opened it.

He frowns.

The wind? There's no other explanation.

But — you're just going to leave it? Aren't you worried?

He thinks about this.

I don't know, he says. Are you?

Suddenly his face collapses and he looks a little tired. He looks at me.

At least I was sober, he says. Christ, at least I was bloody well here.

Chapter 12

ALEX HAS NEARLY FINISHED THE COFFIN. IT LIES ON THE workbench in the draughty outhouse where he works — a huge, sleek thing, carved out of the reddest wood I've ever seen.

He watches me look at it.

Well?

I shiver.

It's beautiful, I say, it's very — big.

Yes, he says softly. Yes, I wanted it big.

He waits, clearly expecting more.

I like how the sides are curved, I say. It looks like it's been blown from inside —

That's the wood. It's the best stuff to work with — you can do just about anything with it.

I run my fingers over it. It feels warm.

Expensive, he adds, and hard to get hold of.

It's lovely, I say.

He tells me that both boys helped him polish it.

They wanted to, he adds quickly as if I might have doubted it.

Rosa comes in. Stops when she sees it.

Is that —?

For her, I say quickly, yes.

She frowns.

It looks more like a bath.

Alex smiles.

Oh well, he says, fine. That's OK. I think that's cool.

Rosa gives him one of her looks.

Rosa — I take her firmly by the shoulders — shush. Go out. Find Jordan — go on, I mean it. Out.

Alex pays no attention.

And look, he says, touching my arm, have you seen?

He shows me where he's sanded a small area on the side and the boys have drawn pictures. Even Connor. A pirate with strange bobbly feet, waving a flag saying Mum. Max has carved his name and a long and steady row of kisses.

He wouldn't do a picture, Alex says. I left him alone and that's what he did — one kiss is for every year he knew her, that's what he said.

We stand there for a few moments. He wipes his hands on his jeans. So, he says, how's things?

All right.

Still seeing Lacey?

I flush.

What do you mean?

He smiles.

Al, I say, for God's sake.

I'm sorry, he says, keeping his eyes on me. But look here, don't you ever think of Mick?

He slides a cigarette from a pack on the bench and lights it.

What do you mean, think of Mick?

He says you got drunk. You and him.

I sit down on the bench.

He told you that?

Yes. It's funny because he said nothing to me about it.

Who? Who said nothing?

Lacey.

Why would he?

No, he says in a colder voice, I suppose you're right. Why would he?

I look at him, standing by the empty coffin, smoking and waiting.

So is it true?

I look at his cigarette.

Give me some of that, I say.

He passes it.

Is it true? he asks me again louder.

Yes, OK, we had a drink. So?

He smiles and says nothing.

We both look at the coffin.

All we need now, he says, is to get her back —

I stare at him.

Her body, he says, to go in it.

Ah.

You know, the undertakers recommended I put some kind of upholstery in it.

Really? I say, enjoying the dirt-taste of smoke in my mouth.

Oh you know — they're so conservative these people, wanting to do things in a certain way. I'll have that back now, he says about the cigarette. You shouldn't smoke you know.

Neither should you, I say. Handing it back.

He takes it. His fingers are filthy, the nails yellow.

No, he says, but you really shouldn't. I'm expendable.

What a ridiculous thing to say. Your boys need you.

He looks at me.

They needed their mother, too.

You know what I mean.

He sighs a long sigh and stubs out the cigarette.

There, he says, OK?

Ignore them, I tell him, the undertakers — you don't have to do as they say.

Oh I did. I am. I told them — it's only going to be bunged in the ground for fuck's sake —

Quite.

He smiles.

But then I went one better, he says. I told them I'd make my own lining anyway. And do you know what I'm using?

I shake my head.

Con's old baby sheet. The flannel one he used to drag round when he was little —

I swallow.

The one he had to take with him everywhere, remember? You've still got that?

Upstairs in a chest. Lennie must have put it away for, well, I don't know for what.

It's not something you'd throw away, I tell him quietly.

Women, he says. Typical Lennie. I mean, I wouldn't have kept it.

I shake my head.

But it's come in useful now, he says.

But is it big enough? I ask him. It's not very big, surely?

He laughs.

Do you think she'll mind what the fuck size it is?

No.

He passes me a roll of kitchen towel and I wipe my eyes, blow my nose.

I don't understand you, he says at last.

What? What don't you understand?

You were always there for me, my best friend, I could say anything to you.

Al, I say.

And then —

No. Don't do this.

Lennie dies and —

Al —

You stop loving me. Just like that.

I say nothing.

I'm serious. I really don't understand it, he says.

It's not like that —

Well what is it like? Tell me, Tess, I really need to know. What happened?

What happened to what?

To us.

Nothing, I say, nothing happened.

I'm squatting by the freezer, trying to pull out two frozen pizzas without spilling ice and peas everywhere, when the phone rings. Fletcher nudges at me and I push him away.

I hear Mick talking for a moment, then he comes in and hands the phone to me.

For you.

I take it and feel him watching my face. Fletcher tries to poke his nose in the freezer.

Oi, says Mick and grabs his collar.

Good news, Lacey says, I just told Mick. They reckon they'll release the body within maybe ten days —

Oh — I turn my face to the cold blank square of the window — that's good.

I mean, they haven't named a day, but they reckon it's safe for Alex to make arrangements.

Arrangements?

For the funeral.

I take a quick breath.

Oh God, I say, I can't believe it.

I know.

I'm silent for a moment.

It'll be tough, Lacey says, especially for the kids. I mean now, after all this, to see her buried.

He wants that? Not cremation?

Yeah. I just don't think he wants anything further done — to her —

He pauses and I hear his breath.

And you, he says more quietly, are you OK?

Oh yes, I say as brightly as I can. Fine, we're all fine.

I meant you.

Yes.

You knew I meant that?

Yes, I say again.

Mick looks at me.

Yes, thanks, I say again.

Mick gets the airline to extend Bob's ticket, for reasons of compassion, though a small supplement has to be paid. Which Mick says is totally out of order — he'll probably write and complain when all of this is over. He says this, but we both know he won't. He doesn't let Bob know about the supplement of course. Bob phones his neighbour who says he is only too happy to take care of the dogs.

The boys won't recognise me when I go back, Bob says sadly. I'll be a stranger to them.

He shows Jordan a photo — two hefty, elderly chocolate Labs gazing at the camera from a driveway strewn with golden leaves and pine cones.

Give them lots of treats, Jordan advises. Spoil them. Mum and Dad always bring us something if they go away.

What do you mean if we go away? says Mick. We never go anywhere.

You did once, Jordan says. You went to London.

Oh, says Mick, yeah. For one night.

Get them some treats, says Jordan again and he goes over to Bob and puts a hand on his knee. Bob acts like it's perfectly normal to be touched this way but you can see he likes it. He picks up the small, grubby hand and holds it in his own. Jordan leans against him.

Aha, he says, but I have to be careful of their teeth. And their weight, you see. Too many treats and the goddamn doctors would be onto them just as they are onto me —

You should never give a dog chocolate, Jordan says. Not human chocolate —

Is that so? Bob says. Well, I must say I didn't know that. Where did you hear that, boy?

On the internet, Jordan says. You can find out all sorts of stuff on the internet, like do you know what the word for a girl dog is?

That's enough, Jordan, says Mick, but it's OK, Bob is already laughing.

Normally plots at St Margaret's are expensive and extremely hard to come by, but Canon Cleve has somehow managed to get Lennie a place. She's going to be buried on the west side, not far from the ancient yew whose dense black branches spread into the playground on Tibby's Green.

Rosa seems exceptionally pleased. That yew is her favourite tree.

I once left something extremely precious in it, she says, and when I came back it was still there. After a whole week!

Really?

Yes — she looks triumphant — it's the tree. It has these powers —

Powers?

She smiles.

You wouldn't understand. But basically it looked after the thing for me.

Great, I say. So what was it? What did you leave?

My lucky stone, she says; the one with a hole in it. I left it in the hidey-hole. Lennie knows which one.

She talks about her in the present tense, I tell Mick later, as if she's not gone at all.

I know, he says. I've heard.

But — isn't it weird? Why's she doing it? Do you think it's OK?

It's a habit she's got into. Once the funeral's over, maybe that will change things.

Maybe, I say.

Everything's weird at the moment, he says. This is such a weird time — a time of nothing happening. Nothing and everything.

I look at him in surprise.

What? he says.

Nothing. Just — you're right. I know what you mean.

The best thing, I overhear Rosa telling Jordan in the bathroom that evening as he cleans his teeth, is she can see the playground from there. There'll be stuff to watch, she won't be lonely.

Out on the landing, I stop and listen.

Jordan says something I can't hear because his mouth is full of toothpaste.

And the tree will shelter her, Rosa adds with some authority. It's always good, you see, to be under a tree.

I go into the bathroom. Rosa is standing naked except for her knickers, school clothes strewn around her on the floor.

She won't actually be buried under the tree, darling, I tell her. Not right beneath it anyway.

Rosa's face falls. Jordan looks at me carefully and then at her.

Oh? But why not?

You can't dig under an old tree. Think about it. There are all these big roots and they spread a long way.

Rosa shoves her hand in her knickers and glances in an agitated way at Jordan. Jordan spits in the bowl and glances back at her. For a moment they don't look like my kids at all.

What? I ask them. What's the matter with you two? What is it?

Rosa is already shutting off from me, staring away out the window. But Jordan wipes his mouth on a towel and turns to me.

She says under it.

What? Who? Who says under it?

Rosa turns from the window and takes off her knickers, then flings them in the laundry basket as if she's scoring a goal.

Shut up, she says to Jordan. He's just being stupid, she explains. The thing is, we just want her to be buried in a happy place, that's all.

She smiles at me in a cheery way. As if I'm stupid.

She will be, I tell her. I swear to you, she will be.

Rosa shrugs. But Jordan gazes at me and I hate how tired and grey his face is.

You're a tired boy, I tell him and I hold out my arms and he comes.

Do I have to have a bath? Rosa asks. She bounces a couple of times in front of the mirror, watches the budding pouches of fat on her nipples jiggle up and down, watching us, too.

Not if you think you're clean. I nestle Jordan on my lap even though he is too big.

I am clean.

Then don't have one.

You don't mind?

Not really. Not today.

Rosa looks pleased with herself.

But will we go to the funeral? Jordan asks me.

I look at his face.

Do you want to?

Yes, says Rosa quickly. Of course! Yes!

And you, I ask Jordan, do you?

Yes, he says.

Then of course you will, I tell them. If you want to.

Mawhinney clears a space for me to sit down. He looks pleased to see me.

Just the person, he says.

He takes an armful of papers and moves them out of the way — and then the files and dirty coffee mugs. The room is more chaotic and untidy than when I last came here.

Sorry, he says, indicating the mess. We're getting sick of this makeshift office.

I don't blame you, I tell him.

Through the window, it's a bright day, the sea rough and striped with sun.

I say no to his offer of coffee.

Look, I tell him, there's something I left out, when you first came and talked to us. A small thing, or I thought it was. But I realise I should have told you — even though I shouldn't think it will change anything —

Oh? Mawhinney looks at me pleasantly.

I'm really sorry, I tell him. In fact I'm embarrassed.

He smiles.

It's this, I say. I have a beach hut on the front. I've had it for years —

Oh lucky you, he says quickly. They're great, those beach huts.

I look at him, try to smile.

And hard to come by, he adds.

Well, yes.

I stop a moment. He picks a paper clip up off the desk, smiles cryptically. Why do I feel he's playing with me?

Suddenly, he tips his head back and laughs. Then he leans forward and touches my arm.

It's OK, he says. It's just — I'm sorry, I've just spoken to Alex.

What?

I think I know what you're going to say.

Really?

He just told me —

I stare at him.

Alex? Told you what?

I'm glad you've come in. I was about to come and talk to you myself.

I don't understand, I say. What's he told you?

That you were there in the hut that night. You and Alex. That you saw Darren —

Darren? Sorry — what — Darren?

Isn't that what you were going to tell me?

Yes, I say. Well, no. I mean yes about the hut. But no, we never saw Darren.

You can see this foxes him. He puts down the paper clip he's been fiddling with and looks at me, perplexed.

Darren Sims?

No. Definitely not.

He says you did.

Alex said that?

Well, yes.

Well, I didn't.

You're sure of that?

Absolutely. I never saw Darren, I tell him, definitely not. I don't know when Alex could have seen him either. I mean we were together all that time.

Now Mawhinney looks displeased.

He told me he saw him outside, he says. That he was outside the hut hanging around as he left.

Well, I say, shaking my head, he never told me —

I have to say, Mawhinney points out stiffly, that this is quite important. I can't go into details but we have stuff on Darren. One or two possibly crucial things.

I try to laugh.

But Darren didn't have anything to do with all this.

Mawhinney looks at me sharply.

I can't discuss it with you I'm afraid, he says, but I do need to know whether you saw him —

Well, I didn't.

He folds his arms and looks at the clock.

Would you sign a statement to that effect?

Yes, I tell him. Yes, of course I would.

Lennie's funeral is finally fixed for next Friday at two. Before then the church has got to be swept and waxed and polished. Rosa and I go along after school to help, taking Livvy with us.

Polly's in charge of the flowers. She's getting them in specially from Yoxford. Which has annoyed Lyn Hewitt, the florist from Winton's. White lilies and Michaelmas daisies.

The lilies have got to be cut as late as possible on the Wednesday in the hope that they'll stay fresh till the Friday.

They won't, Lyn tells Barbara Anscombe, who relays the information back to Polly. They'll be brown around the edges by the start of Friday, you'll see.

Liv is cutting a tooth and very scratchy, needing to be held all the time, but Rosa's very good and helpful. She goes around with a soft yellow duster and does the back of every pew with Pledge and then collects up the kneelers to give them a good dust-bashing out in the porch.

Everyone notices how helpful she is.

I wish she could be like that always, I tell Polly. Or at least more of the time. I'd settle for that.

Oh, she's a good girl, Ellie Penniston says. Reminds me of my niece at the same age, such a lovely girl. She died too, you know, asthma attack.

I'm not dead! Rosa shouts from the porch.

She carries five kneelers at a time back into the church, struggling under the weight. Then she trails a duster over the walnut chest by the altar.

Not you, darling, I tell her. She means Lennie.

Livvy starts to cry. I scoop her up.

Does everyone know someone who is dead, do you think? Rosa asks me as we stand and pile up the hymn books and prayer books and watch the pale band of sun slip through the plain glass of the altar window.

Not everyone, I tell her, but many people, I suppose, yes.

Maggie sees us and comes over and gives me a hug. She says she's glad the funeral's happening at long last.

It's like everything's been on hold for so long, she says. I feel we just need to let go and say goodbye.

Rosa stares at her but no one notices.

I don't know, says Polly who's sitting in the choir stalls, going through the rota. I just don't know if I can face it all again. Just when life was finally getting back to normal. It sounds selfish, but I feel I've had enough grief to last me a lifetime.

If only they'd caught him, Sally says. You know they've been talking to Darren Sims again?

No, I say, I didn't know that.

Why are they talking to Darren Sims? Rosa asks me. Do they think he's the murderer?

Of course not, I tell her. It's too grown up to explain.

In my arms Liv has fallen asleep. Her weight hurts my shoulders. I ask Rosa to get the buggy from where we left it at the back of the pews. Liv's cheeks are scarlet and a glittery rope of dribble runs from the corner of her mouth to the bib around her neck.

As I lay her in the buggy she startles and her fingers fly up and grab at a handful of air.

Alex is opening a can of beans. The kitchen smells of burnt toast. Washing-up is piled in the sink and about a week's worth of papers are on the table. He is trying hard to be a father on his own.

I don't allow myself to feel pity, not today. I ignore the mess and pull out a chair, move a bunch of dirty dish towels off it and sit down.

Hey, he says, that's Lacey's chair.

I look at him.

Joke, he says.

I keep my eyes on him.

I went to see Mawhinney, I tell him.

He looks at me coolly. Oh?

Yes, I tell him.

And?

And I don't understand —

Don't understand what? He turns down the gas under the pan.

All this stuff I find you've been telling him.

He frowns and pulls the toast out from under the grill. Turns it over just in time.

Really? What stuff?

Yes. Really, Al.

What do you mean, Tess? What stuff?

That we saw Darren Sims. Hanging around The Polecat. Is that what you told him?

Oh that, he says vaguely, yeah, well I probably did.

Probably?

OK. Definitely did.

He gives a little laugh.

Why?

He leans against the counter and looks at me.

Well, he says, slowly as if I'm a little stupid, because I did see him, believe it or not.

And me? You told him I did too?

I don't recall. Maybe. I might've said 'we'?

You did.

Ah —

According to him you did.

He says nothing, stirs the beans. The back door opens and shuts.

Now that really is Lacey, he says.

But I don't turn around. I don't do anything. Behind me, I feel him come in.

Tess is just interrogating me, Alex tells him.

Lacey doesn't say anything. I turn and look at him. He is standing there holding his keys and a bunch of papers. Something inside me tightens, curves. I turn back to Alex.

So did you? I ask him.

Did I what?

Did you really see Darren that night?

Alex looks solemnly at Lacey.

Yes, Tess, I did.

And you never said anything to me?

I don't know, he says, I really don't remember every-thing about that night —

I'm telling you, you didn't.

Do you want me to go? Lacey asks, still standing there.

No, I say quickly, of course not.

Alex puts two plates on the table.

Jesus, he says, I mean maybe I'm the one who should go?

Don't be so fucking stupid, I tell him.

He blinks.

He butters toast. Scraping butter on, scraping it off.

Come on Tess, he says, what's the big deal? You don't

have to protect young Darren from anything. The police are only interested in evidence. But if he was hanging around, then they need to know.

If, I say and look at Lacey. I fold my arms and watch as he sits down at the table. I am glad to find I don't blush.

Alex goes to the stairs and calls the boys.

When I left you, he says, when I left the hut to go home. He was waiting on the shingle in the dark. I thought you saw him too.

Well I didn't.

OK, so you didn't. Sorry.

When I came out, there was no one there.

Alex shrugs.

So he'd gone —

Anyway, I tell him then, I don't see what's wrong with him hanging around there. I mean, so were you.

Chapter 13

SCHOOL WILL BE CLOSED ON THE DAY OF THE FUNERAL and so will just about every shop or small business in the town.

Alex is hoping that Lennie's body will be released on the Wednesday and will spend that night and the following one at Sharman's, the undertakers in Halesworth. From there it will be collected and brought into town, but it won't go straight to St Margaret's.

It will come in down Station Road, Alex says. But, instead of going straight down the High Street in the normal way, it'll take a right across Barnaby Green and down Spinner's Lane before taking the road out past the golf course and up to Blackshore. There, it will make its slow way along the rough shale track, past the black-tarred, paint-peeling fisherman's huts and the chandlery stores, past the ferry and the crumbling harbour walls and the edge of the caravan site and, finally, across the sand dunes and onto the beach.

Timetables have been checked. The tide will be out, so the hearse will, apart from where it has to skirt the groynes, be able to travel over firm, damp sand as opposed to the shingle which, the undertaker worries, might play havoc with the tyres.

After about a mile, when it reaches the Tea Hut and the Sailors' Reading Room it will have to stop because there's no way for a car to get up there. Then will come the even harder, even stranger bit. Six men — Alex, Mick, John Empson, Geoff Farr, Kenneth Peach and Jack Abrahams, with Jim Dawson and (possibly, though yet to be confirmed) Vic Munro standing by as reserves — will carry the coffin up the steps and onto East Cliff and back along the High Street, cutting across Bartholomew's Green to the church.

Most of the town will be waiting, either in the church or outside it in the graveyard. It's lucky that St Margaret's — the finest medieval seaside church in England, the guidebooks call it — is so vast. Everyone can squeeze in. And just about everyone, it's thought, will want to.

Alex says this strange journey was Con's idea. That he wanted to give his mum a last look around the town. A way of giving it back to her, he says.

Rosa approves of the idea.

I want to go too, she says.

Darling, I tell her, you can't.

Anyway, it's not straightforward. There are problems.

The weight of the coffin for one thing. Alex never gave a thought to this when he made it — unused as he was to making coffins — but oak weighs far more than pine. Will six men be able to get it all the way up the steps to East Cliff without a struggle? Those steps, cut into the side of the cliff, are famously steep, and hard to negotiate at the best of times. An accident — with Lennie and the coffin crashing all the way down onto the prom — would be unthinkable.

There's the handrail on the left, Mick says, but nothing on the other side. And if you can't hold on, you need at least to be able to look up.

And those guys are all so old, I point out. Well John and Ken anyway and Maggie says that Geoff sometimes gets the shakes.

It might frankly be easier, Mick says, to carry the bloody church to the coffin.

The only way round all of this, Alex decides, is to practise. At nine one night the six pall-bearers meet in The Anchor and then go on to his studio where, in a kind of weird parody of a wedding rehearsal, they shoulder the empty coffin and carry it all the way down to the beach and then up and down those same steps. In the moonlit dark. Several times.

Will we see her? Jordan meanwhile wants to know. Will you be able to look at her when she comes in the church?

No, darling, I tell him, she'll be in the coffin — you know, the one that Alex has made? No one will see her, but we'll all know that she's there.

She's not there any more, Rosa quickly points out. Her soul is gone, you know. When you're dead your soul floats up and leaves your body —

Jordan is silent, holding himself tense and thoughtful.

I miss her, he says softly. I wish we still went round there.

But we do, I say. We do still go round there.

No, he says. I mean when she was there and used to give us tea and things.

I hug him close to me and kiss the hot top of his head.

He means she made things normal, Rosa says. That's what he means, don't you, Jordan?

Alex says that at first Max and Con were upset when they heard that the funeral was happening. They cried because they were getting their mum back and also because they knew they were losing her all over again.

Early on, at Lacey's suggestion, he took them to a post-traumatic stress clinic in Norwich. They went once and then gave up.

It was useless, Max said. They made us play with dolls and look at books. They ought to at least have Nintendo if they want kids to go to those places.

Mick and I laughed.

The three of them ended up drinking hot chocolate in Starbucks and then going shopping to HMV and Virgin instead which, as even Lacey agreed, was probably more therapeutic in the end.

We work things out in our own way, Alex told the counsellor. I've got people to talk to and so have the boys.

Now, to Alex's annoyance, the woman has sent him pamphlets entitled *How to Grieve* and *Letting Go and Saying Goodbye*. Alex puts them straight in the bin.

When asked what he and the boys are planning to do with themselves the night before the funeral, he says they're going to hire a video and get a takeaway.

Work drags along. I haven't a clue whether I'm really helping patients or not. I almost haven't the heart to charge Edna Richards for her treatment, so unsure am I that I really picked up anything or had any real effect on her body.

After I close, I go slowly up the High Street with Liv in the buggy and get the evening paper from Curdell's. The place is busy for a Monday afternoon. At the counter, near the racks of postcards and boxes of Bic lighters, Jan seems to have a crowd of people, all standing around and chatting. I realise they're talking about Darren Sims.

It was on him, someone says. He had it on him.

Down in a ditch towards Blackshore, says another voice.

They don't think it's connected, says Caroline Antrich.

But they haven't arrested him, have they? Jan asks.

No one seems to know the answer to that.

Darren's only seventeen, someone points out.

Eighteen. Eighteen in December.

Seventeen, then.

That's a juvenile — is that a juvenile? asks Jean Almond.

I don't care what anyone says — a pain in the arse and all that but — not capable of violence, no way —

Stupid place to hide it, though.

Or not —

Some kids found it — playing around the ditches.

How'd they know it was Darren's then?

No idea. Fingerprints or something I expect.

I push Livvy up Lorne Road and onto Gun Hill. From up here by the cannons, I can look down on the beach, the sky, the sea. It's very windy, it nearly always is up here — a real, ferocious, flattening kind of wind. A few kids are trying hard to play cricket, but they'd be much better off flying a kite. Jordan would so love to bring his Demon Racer up here right now. Last time we tried there was barely any wind and he was so disappointed.

I haven't been a good mother lately. I know this. That day, when there was no wind, Jordan cried bitterly. It took an hour to get him out of his sulk. I can't remember what it felt like, now, to live in a time when we still worried about the weather and when a sudden lack of wind could feel like a tragedy.

I sit down on a bench and watch the rough aliveness of the sea, brownish and edged with a ruff of foam. Liv's awake, smiling. A tooth has finally come through. I still can't get used to that small serrated stump poking up from where before there was only wet pink.

I wipe my tears on my coat sleeve. It's so old, this coat, that it's barely worth paying the money to get it cleaned.

Jordan swears that all he did was tell Nat that Darren had found something in the ditch.

He made me, he says and his face is sullen and pinched. He forced me to tell. He said he'd hold me down and spit in my face if I didn't.

And did he go to look? In the ditch? I ask him.

Jordan says nothing.

Did you tell him where? Did he go there?

How should I know? he says. He's always going off and doing things without me.

Of course Nat isn't in his room. The curtains are still half closed, trapped between the radiator and the bed which is not only unmade but has its covers falling off, onto the floor. I drag the duvet right off and leave it on the floor. Kick a pair of trainers across the room. Things he will barely notice.

There's a smell of varnish or paint. Plates covered in crumbs are stacked next to PlayStation games and glasses containing the dregs of orange juice gone sticky and dark. All his clothes, clean or dirty — school uniform, socks, pants, tracksuit bottoms, endless T-shirts with logos — are trailed across the rug which is rucked up and thick with fluff and dog hair. Fletcher isn't allowed upstairs, but somehow he has perfected the knack of getting himself up those stairs and into Nat's room and slinking on his belly under the computer table and lying there, half hoping to be invisible, half waiting, guiltily, to be found.

It ought to be simple, just to go down there to the kitchen and ask Mick whether he knows where his son is.

He glances up from where he's sorting the dirty washing into whites and coloureds.

I saw him with his coat on earlier, he says.

So he's out?

I don't know.

You're his father.

I know that.

Well, don't you care enough to know?

I go over to the sink where the tap's dripping and turn it off. Push down the lid of the bin which is jammed full and starting to smell.

What's happening to this place? I ask him.

What do you mean?

Everything — stinks.

You could empty the bin for once, he says. Where've you been anyway?

I took Livvy for a walk after work, OK?

Mick shrugs.

Fine by me, he says. And I know what he means — that it would have been, it used to be.

I sit at the table and put my hand on Fletcher's soft head.

He's almost thirteen, Tess, Mick says. I don't ask where he's going all the time.

Thirteen is nothing, I say. Thirteen is still a child.

That's not what you would have said — before.

Before?

Before all this.

I sigh.

Look, Mick says more gently, he's perfectly safe.

You've no idea, I tell him, whether this place is safe any more.

Don't be so on edge.

I'm not on edge, I tell him but my hands are trembling.

He looks at me.

I'm not, I say again.

Nat says he was just in the playground.

What, playing football?

No, he says, not playing. Just hanging out. And I never touched the knife, I never even saw it. I just went and told Darren he should tell someone, that's all.

How did you know it was a knife?

Nat looks at me.

Well, duh-brain, I asked him of course.

You went and asked Darren what he'd found in the ditch?

Nat rolls his eyes.

Yes of course. Why not? What's wrong with that? Was I committing a crime or something? He was dying to tell someone, you know.

Nothing's wrong with it, I say, but — well, why didn't you come and tell us?

He gives me a look as if to say that should be obvious.

Because you'd just have prevented me, that's all, he says.

Prevented you from what?

Dunno. From everything.

Nat, we wouldn't.

Oh yeah, you would. You do it all the time.

I look at him and feel a kind of hunger — for what? For the days when if I tried to hug him he didn't spring away from me? For the days when he didn't use to lock the bathroom door? For the days when he still smelled of his own sweet baby self, instead of the different, contaminated smell of the outside world?

He meets my eyes and his own are fierce, challenging. What? he says.

Nothing. I didn't say anything.

I didn't mean him to get into trouble, Nat says quietly. I didn't know they'd think it was his.

I touch his skinny, nerved-up shoulder.

It's OK, I say. I can tell them, you see, that I know he found it. He won't get into trouble, not if I talk to Mawhinney, he won't.

Four times, Rosa tells me when I ask if they've really seen Lennie. We've seen her roughly four times.

Roughly? Rosa, for heaven's sake, what does that mean?

She screws up her eyes so tight that her freckles blur together.

I mean I'm not exactly sure of how many times. Sometimes I see her in my sleep. I don't count those.

And who's we?

Jordan and me. Let me see — she counts on her fingers — once on the beach near The Polecat, once at the end of the road where school is, and twice here.

What? Here in the cemetery?

Yup. Jordan and me were swinging on the big tyre and we looked up and saw her sitting just over there. She was there for ages, just staring at us the whole time we were swinging. I'm not lying, I swear we did. Ask Jordan. He saw her too.

I look at Rosa and she widens her eyes.

Even if you don't believe me, she says, it doesn't matter. It makes no difference. She'll still keep coming and I'll still see her.

I don't mean a ghost, she's saying to me as the wind blows and the church clock dongs the hour, I'm not stupid, you know. I know that ghosts don't exist, they aren't real.

Well, I ask her, what, then?

It was just Lennie. It wasn't scary or anything. She looked really normal.

What was she wearing?

Rosa narrows her eyes.

Um — jeans. I can't remember what on top. And trainers, the ones with the silver bits on them I think.

I take her small hand in mine.

Darling, I say, Rosa, listen. This doesn't mean I think you're making it up, I promise, but, well, do you think what you saw was in your head?

As if expecting this, she smiles and shakes her head at me in a benign and patient way.

In your imagination, I mean.

If she was in my head, then she wouldn't have been real.

People see things, I say, but she smiles again. She's not falling for that one.

Well then, I ask her, trying something else, why do you think you saw her? It's not normal is it?

It's not normal, no.

So — why? What do you think she's doing?

Rosa thinks about this.

Just being sad. I think she's sad.

Do you?

Yes. She looked like she wanted to be with us. And like she was missing us and — seeing her made me want to cry.

Because you miss her?

I do miss her, yes, but that's not why I wanted to cry.

Why then?

I don't know, Rosa says slowly. Maybe it's that I don't want to think of her being all alone.

Our lives are all around us. That's what I know now. The beginnings and the ends of them, some wrapped tight, pulsing, unknowable — others floating free.

Time is a made-up thing. Everything happens at once. I know that now. It's all the same — life, death and life again. Children know this. That's why they complain if you make them wait for anything. Waiting is dead time, nothing time, they know that. Waiting is a punishment, finally over when the moment comes.

Even after Lennie, life goes on. You think it shouldn't, but it does. Smoke topples out of chimneys, babies startle, kids shriek, cars draw up and stop and go away again, men get tired of things, the sea crashes snarling onto the shingle and then retreats, sparrows jump up and down off branches and out of trees, dogs sleep.

So why won't she let go?

Maybe she wants her heart back, Rosa says. Maybe that's what it is. I know if I was her that's what I'd want.

We sit on the low flinty wall that separates the cemetery from the playground.

So, I ask Rosa, if you can see her, why can't I?

Don't know, she says, her eyes far away as she chases a ladybird up a stalk of grass with her thumb. Maybe you could. But I doubt it.

Why?

She's silent, concentrating on the insect. I can see every single light-blonde hair all the way up the nape of her neck, the faint beginning of colour where her cheeks curve, the swirl of baby hair that turns into a cowlick at her temple and is charming now but will probably annoy her when she's older and vainer.

You don't want to see her, Rosa says.

It's not a question. She has the insect on her thumb, watching as it crawls over her grubby thumbnail. Tilting her head, careful not to lose sight of it.

I do, I tell her, but I hear my voice — adult, tired, without conviction.

No, Mummy, she says. Let's face it. You don't.

I smile.

You've got your mind on other things, she says. All the time. You're always looking out for something else.

She takes her eyes off the ladybird for one single second to look at me with narrowed eyes.

Am I? I ask her, surprised.

Mmm, she says.

Something?

My heart bumps.

Or someone, she says and she turns and smiles at me with eyes I don't recognise.

The ladybird flies off — a black frizz and whirr of wings. Rosa tuts.

Oh look, she says. Look what you made me do.

Mawhinney says I needn't worry about Darren. He says the knife has been ruled out anyway by forensics. It's not connected with the murder, he says. It's just a knife. A co-incidence. So that's that.

I try to make him understand that I'm not worrying, that I just want him to know that it wasn't even Darren's knife to start with. How I know he found it — how Jordan and I ran into him just after he'd found something, that day when we were walking Fletcher at Blackshore.

What I mean, I tell Mawhinney carefully, is Darren wouldn't even own a knife.

Mawhinney looks at me and laughs.

Rosa and I walk down Fieldstile Road, turn right onto North Parade and then head down onto the beach.

No one's there, not a single person, not even a dog. I sit hunched on the windy shingle while Rosa mooches up and down at the water's edge, head down, looking at pebbles.

Every now and then she squats — legs bending easily beneath her — and picks up a stone, turning it over, but mostly leaving it. Or else stands and hurls it so it skims the dark water, bouncing along the way Nat must have taught her. When that happens she glances back to see if I've seen. I raise my hand and wave to show her that I have.

The sun moves in and out of the clouds, drawing long black shadows across the beach, throwing light at everything, then snatching it all back up again.

Rosa comes crunching up the shingle, holding something up to the light.

Amber?

No.

I take the pale brown stone from her. The wet makes it pretty but as soon as I wipe it on my jeans it dulls.

Too heavy, I tell her, you know that. Amber's light.

Amber's a type of plastic, Rosa says.

Right.

My kids are obsessed with finding amber on this beach. Not that they've ever found any. The only person who has is Mick. Mick, who rarely looks, yet once casually picked up a honey-coloured, translucent lump the size of a 10p piece — only to lose it again through the hole in his coat pocket. The children have never forgiven him.

Rosa holds her brown stone up to the light. Weighs it in her hand.

It's quite light, she says hopefully.

The sea is dull. Then sun comes out, glitter rushes across its surface and everything turns yellow. Then back to dirty as the shadows fall.

The shadows on the beach get longer, colder. I pick up my bag.

Look, I warn her, you mustn't go telling people about this. Not Bob for instance. It might upset him. And the boys — you won't tell Max and Con, will you?

Oh, Con knows, Rosa says quickly. Con's seen her too.

Oh Rosa, I say, come on —

He has! Rosa wails. Oh, how can I get you to believe me?

As a baby, Rosa was the quiet one. She'd lie in her cot and fix on something motionless like the curtains or the sun coming through the blinds and just stare and stare. Then suddenly she'd chuckle, as if she'd just seen something extraordinarily funny that none of the rest of us could see.

Now she's crying, from frustration and anger.

She's not here, I tell her as gently as I can. She's gone, Rose. You know that. Lennie isn't coming back, not ever.

She doesn't look at me but she doesn't argue either.

It's not fair, she says, still feeling the weight of her stone.

That's right, I agree. It's not.

She chucks the stone away so it lands with a plick in the shingle, immediately indistinguishable from all the others.

Chapter 14

LACEY PULLS UP BESIDE ME OUTSIDE PARSONS' TEA ROOMS, in full view of most of the High Street. He winds down the window. He looks tired and cross and his hair is all sticking up.

Can you come for a drive? he says.

What, now?

Yes, he says, I really need to get out of this place.

It's a cold and blustery day. I know that Alison Curdell is watching us, standing on the steps of the post office and twiddling her hair. Next to her the sign saying Antiques & Curios blows over, caught by the wind.

I'll have to phone Mick, I tell him.

He passes me his mobile as I get in and clunk the door shut. The car has dark red leather seats and smells of sherbet or something acid and familiar like that. There's a white paper bag of sweets open on the dashboard.

I didn't know you had a car, I say. I mean here with you in town —

It's not my car, he says.

Oh.

Mawhinney arranged for me to borrow it.

What shall I tell Mick? I say.

I don't know, he says without looking at me. Don't ask me. Tell him whatever the fuck you like.

I bite my lips and look at all the numbers and symbols on the phone. What shall I tell Mick? Suddenly it seems like a question I've been asking myself all my life.

The answerphone is on. I tell him a lie — to do with Maggie Farr and Polly Dawson and some tins of something.

I ask Lacey how to turn the phone off and he takes a hand off the wheel and does it for me. A click. I watch his fingers, long and quick. I know how to turn a phone off. I just wanted to see him do it.

What? he says.

Nothing.

Why are you upset? I ask him.

I'm not.

You are. I can tell you are.

Oh, he says, I'm just a bit fed up that's all. It doesn't matter.

As we drive up to the A12, I watch the hedges speeding past the window, the skeletal cow parsley, the flattened leathery dead thing in the road. Brownish fur, bit of dark red blood. Once an animal, now a part of the surface you drive over.

So, Lacey says, the funeral's on Friday.

That's right, I agree. But you know, I'd rather talk about something else.

On a table by the road someone has made a sign saying Fresh Veg. There's a bunch of carrots and a marrow. Also some purplish-pink chrysanthemums in a black bucket.

Fair enough, he says.

I think he seems angry with me. Then I think if he was, he wouldn't be asking me to come out with him. Then I think, this is madness, what am I doing, coming out with him?

At the crossroads, Lacey waits to give way and then turns a sharp left. Lorries shoot past on the other side, heading for Lowestoft or Yarmouth. On my left the marshes stretch, black and wet, and from the right comes the sweet pong of Blythburgh pig. Put British pork on your fork, the signs say. Signs that reduced Jordan to tears of disgust the first time he saw them.

I hear they're bringing in new staff, Lacey says. On the investigation. An attachment from the task force.

What's that mean, then? I ask him and he shrugs.

It doesn't mean anything really — just some fresh blood. But anyway, I think Mawhinney is a bit pissed off.

Really?

Yeah. He takes things personally. I think he genuinely thought he had something on Darren Sims.

But he doesn't?

No, Lacey says, Darren's not involved in this.

You're sure? I ask him and he flicks me a look.

Are you? he says.

Yes, I say. Yes. Of course I am.

At the turning to Blythburgh, Lacey stops and puts his hand on the indicator.

Which way? Left or right?

I'm in charge?

Yes.

Left, then.

He turns so sharply that the wheels make a noise on the verge. A van behind hoots to complain.

Where are you taking me? he asks.

I laugh. You'll see.

Where?

Just a place I know. A funny place. You'll like it.

But then before I can say anything else, he pulls in at the side of the road by the sign for Toby's Walks and stops the car.

I know this place. Two centuries ago or something, a young girl was murdered here. It's in the guidebooks — long enough ago for people to find it exotic, exciting. Now though it's a nature reserve, with walks mapped out and little signs for where the marshes are, and benches for picnicking. A lot of birdwatchers come here. They say in spring you can hear the first nightingales if you're lucky.

I stare ahead at the vast black conifers and bracken. If you listen hard there's always a gentle tick-ticking. I don't know what it is — just the sound that the forest makes, the forest floor.

Why have we stopped? I ask Lacey.

He doesn't look at me.

I don't know, he says, I'm sorry.

I laugh, but only because I'm nervous and I don't know what else to do.

I'm lost, he says. He says it with a serious face but when I dare to glance over at him, he says, No, not like that. I mean, lost in other ways.

You know what I mean, he says after a pause.

Don't say things like that, I tell him.

What do you want me to say then? he asks me. I mean it. What do you want to talk about, Tess?

I don't know, I say.

The truth is I can think of nothing to say that would be right.

He says, Do you want to talk about how much I like you?

I take a breath.

About how I can't sleep or work or think or do anything that isn't about finding out how I can next see you?

No, I whisper, not that.

He doesn't smile.

Well, what then?

I don't know. But not that.

I look at him — at his face with its pale skin and dark eyes, the sharpish nose, the arrangement of features that aren't anything much at first glance, but for some reason get better the more you look at them.

He shrugs.

I'm only doing what you said, he tells me.

What?

What you said you had to do. Spending time and waiting for it to wear off.

Oh.

Except it won't, he says. You know that. My feeling for you isn't like that. It won't just go.

Oh God, I tell him, I shouldn't have come.

He puts both hands on the steering wheel.

I would have made you.

Would you?

Yes, I would.

I keep thinking he might touch me but he doesn't. He just keeps both of his hands on the wheel.

I don't know anything, I tell him. I mean, what to do, what to think —

You're in a difficult position, he says quietly, because you want to please everyone.

I think about this.

Is that what you think?

I don't know, he says. I'm finding it hard to know what I think either.

He winds down the window. There are pops, creaks and rustles in the bracken. Animal sounds. A magpie flashes black and white in the clearing ahead.

A girl was murdered here once, I tell him.

Is that what they say?

Centuries ago. It's supposed to be haunted or something.

Oh, he says. Haunted by what?

I don't know, I say. A ghostly girl in white?

Lacey laughs and after a moment so do I.

As we drive up into Westleton, he has to slow for a brown pheasant which picks its jerky way across the road and into the hedge. A sign by the side of the road says, Apples And Kindling For Sale, £1.20 a Bucket.

I decide to tell him about Rosa and Jordan and Connor and how they say they've been seeing Lennie.

Yes, he says slowly, Alex told me that.

Don't you think it's weird?

He rubs his eyes and then smiles.

I think it's that daughter of yours. She has a big imagination —

You think so?

Huge.

I think about this — about Rosa. The Rosa-ness of her.

It's funny, I say. When you first have kids, you think you know what their limits will be, how they'll turn out.

Do you? he says.

I mean, you know they aren't you, that they're their own people. But you don't really believe they'll have all this energy and thought that is nothing to do with you.

He smiles.

Your Rosa certainly has that.

What?

Energy.

I look at him.

Yes, I say, she does, doesn't she? And it's nothing to do with Mick or me. Sometimes we can't control it at all. It's a force of its own.

An alien force, says Lacey, and smiles again.

Yes, I say quite seriously, an alien force.

After a moment or two he says, She had a big thing about Lennie, didn't she?

It's raining slightly and the road ahead of us turns dull.

Yes, I say. She did.

The bookshop is in an old chapel with a corrugated roof and dense thickets of nettles and brambles growing on either side. Opposite is a post office and general store combined, where you can buy shampoo or stamps, painkillers or home-made coffee & walnut cake.

In the shop window, among all the ads for Bed & Breakfast and babysitters and stuff for sale, is a Suffolk Constabulary poster with Lennie's face on. I don't have to look at it, I already know what it says. It gives details of what Lennie was wearing and carrying on that night. I know these details now by heart: jeans, a red satin shirt, a silver bracelet, a soft, dark red leather clutch bag with a yellow smiley face sticker (stuck on by Con and never removed) on it.

Unlike the post office, the bookshop is always open. Always open and always deadly quiet except for the twitter of the starlings that nest in the roof. Inside, old books are piled everywhere and in all directions — on the floor, up to the ceiling and up each and every wall, some of the piles so high you feel they might curl right up over the arched ceiling and come creeping down the opposite wall.

Other stuff is also piled almost to the ceiling, tin boxes, broken chairs, old bedspreads, spider plants spilling over.

Lacey looks around him.

You like books? he says.

Yes, I say, I do like books. Do you?

He says nothing, just laughs to himself.

Some are stacked in formal glass cabinets, others crammed into cardboard boxes that are in their turn balanced on old wooden step ladders or spilling out of metal filing cabinets.

There's quite a bit of handwritten labelling and a system of sorts. Health, cookery, DIY, crime, history, France, Egypt and nature studies. And religion and philosophy and fiction, as well as Rupert Bear and sci-fi and 60s TV programmes. On the dusty brick walls are strange canvases of twisting, fleeting figures and shapes, all done in oils, many of them for sale.

Up in the area that you might call the till — though certainly nothing like a till is in sight — is an upturned Carr's biscuit tin and a broken wooden spoon. And next to it, a felt-tipped sign done on corrugated cardboard: Bang With Stick On Tin For Attention.

Shall I bang? Lacey asks me.

No! I whisper. Don't you dare.

The owner doesn't seem to be around. He never is. There's no one else in the place at all and no sound except for rain coming down outside. Or maybe it's inside as well, for some kind of creeper grows through the upper windows which seem to be pretty much wide open to the elements. Above our heads, bare light bulbs hang, attached to strings at different levels.

I undo my coat.

Have a look around, I tell him.

OK.

I'm going to fiction, I say. I think he might follow me but he doesn't. I glance back and see he has picked up a book and is leafing through it already.

Hey! he calls softly after a moment or two. Tess! Come over here.

He's not where I left him. Following his voice, I make my way between birdlife of East Anglia and Norwegian cookery. He is in the furthest corner of the shop, a little book-lined room all of its own, with a metal step ladder on wheels and a stack of empty cardboard boxes in the corner.

Look, he says. Come here.

What? I say softly.

He's holding a book in his hands.

This, he says. Looking at me and waiting.

I stand there, too hot now in my coat.

What? I say. Look at what?

Here, he says. Come here.

And I move right over to him. The book is small and heavy and old, with a shiny tassel of a bookmark.

I hold out my hand.

Let me see —

But he doesn't give me the book or pass it so I can look. Instead he puts it gently down and reaches forward and opens my coat. Pulls it wide open and holds it by the stiff wool lapels — and pulls me closer.

No, I say, laughing and resisting.

Yes.

No, I say more seriously. You mustn't.

Oh, Tess —

I can't do this.

You're not doing anything. I'm doing it.

I look up at the shelves. A sign above me says, Miscellaneous Theories.

He doesn't let go.

Are we in Religion? I ask him.

I feel him looking at me — at my shoulders or my neck or my face.

I blush hard.

Why are we in Religion? I whisper as he pulls me closer still and I smell the unfamiliar smell of his breath, see the shadows on his skin, the way the hair brushes his ears.

It's the quietest, he says.

Oh.

I put my face near to his neck. A pulse is banging there. I've done it now, I think.

But the whole place is quiet, I tell him.

I know, he whispers and he puts a hand on my head, pulls me to him, but this bit's the quietest.

His skin is warm.

I've never done this, I say as I feel the worry and the confusion of it and the mixed-up swish of both our bloods banging against each other.

Why? What are we doing? he says.

I don't know.

Afterwards, we go around the corner and stand by the duck pond and watch the ducks. There's a bench and a weeping willow and a wire-mesh litter-bin. We stand right next to each other, but don't touch.

Ducks love the rain, I say.

Yeah, says Lacey.

I realise I've never been here without my kids. I've never stood on the edge of this pond and not had to grab the hood of some child or other to stop it falling into all that weedy water. I've never in all these years with Mick pressed my face into the neck of another man.

Mallards are paddling up with their bright legs and eyeing us beadily.

Oh, I say, I wish we had some bread. We should have brought some.

You don't really think that, Lacey says.

No, I agree.

The rain is pelting down very hard now. I shiver. I'm terrified but I don't know what of.

I'm going to kiss you, Lacey says quietly. Not now, but later. Don't say anything because I'm going to do it whatever you say.

My heart swerves.

Not here, I tell him quickly. Don't do it here.

But I don't say what I should: don't do it at all.

When I get home, Alex is there with Mick. Nat too, sitting at the table and refusing to eat.

Hi, Mick says.

He says it perfectly calmly. Maybe he hasn't noticed how long I've been gone. Alex just looks at me. He looks stoned.

Liv is wriggling on Mick's lap. Sockless, the front of her sleeper damp with dribble. I can see from her frantic face that she's been fretting for ages. As I reach out for her, she cries loudly in a sorry-for-herself way.

Sorry, I tell Mick, undoing my shirt.

I don't know what you're apologising for, he says.

For being so long.

You got wet?

I can feel my hair wetting my shirt, my shoulders.

It's pouring.

And you've been out in it.

Yes.

Alex laughs. I shove a damp breast pad in my pocket, feel the dragging sensation deepen as Livvy sucks.

Smell this. Nat thrusts a spoonful of yoghurt in my face.

Why?

He says it's off, Mick says wearily.

Hold on. I try to adjust my arm around Livvy so I can take the spoon from Nat. I can't just smell it.

I taste it. It's slightly fizzy.

It's way past its sell-by, Nat says. Admit it. He wants to poison me or something.

Nat goes and the door bangs. The room is quiet again. Alex starts to roll a joint.

So. Al went to Halesworth, Mick says.

Oh, I say, realising I've forgotten all about Lennie, the funeral. Oh my God — and?

And they haven't released the body yet.

Alex says it in a blank voice, blank and triumphant.

No? I say. But surely —?

Tomorrow morning. Or that's what they're saying now, he says.

Can you believe it? Mick says.

But I thought it was supposed to be today?

It was, Alex says, but there was a cock-up. So tomorrow it will have to be.

Soon after Alex has gone, Jordan appears in the doorway, one hand sliding up the doorframe, the other delving down inside his pyjama bottoms.

Go to bed, says Mick. Straightaway Jordan looks at me.

You heard, I tell him without looking at Mick.

But he doesn't move, just gazes at me, eyes shiny with exhaustion. He's at the age when kids look old enough during the daylight hours, but then go back to being little all over again at night.

I sigh.

You want me to take you up? I ask him.

Yes, Jordan says and carries on looking at me steadily.

Mick makes an exasperated noise.

Well, of course, he says. I mean if you offer him that —

You're a hard man, I say to Mick. I say it half joking but the voice I use is not very jokey.

He looks at me as I clear the plates off the table and put them by the sink.

What's that supposed to mean?

Nothing, I say. Come on, boy.

On the stairs, I prod at Jordan's small hard bottom till he giggles and collapses back against me. Relieved, I breathe in his warmth and his bed-smell.

At the doorway to his room, he yelps.

What?

Ouch-y. I stepped on Lego, he says.

Shouldn't leave it lying around, then.

I didn't. It was Rosa.

I put him in bed and he immediately tugs the duvet up to his chin. As I kiss the bridge of his small nose, he reaches out for a handful of my hair. Holds it.

Where were you today? he says.

Oh, nowhere much. I had to see Maggie and a couple of other people. Just jobs and things. Why, what did you do?

I got worried, he says, yawning.

But why? Didn't Daddy say where I was?

He did but I was still worried.

Why, darling?

He says nothing. Just looks at me and his mouth stretches down at the corners like it does when he's going to cry.

What, darling?

His mouth stays down. I stroke his face — slide the palm of my hand all over it, feeling all the curves and dips and softnesses. He shuts his eyes. A tear squeezes down the side.

You weren't here, he says.

I'm here now, I tell him.

He gives a little sob.

I was worried, he says again.

Worried about what?

That something might happen.

Oh Jordan —

He sobs again.

Nothing's going to happen, I say, kissing his face. And I'm not going anywhere.

He says nothing.

OK, sweetie?

He blinks.

OK?

I might have to tickle you, I tell him. If you're not going to answer me, I might just have to do it.

And I do and I feel the wriggle of him, crazy beneath my fingers. I drink in his toothpaste-and-saliva breath. But in the end I stop, because he's just not laughing. Or at least, he is, but not quite enough.

Downstairs, Mick is sitting with the last of the wine. Fletcher is asleep at his feet. Mick has his shoes off and his feet are stretched out in their thick woollen socks. One of the dog's front paws twitches ever so slightly.

OK? Mick says.

He's just overtired.

I knew you'd take him up.

You think I shouldn't?

It's getting into a habit with him, that's all.

I shrug.

I just felt bad, I say. At being out so long today.

What do you mean? he says, staring at me. You're allowed to go out.

Yes, I say, but for so long.

I don't look at him. I don't know what I'm trying to tell him — whether I'm trying to tell him anything. The more I try to tell the truth, the more it feels like a lie. He sighs and pulls out a chair, puts his feet up on it.

I told you. You're a free agent, Tess. Please don't make me into this person who always wants you home. It's not fair.

Yes, I say, but the baby —

She was OK. And as you say, we could start her on some formula.

He twizzles his wine glass round and round on the table.

Friday, he says at last, is going to be difficult.

Yes, I say, I know.

He stops turning the glass, finishes the last mouthful of wine.

And after Friday, he says, I'm not sure exactly how life is going to be either.

I sit down.

How do you mean?

He looks me in the eye.

I mean us, Tess. Our family. You and me.

He runs his hands through his hair. It's getting long again — even though he always has it cut extra short, in a style I hate, just to save money. He has good hair. I watch as the thick, gold band of his wedding ring runs through all that hair.

I shiver, listening to the wind. Pull my cardigan round my shoulders.

I'm sorry, I say, I'm tired. And I don't know what you mean and I don't know what to say.

He looks at me.

It's just — I've run out of energy for saying things, I tell him.

Anyone would look at this family, he says quietly, and think we were happy.

I shut my eyes.

That's a weird thing to say.

Is it? he says.

You know it is. We're happy, aren't we?

You tell me, he says and he sounds almost angry. You tell me, Tess — do you like this? How is it for you? Are we?

I sit there and I can't speak. Panic shifts things around in my chest.

We've all been having a terrible time, Mick, I say. It's no one's fault.

I hear myself and think I sound like Lacey.

This goes beyond that, he says.

Does it?

I think so.

He hesitates.

If you want me to be different, he says, if you want me to change, you have to say how.

Yes, I say.

Yes what?

Just yes, I'm listening.

He stops a moment.

But you have to give me a clue, he says. Otherwise it's just not fair. The odds are just too stacked against me. Do you see that?

I nod.

I'm going to think about going back to work, he says then. The paper would have me. We could come to an arrangement. I talked to Blake.

You did?

Mick nods.

Today. I called him.

You want to do that? I ask him.

Maybe, he says. Maybe I have no choice.

What do you mean, no choice?

He's silent.

We're managing, I tell him. We have enough money.

It's not just money, he says after a moment.

I don't want you to change, I tell him. I'm about to continue and tell him that he doesn't have to go back to work either, when he stops me.

Don't, he says. Don't say anything now. I mean it. I'm

not asking you for that. But do me the favour of thinking about it. We have to get through Friday. We have a lot to get through, you and me.

OK, I say.

You're important to me, he says and gives me a bruising look. He pushes back his chair and the dog wakes up, stretches.

We should get to bed, he says.

Yes, I agree. Bed.

Sometimes, when I carry Liv around for too long, I'm left with a memory of her in my arms, a heaviness you can't quite shake off. Or perhaps a lightness, an emptiness. That's what I'm feeling now, except the memory is of Lacey. His touch, his breath, the feeling of what might happen next.

Mick looks at me and I flush. If he looked inside me, he could probably see it too. If he wanted to.

Chapter 15

NEXT MORNING, LENNIE'S BODY IS BROUGHT TO HALES-worth. It is brought in an ambulance and put in the coffin that has been waiting for days now at Sharman's. Alex is there alone when they bring her. He won't have Mick, he won't have Lacey. He doesn't invite Bob either. Instead Bob comes over to us early. He does this a lot — he likes to see our kids before they go off to school. Especially Rosa.

Passing through the hall, I hear this:

Why do dogs always look like they're about to cry? Rosa is asking Bob.

You're right, I hear him say, I guess they do look kind of tragic.

Tragic, yes, Rosa agrees, as if they're about to cry. Do your dogs at home look like that?

I've almost forgotten, he says, what they look like at all.

It hasn't been that long —

Well, it's been a while.

But you'll go home soon, right? After tomorrow you can go any time?

I guess so, he says.

There's a pause and then:

I don't really want you to go, Rosa says.

Silence.

I've got used to you being here.

So what's that you're drawing? Bob says then. Shouldn't you be getting ready for school.

Not yet, Rosa says. In a minute. Fletcher — it's Fletcher, can't you see —?

I can almost hear Rosa bite her lip and hold her breath. The big dark slope of her silence as she concentrates.

It's great, I hear Bob say then, a great picture. The eyebrows especially — you've got them exactly right.

Sad eyebrows, Rosa says, sad everything.

That's right.

I could draw your dogs if you like, Rosa says. If I ever get to meet them, that is.

That would be nice, Bob says. A special portrait. Maybe I should invite you over.

Yes, Rosa says, please do. Well, just ask my mum and send me a ticket. Or if you want, just the money.

I hear Bob almost laugh.

He's got a big tongue, that dog, Bob says.

No, Rosa says a little impatiently, that's not a tongue,

that's a heart — Lennie's big heart in his mouth. Can't you see? Don't worry, he's not going to eat it —

In the hallway, I hold my breath. Fortunately Bob is laughing.

You're a funny little girl, he says.

Well, and you're a funny man, Rosa says. Do you want to sit together? At the funeral?

Another chunk of silence.

If we're allowed, Rosa adds. We might not be allowed.

That afternoon — Thursday afternoon — turns suddenly beautiful. The sky, which was inky with threatening storm, clears and bright white sunshine soars across it. The sea sparkles. It isn't warm exactly, but you couldn't say it's cold either. No-coat weather, definitely.

I've done a morning at the clinic, but my last patient cancelled. I go home early to find Mick still barely dressed, padding around the house in slippers and cardigan, like an old man. He hasn't even shaved.

Are you OK? I ask him.

Fine, he says.

Really? You don't look at all fine.

He shrugs and doesn't answer but I catch him frowning once or twice. I don't know if it's me, or just his own thoughts unwinding in his head.

He says he'll walk Fletcher after lunch and go on to get the kids from school.

Are you sure? I say. Normally when I haven't got clinic in the afternoon, I do it.

Stop being guilty all the time, he says. Would I offer if I didn't mean it?

Liv is in her cradle seat in a corner of the sitting room. The seat has a row of blue, mauve and orange plastic beads strung in front of it, but Liv is much more taken up with watching Rosa's kitten who's batting a piece of scrunched-up paper across the floor.

She keeps her eyes on the kitten, both fists pushed in her mouth. Kicking her feet sharply every time the kitten jumps.

I pick up the kitten in one hand and in the other the piece of paper which, I see, is covered in Rosa's neat meticulous drawings, her handwriting. All her drawings are like this — sturdy, detailed and repetitive and packed with information. She's like a cave painter, her art teacher at school says.

I open up the scrunched paper and the kitten yowls. I drop her.

On the paper are a succession of pink crayoned hearts and the words, A Map Of Where To Find It — followed by Rosa's initials and her age. Underneath are piles of long wavy blue lines and a picture of a woman standing on top. A person standing on the waves. At the bottom, Rosa has written: Keep Out.

I put the paper back on the table and pick Liv up. She smiles and almost laughs when I bundle her into the buggy. It's like she knows where we're going. It's like she does, even if I don't.

*   *   *

We go down the High Street, in the direction of Gun Hill. It's still bright but very windy. Things falling over, bins and signs banging. Outside the grocer's a woman is yelling and yelling at her child to get into the car. In the road is a pile of manure left by the brewery drays. By the post box, an old man with a stick stands very still and bent over and further on an even older woman travels down the street in a little electric disabled car with a flag on it. She waves to a boy who comes out of Somerfield and picks up cardboard boxes and takes them back into the shop.

I want Liv to fall asleep but she doesn't. She sits up as straight as her almost five-month-old back will allow, straining and following everything that's going on.

We go past the Marie Curie shop, where Maggie is possibly sorting black bags of stuff in the back, and the butcher's. No one in there at all. At Suzanne Hair Fashions, Sue Peach can be glimpsed through the glass, foils in her hair, holding a cup of something.

At the foot of Gun Hill I hesitate, as if going up there is really an option. Then, after thinking about it for a second or two, I turn the buggy and head along North Parade towards the pier.

Though I don't know that's where I'm going till I get there. Or maybe that's wrong. Maybe I do know.

It's really not cold but still the wind along the front stings your cheeks and makes your eyes water.

I feel happy and excited for the first time in a very long

time. Because it is a weird day, a mad, glittery day, uncanny and unseasonable. Because the sea has a million different colours slipping over its surface and my heart just nearly explodes when I see it — all that water and the pier, with its tangled mass of metal. And because Rosa may well be right. From where I stand it could just be a huge spidery animal crawling, belly slung low, into all that water.

He's perched on a filing cabinet over by the window, drinking something from a polystyrene cup. Tipping his head back, watching the sea.

I stare at him.

Why are you here? I ask him.

He turns and looks happy and pleased and careful.

Why are you? he says.

I really don't know, I say because it's the truth, and I go bright red and take a step back. He laughs. From the other side of the room Mawhinney's watching us. Mawhinney and a thousand others. The whole room buzzing — more police than I've ever seen in there.

Good news actually, he says. They think they might have something. The National Police Computer, a profile that fits. It's something, anyway.

My heart contracts.

They've found a man?

A suspect. A better one than Darren Sims, anyway. Mawhinney's over the moon.

My God, I say.

I know, he says. It's a shock isn't it.

Look, I say, do you need to stay here?

He looks at me.

What, now?

Yes, now.

No, he says, not really. They're finished with me. Though I'll have to see Alex later.

Come for a swim then, I say.

He looks at me as if I'm mad.

A what?

Over by one of the computers, Mawhinney is talking to a blonde woman in uniform.

A swim? I say. Or if you want, a paddle.

He chucks his cup in the bin and folds his arms and laughs.

OK, he says.

OK?

He glances over at Mawhinney, who is bent over the computer now as the woman scrolls along the screen.

Yes, crazy woman, Lacey says. Come on then, yes, let's go.

Maybe I do really mean it about the swim. Or maybe it's only a way of getting him inside The Polecat with me. Whichever it is, as I dig the key out and put it in the lock and turn and yank it open, my hand is trembling. He lifts the buggy up the two wooden steps and we're in.

Sand underfoot. The grit sound of sand on wood.

The curtains in the hut have bold oranges and lemons

on them — leftovers from the sixties, from someone's mother. I tug them now along the little stretchy curtain wires and light falls in. The windows are dirty but the light outside is bright. A spider has spun its web across one of the corners and in pulling at the curtain I break it. It falls and hangs for a moment on a thin string — a tiny, balled-up, bouncing dark red thing — before dropping to the wooden floor where sand, dust and, I suppose, old sandwich crumbs combine.

My little hut, I tell him.

Lacey looks around.

It's a mess, I know.

This is it? he says. Where you come?

I haven't been here in a while, I tell him and I can't tell what he's thinking. Not properly since —

We take a step back from each other. Suddenly I'm embarrassed.

It's tiny isn't it? I say almost in a whisper, because it is, the walls are coming closer every minute. I used to think it was big, I add, when I first got it.

Bigger than you think, he says, from the outside.

Some are much better than this, I tell him. Some have — oh, I don't know, some go back further.

He looks at me. I touch my hair, my face.

The ones towards Blackshore are bigger, I tell him.

He says nothing.

We've been meaning to do it up, I say.

Have you?

Yes.

I look at his eyes. My chest and knees have gone hot.
Will he kiss me?

Livvy sneezes — once, twice — and the moment breaks.

It needs a paint and a clear-out, I continue, moving an
old broken table football game of Nat's out of the way.

What do I wear, he asks me then, for this swim of yours?

Over there — I indicate the endless stiffened costumes
hanging over on the wire coat hangers — take your pick.

He looks at them.

Unless you don't want to.

Are you going to? he asks me.

Of course I am, I tell him and I pull up my shirt to show
I'm ready underneath, costume on.

He grabs the trunks nearest to him, old and baggy, Mick's
from about five summers ago. His face is impossible to read.

Shut your eyes, he says.

The sun's still out, but there's no one around, only an
elderly couple throwing a piece of wood for their dog and,
further down towards Blackshore, a couple of guys dragging a dinghy with flapping orange and pink sails out of the
water.

We crunch down over the shingle and I spread a blanket with a towel on top and put Livvy on it. I try to put two
other towels on either side of her, but she immediately starts
fussing, wanting to get onto her front.

My swimsuit is way too small — it's from back before
Jordan was born — and I had forgotten how it's all shiny
and baggy and wearing out at the sides. Also how the legs

keep riding up so I have to pull them down all the time. Driving me insane. It seemed OK when I put it on, but I never go swimming with anyone but the kids. Now I realise I must look terrible in it with my bottom hanging out and my thighs all cheesy white and marked with tiny dark veins.

I hope he isn't looking at me. He's not. He's frowning at the sea. So I look at him. He's good without his clothes, just fine — pale but kind of streamlined and purposeful. A pencil sketch of a man. I like him. As I knew I would.

He turns to me and laughs.

Are we really going to do this? he says.

I don't know, I admit because part of me is losing heart. My arms are goose-pimply, though the air is actually surprisingly warm.

But he wades straight in.

You think I'm just a city boy, he calls over his shoulder without stopping, still going in.

I laugh.

I never said that.

You think it, though. You think I can't get wet.

I don't, I swear I don't.

Come on then, he says. He is in up to his knees. He grabs little palmfuls of water and rubs them on his thighs, his waist, his chest. Shudders and laughs.

I wade slowly towards where he stands. The first moment of putting my feet in is a shock but at least the waves are gentle, little washy, slappy ones, tipping their icy weight over my knees but never higher.

He holds out his hand.

This is mad, I say.

I glance back at Livvy who has rolled right onto her front but seems happy enough, lifting her head to wink at the sun. I take it. I take his hand.

He squeezes my fingers.

It was your idea, he says as I gasp at the cold, I'm just reminding you of that.

I don't know what got into me, I tell him. I've never in my life swum in November.

Suddenly he lets go of my hand and dives off under the water. Comes up gasping a little way away. Head all slicked blackly down and smiling.

I can't do that, I tell him, laughing. Don't expect me to do that.

He swims off away from me, a steady crawl with his head right down. Meanwhile I move myself along, feeling the shingle shift and roll under my feet. Occasionally a pebble drifts across the top of my foot, lifted and pulled by the motion of the water. I try not to think of what's down there — the pincers and tentacles creeping over the cold and eerie sea bed.

Now the water is up to my waist almost. I can feel it, the brown swollen weight of the water all around me. Back on the shore, Livvy is suddenly small. The sun slides under a cloud and in a second the whole sea looks dark and achingly cold. The loneliest place in the world.

I turn. I can't see Lacey.

Where are you? I call.

I can't see him anywhere.

Hey! I shout. Hey!

Then, under the water, a hand is on my waist and he comes up beside me. Water falling off him.

Oh, I say. Because the sea is still dark.

What is it? he says.

Shall we get out?

You haven't got in yet.

No, I say, but I think I might have had enough.

But it's a waste, to get out now.

And he puts both hands around my waist and pulls me down so quick that I gasp aloud at the shock of it.

But before I can even take a breath, he takes my whole face in his hands and kisses me so hard and deep on the mouth that all other sensations are swallowed in that single one. His mouth on mine, hot falling away from my body, limbs gone. Livvy gone, the shoreline gone, the brown water gone. For a few liquid seconds, there's us and me and him and only the pure smooth terror of that kiss.

And then the sun comes out again and turquoise shadows chase over the water and the whole world lights up.

I put my two wet hands on his two wet arms and glance towards the shore.

It's OK, he says. Don't worry — I can see her.

No, I say, I didn't mean that —

He touches my face. What, then?

I like it, I say and he smiles.

Again, I say. Please — do it again.

He still holds my face, but he stops, looks at me.

You're not afraid of someone seeing? he says.

Yes, I tell him because it's the truth. A little, I am.

He puts his arms around me and my teeth bang as he looks at me but it isn't from the cold and wet or only partly anyway. It's because I've done it now, the thing I never thought I'd ever do. It's happened, I've done it and I'm terrified because it changes everything.

In The Polecat, there are plenty of towels, but all of them smell stiff and musty. The blankets are better, cleaner. There's even an old goose-down duvet, thin and scrunchy and lacking a cover.

Livvy fell asleep on the beach, but I managed to get her back in the buggy without waking her. This is a rare thing. Normally she sleeps so lightly — the slightest touch startles her back.

We dry ourselves without talking and put back on most of our clothes. Then I lock the door and he helps me pull the two old mattresses, children's ones — lumpy and with a pattern of stars and planets on them — down onto the floor and cover them with the blankets.

We still don't speak. We just get under the duvet and lie there in each other's arms. And it's the best thing yet, just lying there so close and listening to his heart, his breath, and on top of that my own and then the soft, quick in and out of Liv asleep.

This is exactly what I was afraid of, I tell him when we've been lying there in silence for a while.

What? he says.

That it would feel this good.

* * *

Moments pass. We still have all these clothes on us, layers and layers of them, but I can feel him pressing against
me, getting closer.

I can't, I say, suddenly panicky. I can't — do it.

He moves his head so he can see my face.

Can't do what?

I am trembling so much that my voice shakes.

Sex, I say. I can't have — sex — with you.

He laughs.

Hey. He kisses me near my mouth. Hey, shush, it's OK.

I kiss him back. I kiss his shirt and then his jumper.
Wool that smells of him.

You don't have to do anything, he says.

No, I tell him, you don't understand. I don't mean because I shouldn't — though I shouldn't. I mean, I haven't
done it for about a year, I don't know if I can any more.

He pulls back a little and looks at me.

Since the baby, I tell him as flatly as I can. Well, since
before. I mean, Mick and I — we just haven't.

I wait for him to speak but he says nothing and I can't
see his face. He feels for my fingers and covers them with
his, interlacing them, squeezing, holding.

So there you are, I tell him in the calmest voice I can do,
I'm — frigid.

He laughs.

No, I tell him. It's true. You don't understand — you
couldn't, you're too young. I'm this old, frigid woman and
you're young and —

I'm not so young, he says.

You wouldn't know, I tell him, how having kids changes you.

He says nothing.

I'm thirty-nine, I tell him, I mean it. I'm not like your —

I don't say it.

Not like my what?

Your — young girls.

He laughs again.

I thought plenty of old women had sex, he tells me. I thought they liked it.

Hmm, I say.

From behind me he grasps my hands by the wrists, holds them, circles them, strokes them. I feel a stirring of something and then it tapers off and I feel my eyes close. Maybe for a moment or two I sleep.

It begins to get dark and Livvy wakes and cries and I feed her. She's a good baby, a good girl. None of the others would ever have been quiet and easy for half so long.

When Nat was the same age he'd cry and cry, hardly drawing breath, and would only stop if Mick held him upright against his shoulder, triumphant and beady-eyed, for hours on end. Livvy has never demanded half as much.

I feed her there on the little lumpy bed with Lacey. And the noise of her sucking loudly and happily with him right next to me feels so strange and easy that I find I can barely speak to him or look at him while it's happening.

You love your kids, he says.

It's not a question, just a statement of pure fact, the way he says it.

Afterwards, I put Liv down on the mattress next to us and I get up and find some tea lights in a drawer. While I strike a match and light them, one by one, Lacey leans over Liv and pulls the cuffs of her sleeper up over her wrists, does up the top snap. He does it carefully, like a person who has never touched a baby before. Then he puts his finger on her hair — just touches it with one finger as if a whole hand might be too much. Seeing him do it gives me a pain somewhere in my body, I don't know where.

All we need now is a drink, he says.

I remember the bottle of brandy.

Alex brought this, I tell him.

What? That night?

Yes that night.

He's madly in love with you isn't he? Lacey remarks so suddenly that I stare at him.

He's mad, I say. He's bonkers, raving mad.

Did Lennie know? Lacey asks me.

That he's mad?

No, about — you.

I don't know, I tell him. No, I hope not.

Why? Lacey asks. Why do you say he's mad?

I shrug.

He just is. Always has been. There's something about him. He's not reliable, you know. Not in any way. Lennie knew what he was like, I can promise you that.

Did she mind?

I shrug, try to think.

She was the practical one, is all I can think of to say.

He's lost without her?

Yes, I say, he is.

He can't function, Lacey says.

I think about this.

No, I say, you're right, he can't.

I hesitate, look at Lacey.

He was never — I mean, you and Mawhinney didn't think —?

No, says Lacey quickly, we didn't.

He thought you did —

He was jumping to conclusions, then.

I smile.

That's it, I say. That's exactly what he always does.

Jumps to conclusions?

Yes. Always.

Why? says Lacey. Why do you think that is?

Why does he do it? I don't know.

Perhaps he likes the drama.

Yes, I agree. Perhaps he does.

I pour brandy into two chipped teacups and we lie back, not touching, watching each other. It's like every time we spring apart we're afraid to come back together.

After a moment he glances at his watch. I already know what the time is, I know it's half past four because I read it upside down a minute ago.

Don't you have to get back? he says.

Yes and no, I tell him. Not really. Not yet. Why? Do you?

I ought to drop in on Alex later, he says.

I watch the walls of the hut bend and change shape in the candle-light.

But not yet, he says.

Tell me, Lacey says, because I have to know. What's it like between you and Mick?

What's what like?

I don't know. Things. Everything.

I already told you —

Not just that — I mean the rest.

I huddle on the end of the mattress, my chin touching the furred cotton of my shirt. I miss Lacey now and I want to get close to him again but I don't know how to.

I feel suddenly miserable.

Oh, I tell him, please. Don't ask me stuff like that.

Do you love him?

Yes, I say, without looking at Lacey. Of course I do. He's a good, good man. How couldn't I?

Lacey lays his arms across his knees, same as I'm doing, and looks at the floor.

It doesn't always follow, he says quietly.

I ignore him.

And he's a good father, I tell him. A really good father.

I take a breath.

But? Lacey says.

I hesitate.

Saying it feels disloyal.

Saying what?

What I feel —

Have a go.

I shrug.

He doesn't make me feel like this, I say.

Lacey reaches for the brandy.

That's just because you know him, he says.

And I don't know you?

No, he says. You don't.

I look at him, so far away from me.

So don't make me talk about it. It feels wrong to complain about him. It feels — lazy.

We are silent for a moment.

That's why I can't — have an affair, I tell him.

He seems to think about this.

Is that what you think I want? he says after a moment.

I don't know, I say. I don't know what you want.

No, he says. You don't.

That's what Mick always says, I tell him. That I don't know what he wants —

That's hardly your fault —

No — but he says I claim to — to know, I mean.

Lacey keeps his eyes on me.

I can't keep myself away from you, he says. That's the truth. I told you. I think about you all the time and I can only really get on and do things that have to do with you.

I put my face in my hands.

This feeling I have for you, he says. It's huge.

I feel the same, I tell him. It's like I can't breathe. It feels like I love you.

But you don't, he says.

Don't I?

No.

It feels as if I do.

Love is just a word, he says. An overused one.

Now that we've got love out of the way, I think I might want him to touch me again. I ask him if he will.

He looks at me but he doesn't move.

Where? he says. Where do you want me to touch you?

The blood comes up in my cheeks all over again.

I don't know. Just — anywhere.

He still looks at me. So much distance between us.

What is it? I ask him. Don't you want to?

I want to, he says. His voice is different — low and cracked.

Well then?

You come to me, he says. Come on. You come over and ask me.

He pulls me onto him, on the mattress. All my skin has gone, dissolved. There's nothing between us, nothing left but us. I kiss him and he kisses me back. At first softly and wetly and slow — and then harder and deeper. We do that part for so long that my lips feel blurred, hot with blood.

When I've had too much, I pull back and try to sit up.

I don't know what I feel about Mick any more, I tell him. And that's the truth.

Though everything I say to him is beginning to feel like the truth.

Oh? he says.

No, I say. That's what I mean. It's true that I love him, but I don't know what sort of love it is or what our future is or what I feel.

No?

No.

And you want to find out?

I don't answer this. I sit back instead and take the brandy cup up from the floor and sip. Feel my lips burn after the kissing.

Do you?

Oh, don't ask me that, I tell him.

He takes the cup from me and puts it down on the floor next to the mattress and then he pushes me gently back and starts to unbutton my shirt.

I don't mind if you use me, he says. I don't mind if you use me to find out.

No, I tell him.

But don't expect me to be heroic, he says softly.

What? What does that mean?

He carries on unbuttoning.

I hold out my hands and touch his face.

I didn't know whether I should do anything about you, he tells me, when I met you. I couldn't decide, you know.

I listen. I listen to him undressing me. I notice that Liv is awake and listening too.

She's awake, I say.

Shh, he says. I tried to stay away. But you kept blushing every time I saw you. It was a dead giveaway.

He pulls my shirt right off and lays a cool hand on the hot skin of my stomach. I reach for it, for his hand, but he pulls it quickly away.

He puts a kiss on my neck. I feel it somewhere behind my eyes as well as up between my legs.

Can't we just hold each other, I ask him as he takes his clothes off.

No, he says, we can't. That wouldn't be enough.

But, I say, I can't — I can't do it.

It?

This — sex.

He smiles.

Tess, he says, it's not such a big thing, you know. What you're doing is, you're making it into a big thing.

But it is — a big thing —

No. Shh. It's not, it's easy —

He undoes my bra — my awful feeding bra — and touches my breasts.

I shut my eyes and lift my hips so he can get my knickers off. Then, just as he thinks he's going to enter me, I stop him and I push him over on his back and I kiss his goose-bumpy balls, the hard furred inside of his thighs. Still tasting of sea. He makes a little noise as I take him in my mouth and lick the salt and the mauveness of the slit that is him. It's good to hear his small gasp of surprise.

Chapter 16

LIV AND I HEAD BACK UP THE HIGH STREET IN THE DARK.
It isn't that late, in fact the evening is just beginning. The
street is deserted but in The Angel they are just moving
through from drinks to the dining room, ready to sit down
among all those pink linen tablecloths and silver cutlery.
Through the low bay windows I can see the black and
white clothes of the waiters, the glint of silver, the sparkle
of chandeliers.

Empty cardboard boxes and crates are piled up outside
Somerfield and Ann Slaughter is putting rubbish bags on top
of the wheelie bin outside The Griddle. She nods to me. Some
kids are shouting and hanging around outside Mei Yuen's.

I try to think what I am going to say to Mick. I know I
can't tell the truth, but I can't bear to lie either. I think I may

just tell him I've been in The Polecat. I think I may just —
But I don't get beyond this thought. Mick must have heard
the gate, because he opens the door and rushes out before
I can even get the buggy up the path. His face is white, his
breath coming in terrible, jagged gasps. Nat hangs back in
the doorway behind him, holding Fletcher by the collar.

He grabs at my arm. Have you got Rosa?

No.

My stomach does a flip.

Rosa? No. Why?

I stare at him.

Mick — what's happened? Where is she?

His face terrifies me.

Oh my God, I say, beginning to cry. Where is she, Mick,
tell me! Where's she gone?

He stands absolutely still for a moment.

Right, he says, I'm calling the police —

Wasn't she with you? I say. When did you see her —?

Inside, Jordan is sitting on a kitchen chair in his pyjama
top and pants and bare feet, crying. His sleeves are wet with
tears and snot. There are tears in his hair. Pasta sauce on his
pyjama top. I pull him onto my lap and wrap my arms
around him.

Rosa's gone, he says again and again, shuddering, sobbing, Rosa's gone.

Hey, I tell him. Darling, don't cry, I swear it'll be OK,
we'll find her.

I say these words over and over while Mick explains.

He speaks slowly and carefully but in between each word his voice tightens as if he can't quite breathe.

Rosa was here at teatime, he says. She was very helpful, unloading the dishwasher and grating the cheese for the pasta. Not in a mood or anything. Perfectly normal Rosa. She ate a big plate of spaghetti.

And fromage frais, Nat adds. Two of them.

He kicks at a chair leg as if his limbs are too large for the space, which maybe they are. The laces of his trainers are undone and fraying.

But — she kept getting up, Jordan says, still heaving with sobs. To look out of the window —

No, Mick says, that was before. That was long before tea, Jordan, please shut up and let me just tell Mummy.

Jordan gives a little sob and I wind my arm tighter around him, flesh on flesh, leaving no space between. As Lacey did to me barely an hour before.

Mick tells me that he went out the back to take the rubbish out, keeping the door on the latch so that Fletcher couldn't escape. Then when he came back in, Rosa wasn't there but he didn't worry because he thought she'd gone upstairs.

And anyway she did go upstairs, Nat says. I saw her. She was drawing in her room —

Pictures about Lennie, Jordan says.

I look at Mick and try to take this in and suddenly I feel sick — my insides sick and light, skin damp.

And?

And that's the last time any of us saw her. In her room, like Nat said. She's been missing since at least six, maybe earlier.

Oh God.

I put Jordan down on a chair. I am trembling so hard I can barely speak.

Right, I say. Right —

Mick pushes his hands into his eyes.

Jesus Christ, he says.

But she wouldn't just go, I tell him then. Mick, she wouldn't. She's not allowed to just leave the house — you're sure she's not here somewhere, asleep?

Mick looks at me as if I'm mad.

We've searched everywhere, he says. What do you think? The garden, the road, we've looked bloody every-where —

And you've checked she's not at Alex's? Or with Bob?

Bob's out looking for her now, he says. On the beach and along the front. He won't stop. He says he's staying out there until he finds her.

I stand up and my stomach tips.

We have to call the police. Or Mawhinney.

Mawhinney is the police, Nat says.

Livvy begins to cry and Mick picks her up out of the buggy. He pats her vaguely, holds her against him.

I was only waiting, he says, for you. I was just desper-ately hoping she was with you somewhere. I mean, where the fuck were you, Tess?

*   *   *

Mawhinney says he'll come straight over.

Mick starts phoning everyone we know, everyone who knows Rosa. I meanwhile pull on a coat and go out with Nat. To the graveyard. It seems to me quite possible that Rosa might go there. Being Rosa. Especially now. Especially the night before Lennie's funeral.

St Margaret's is immense and silent in the half-light from the moon. The white metal gates are pulled across the porch and locked. I try the handle but it won't turn.

I thought they never locked it? Nat says.

Sometimes, I tell him. It's because of Lennie — tomorrow.

The cemetery's dark and windy — just two exterior lights shining their cold beams on the grass. We go over to the spot next to the dark spreading yew where Lennie's grave is already dug. Nat shines the torch in and we both look at the deep drop, the glossy, sharply spaded sides, the black, black earth.

He doesn't say anything. He just looks. I touch his shoulder.

Come on, boy, I tell him. Let's just walk around —

As I walk, I concentrate on keeping breathing, on taking big sensible breaths, keeping focused.

Rosa! I shout, struggling to keep the tears from my voice, Rosa! Rosa! Rosa!

In the darkness the sound of our voices is so huge and strange and loud, the edges of them so blurred, that we have to keep on stopping to wait for the echo to finish.

Rosa! a! a!

We strain into the silence, listening.

Nothing. Just the wind and a faint metallic clinking sound, probably telegraph wires. And if you listen hard enough, if you strain, maybe a dull roar that is the sea.

Nothing else. Nothing coming back.

Nat's quiet. I take his hot hand in mine.

What do you think? I suddenly ask him. Where do you think she's gone?

He says nothing for a moment, then, Well, you know how weird she is, the way she talks about Lennie as if she isn't even dead.

So —

Well, she might be looking for her — I mean, she's pretty stupid when it comes to Lennie.

She thinks she's seen her, right? I say. Nat makes a dismissive noise in the back of his throat, half laugh, half sob.

I try to remember where Rosa says she's seen Lennie. Try to think of what kind of crazy thing she might want to do.

The school? I say to Nat. Or maybe the pier?

He gives me a look. I know what he's thinking. He's thinking that even Rosa would never go there. That no one they know would dream of going anywhere near the pier car park at night — not now, not any more and especially not tonight.

Mawhinney sits in our kitchen. It's 11 P.M. Lacey too. Lacey has come not because he's with the police, but for me. I know this, but I'm not going to think about it right now.

I can't look at him. Tonight — now — I just can't let myself look. He knows what I'm thinking. Where the fuck was I? Where were you, Tess?

Mick has made coffee. He needs to do things, to boil kettles and move stuff around, to have reasons to get up and down from his seat. Now he has the phone on the table. He's been calling people. He is pale and jittery, unable to be still, even for one single moment. It's obvious, isn't it? Only action can bring Rosa back. Anything but sitting, in fact. Sitting and waiting is what makes you powerless. It's what makes disasters happen.

Meanwhile, we all keep looking at the door. Even Mawhinney does, even him, he can't seem to stop himself. Even though he must be used to these moments.

But maybe that's how it is when you've lost someone — that you can't help but believe that at any moment they will come walking through the door and it will all be over. Hugs and tears. Maybe that's how it was that night for Alex, before he called me, before the police came and he had to be told, he had to know.

If Rosa came walking in, right now, I try to think what I would do. She'd be hungry and tired and cross. Snapping at everyone. I'd get her crackers and milk — crackers with goat's cheese on and milk from the fridge without any lumps in. I try to fix on this — on the idea of what she'll ask for.

Mawhinney puts his radio down on the table.

He looks at me. Makes a face. Tries to smile.

The last thing you need, he says. Tonight of all nights.

Yes, I say. It is.

I feel almost calm now. The whole day has been unreal.

And I swear to God that if it could just begin again I would be good — never complaining or making life difficult for Mick. I would never think of myself again, never, if I could just scratch this day clean and begin it again.

Are you OK? Lacey asks me. Can I get you anything?

No thanks, I say and I shake my head and my fake smile blots him right out.

Mick says he was going to call Alex again but then he thought why do it? If Rosa turns up there then of course he'll call us — and if not, then why put another thing on his plate, on this night of all nights?

Meanwhile Bob is still out looking. An old man stumbling along the shingle with a torch. Mick and I agree there's no point forcing him home. What else is he going to be doing tonight? He may as well be out there. Mawhinney has a whole bunch of officers out there, too. He says that in a place this small, it'll be easy. She can't have gone far. She'll be somewhere or other.

Somewhere silly, he says and I know he says it to reassure me. Little girls are strange creatures, aren't they? he says. Very hard indeed to say what's going on in those heads of theirs.

I get up and go to the toilet. My body empties — everything. I am perspiring. I splash cold water on my face, it drips down my wrists, into my clothes. I haven't washed since the sea. My arms and wrists still smell of it, of him.

I haven't been taking enough notice of her, I tell them

all as I come back into the room. Because the truth swoops in on me, sudden and terrifying.

Don't blame yourself, Mawhinney says.

But it's true, I say in a quiet dull voice. I haven't.

None of us have, Mick says.

Straightaway I resent how he has to lump himself in with me.

You've been a perfectly good father, I tell him. You've been great. You know it. You always are, you're fine.

Can she swim? Lacey asks after a moment or two.

Oh yes, I tell him. She's done three badges.

But, says Mick, she's not allowed in the sea alone, obviously.

She'd never try and go in alone, I tell him, horrified. Not now, not at night —

He agrees with me and he looks at Lacey.

She's quite sensible, I hear one of us say.

Mawhinney sighs and writes something down on his pad. It seems to be a phone number, but it could be just a scribble.

Lacey sits with his two bare hands on the table, perfectly still. His face is white and his eyes are pink with exhaustion.

He seems to think of something.

Is she upset? he asks us. Do you think she was perhaps feeling upset about tomorrow?

Mick looks at me.

Well, they all are, he says. All the kids, naturally. But not especially, no, no more than any of the others —

He seems to be about to go on, but then gives up and puts his head in his hands.

Then I remember.

No, I say. She is, Mick — she's been drawing these things —

In a stiff and unreal way, I feel myself get up from the table and move across the room. Fetching the scrunched-up piece of paper that I pulled from the paw of Rosa's kitten.

I open it out to show them. I wait for them to look. It now has a pale brown stain on it — tea or coffee — got from lying on the kitchen table all afternoon probably. But still — the careful words and pictures: A Map Of Where To Find It.

Look, I say. Look, she did this.

What? says Mick, What is it?

It's Lennie's heart, these pink things are hearts. And the sea. And there's Lennie —

Mick stares at me. I ignore him. Mawhinney leans over to see. So does Lacey. They all try to see. Why can't they see? I wait for them to understand.

A Map Of Where To Find It, I tell them.

It? says Mick.

Her heart. Look, I say, raising my voice now, surely you can see what it is —? Can't you? It's a map —

Mick touches my hand.

It's just one of her little drawings, Tess. She's always doing these funny drawings, he tells Mawhinney.

A map of where to find it, I tell them again. Breathing hard, through my teeth.

But Lacey looks serious.

You think that's what it is, he says. That's she's off somewhere trying to find Lennie's heart?

I close my eyes with relief.

Yes, I tell him. Yes, I do. That's what I think.

Mick puts his arm around me.

Oh Tess, he says and I feel his body tremble against mine.

No, Mick, I mean it.

It's a game of hers, he says, the Lennie thing. A mad little game. Come on, you said so yourself.

I shake him off me.

It's not a game, I tell them. It's deadly serious. She thinks she's seen Lennie. She thinks Lennie talks to her. You know Rosa, Mick. I swear to you, she thinks it's absolutely real.

Mawhinney gets up and goes over and starts rinsing out his coffee mug at the sink.

Oh please, I say. You don't need to do that.

He looks odd and wrong standing there at our kitchen sink. His big wrists look suddenly futile as he lays the mug on the draining board and glances around for somewhere to wipe his hands.

I can't bear it. I hand him a tea towel.

Could I — can I have a cigarette off you? I ask him in a low voice. He's never smoked in my presence but I've seen him stop to light up the moment he gets out on those bald white steps of the pier.

He hands me the whole pack, slightly squashed and almost full.

Really, he says, when I try to give them back. You'd be doing me a favour. I'm trying to smoke less.

He hands the tea towel back to me as well. I put it to my face and use it to wipe away the tears that keep on coming.

When he and Lacey have gone, Mick and I go on sitting at the table and I smoke one of the cigarettes. Mick doesn't even mention it. I feel grateful for how it scoots up into my brain and steadies me. Smoke clings to every thought and I'm glad of something to hold. I am almost dizzy with fear.

Halfway through it though I stub it out on a plate.

I can't just sit here, I say.

No, Mick agrees.

We decide we'll take it in turns to go out looking. One staying with the boys who are at last sleeping, the other going out with a torch and maybe with Fletcher and just going anywhere they can think of to go.

Mawhinney has said to get a piece of Rosa's clothing ready. Something she's worn recently. Sniffer dogs are coming from Yarmouth. If she's not found during the night, they intend to cover the marshes at first light.

I slip off my shoes and go upstairs and flick on the light in her room, automatically picking up clothes from where they lie on the floor. School skirt, bobbly school jumper, stained with something. A sock with fluff on it. Her striped pyjama top is there among the felt pens and half-broken cassette boxes. Limp from being worn last night. I hold it to my face. The Rosa smell is unbearable.

And so is the sight of her messed-up but totally empty and unslept-in bed — unbearable. Maria lies hunched at the end of it, her paws folded under her and her two unblinking eyes fixed on me.

From the next room comes the loud up and down of Jordan's breath. I turn off the light and go back down to the kitchen.

Do you think this will do? I say to Mick, dropping the pyjama top on the table.

He doesn't look at it.

I'm going to be so fucking cross with her when all this is over, I tell him.

No you're not.

No, you're right, I'm not.

I go out there. I go all the way back to the pier, to the car park, to all the places that frighten me. The night is thick and empty of light and the sea sounds wild. Fletcher runs alongside, suddenly excited, trying to bite and snap at the lead, wanting to play. I didn't want him with me, but Mick wouldn't let me go alone without him.

I pull him in sharply. Maybe if Rosa could just hear him bark. Maybe —

Black wind rushes past my ears. It's a rough night. Out there, beyond the pier, you can hear the sea chopping and slapping its big wet jaws. A swell that would be dangerous if you were on it. Grey clouds skidding and racing across the moon, drowning out the yellow of its light.

Rosa!

I call for her — I call out for my daughter. I call out so many times I quickly lose count as one minute of calling and calling overlaps into the next. Every time I call, my voice is straightaway sucked in by the wind, and swallowed. My tears too, sucked away. My hair whips all over my face and I use my free hand, the one not holding the lead, to pull it back.

Rosa!

Fletcher barks once. His lonely, mystified bark, the one he does when he's either being left somewhere or doesn't know what's going on. It has a kind of scream at the end of it. He barks like that now, just once, and then once more.

We run down the concrete steps and go crashing over the shingle under the great concrete legs of the pier, the place where in summer kids chuck their used condoms and takeaway cartons. Water hits the graffitied sides of the pier, the breakwater, so hard you'd think it would come loose and float away. Fletcher barks again — he barks so hard and pointedly at the water, you really would think there was someone there.

Rosa!

We wait for a moment looking at the water, but we're looking at nothing.

I stumble back up into the car park. Two cars are parked there at the far end, but otherwise the tarmac expanse is empty. No one uses the car park in November, especially not at night. Wind rattles the heavy chain on the boating-lake gate and an old fish and chip paper is lifted by the wind and hits the side of the phone box.

I shudder and tremble. Circles of cold close around me.

The moon is wrapped up in cloud at the moment that Lacey moves out of the shadows. As his arms come around me, I gasp.

Shh. It's OK, he says softly. Look. It's me.

In his arms, I can't move, can't go forward or back. I begin to cry.

What have I done? I say to him. Oh what? What did I do?

He puts his hand on my head, on my hair.

Shh, he says. It's not you, Tess, it isn't, it's not you.

But — my Rosa!

They'll find her, he says. They will, they'll find her.

I cry louder.

Fletcher whimpers and Lacey takes him from me and, keeping his arms around me or at least on me, he presses me against him and doesn't speak. I know he is trying to keep me altogether, to stop parts of me flying off, and that he's a good person basically and that he knows less than I do and also that he can do nothing for me now.

Where is she? I say desperately. What can have happened?

I want him to tell me but he doesn't answer, he just says nothing. He doesn't say they've found her and he doesn't any more say it will be OK, he just says nothing and stands with me there.

Chapter 17

ALEX RINGS EARLY THE NEXT MORNING. HIS VOICE IS jagged and upset.

Where is she? he says. I don't believe it. I mean — where the fuck could she possibly go?

I try to speak but I can't. My head is hard and tight. I'm afraid of what I might say.

I don't know what to do, he says. How to help. Tell me, Tess —

We've lost her, I hear myself whisper. Al, I just know it — she's lost, gone.

Look, he says. Listen to me —

I try to listen. But I don't know what he says. All the time, other things creep in. Down the street is the clink of

Doug the milkman delivering, just like any normal day. Birds doing things in the roof. Outside the window the sky is white, stripped bare by wind.

I'm half dressed, trying to drink a glass of water. If I don't drink, I won't be able to feed Liv, it's as simple as that.

We're just — waiting, I tell him, my voice shaky with tears. Oh God, Al, oh God.

I should have come round, last night.

There was no point.

Have you slept?

No, I say. Have you?

A little. I think so, yes.

He's silent for a moment.

Christ, he says. Jesus, Tess, I mean it. What's Mawhinney saying? Where could she have gone —?

They're all out there looking, I tell him. So many of them. He says if she's out there they'll find her —

Alex takes a breath. Or maybe he's smoking. In the background I can hear Connor saying something to Max.

I'm sorry, I tell him.

What do you mean?

Today. That it had to be today — to have this — today.

Don't be so fucking stupid, he says.

A beat of silence. Tears are creeping down my cheeks again.

Look, he says, I've got Patsy here with the boys. Bob's shattered — I don't know what time he got in. Do you want me to come round?

There's nothing you can do, I tell him.

Be with you?

I don't need that.

Where's Mick?

Out there, with them.

When's he coming back?

I don't know.

The funeral will go ahead. It can't be postponed and no one wants it to be. Everyone's ready. The town needs it to happen now.

For Christ's sake, Alex says when I tell him Mick and I are still coming, neither of you need to be there. What does it matter? It will all happen with or without you —

We'll see what happens, is what Mick says.

I know what he means. He means that the afternoon is an unthinkably faraway place. So much could happen between now and then.

I start to think things. I think, if Rosa's just run away, if she's perfectly OK and just being naughty and hiding or something, then she will be there, she will somehow come to Lennie's funeral, I know she will. She has a watch. She knows when it is. She, more than anyone, would want to see Lennie buried, there beneath that spreading yew.

I want to be there, I tell Alex, panic mounting. I have to be there.

Tess, he says, why?

For Lennie.

You know what Lennie would want, he says.

*   *   *

The boys are watching a video, but only because I made them. Their faces are turned towards it, but they keep looking around them — Jordan at me, into the kitchen, Nat out of the window.

Jordan woke up this morning with a stomach ache and asked immediately about Rosa. Nat wants to go out looking for her again and he's angry with me because I won't let him.

Liv is asleep, but not for long. She's hungry and my milk is going. Fast. I can feel it. When I tried to feed this morning at about five thirty — weepy and tired — I was shocked at how little there was, just a thin blueish spurt and then a dribble, then nothing. Liv sucked so hard it hurt, then burst into furious cries. Then so did I. So, almost, did Mick.

Now my breasts feel small, useless.

It's the anxiety, says Maggie Farr who has kindly come over with a tin of formula. Tess, seriously — no one could keep on feeding through all of this.

If I can just keep drinking, I tell her.

You need to eat as well.

I'm trying to eat, I say but it's a lie. When Mick made me a sandwich last night I almost choked on it. My body is rejecting everything.

Mick has already put the bottles in the steriliser. Seeing that pink and blue tin of powdered milk and knowing what it means makes me cry all over again.

I don't want to get into all that, I tell Mick.

All what?

I don't want to start boiling kettles and sterilising.

He looks at me with a strained face.

But you said —

I know what I said.

You won't manage, he says, if she's hungry and crying.

I know, but I didn't want to stop yet. I wanted to keep going a bit longer.

She's quite old enough, Tess —

It's so final.

Tess.

I just don't want it to be — like this.

By lunchtime nothing has changed except that Liv has done it, she's taken a bottle. Mawhinney and his men are still out. Mick goes to take a shower and Maggie sits with me in the kitchen. I can't speak or think but Maggie doesn't seem to expect it. All I want to do is to sit by the phone and wait and Maggie lets me do it.

My two girls, I tell her and then I stop myself. Words, bursting up to the surface, but pointless. My two girls.

Maggie takes my hand.

She has on her black clothes already, even though Alex has expressly asked for people not to wear black. The brighter the better, he says, especially as Lennie hated black. A colour that sucked out the light, she said it was.

Maggie's black dress has red piping.

A compromise, she tells me. I know, I chickened out. I couldn't dress in bright colours. I just don't feel it, I just can't.

Tears slide down her face. I lean forward and tuck in her label which is sticking out at the back.

I feel I'm doing more harm than good being here, she says.

No, I tell her. No, it's not true.

She makes us some coffee. She makes it too weak because she's not used to making it in an espresso pot. She opens her handbag and gets out her sweeteners, clicks a couple into hers. We sit there and neither of us touch our cups.

There's washing-up piled in the sink. Maggie is so desperate to load the dishwasher and start washing pans that she keeps on touching the apron that Mick has flung down on a chair. Eventually I give in and let her. It's easier.

Rosa knows when the funeral is, I tell Maggie. And where.

Yes, Maggie agrees, but she carries on standing with her back to me. I long for her to turn so I can see if there is hope on her face.

When Maggie has gone, Mick comes back down. He has on his dark clothes, the suit we got dry-cleaned, the white pressed shirt that belonged to his father. I can feel him looking at me, trying to decide whether to say something or not. I feel him decide not.

The service is to begin at two. Lennie's body, already on its way from Halesworth, is to start the slow and winding journey towards Blackshore at one. The bells will start ringing then. An hour of bells. A sound not heard in the town since the last lifeboat tragedy, two decades ago.

Alex phones and I know what he's doing is telling Mick for fuck's sake to forget being a pall bearer, to go and carry on looking for Rosa instead.

I hear Mick start to argue.

There's all those police out there, Al, I hear him say. It makes no difference whether I'm with them for that hour or not.

Mick pauses while Alex says something, I don't know what.

I'm already changed, he says uselessly.

He's silent a moment, listening to Alex. Then he says OK, then he puts down the phone.

I look at him.

Are you doing it?

No, he says. No, of course I'm not.

I hear him cross the hall and go into the downstairs toilet. I hear him shut the door. I hear him being sick.

After a misty, rainy start, the day has brightened and it's a lot like yesterday, with great sudden floods of sun swooping over the rooftops.

I make the boys eat a plate of sandwiches. Peanut butter and honey, anything they'll eat. I make too many — I am programmed always to make food for three. Jordan insists on putting two sandwiches on a plate for Rosa. He gets the clingfilm out to cover it and drops the box. The film unravels and gets in a mess. He begins to cry.

I wipe his tears and tell him it's OK. His hair is cool against my face. Together we smooth the clingfilm back over the plate and put the sandwich next to the bottles of formula in the fridge.

Nat sighs and looks down at his plate. His eyes are circled with tiredness.

What is it, Nat?

You know I don't like crunchy peanut butter, he says.

The bells have started. Mick comes down again, in jeans now, and finds me standing in the kitchen and holding a dishcloth and staring at the wall. He takes the cloth from my hands and gently pushes me into a chair.

No, I tell him, I don't want to. I don't want to sit.

Come on, he says.

I thought you'd gone, I say. Aren't you going? Out again?

In a minute, he says.

He stands there.

Tess, he says and his face is terrible, dark with grief.

What?

I need to know, are you going to leave me?

I stare at him.

What?

Am I losing you?

Why? I say. I am thinking of Rosa and unable to follow what he's saying.

Just tell me. Please. Is that what's happening?

I lay my head in my arms which are spread on the table.

I lost her, I say. It's my fault.

I did, he says. I had her. She was with me. I lost her.

No, I tell him. It was me. I didn't think — I wasn't paying attention. I was out, I was with —

He shuts his eyes.

You don't have to tell me, he says. I don't want to know what you've been doing.

So —

I just want to know about you and me, if we'll go on —

What do you mean, go on?

As a family, you and me.

I begin to cry, hard deep sobs.

Do we have to talk about this now? I say. Is this really the moment?

His face changes.

But Tess, he says, there are no other moments — we don't get any of these moments. Tell me, when are they? When do we get to talk?

After a moment or two, he sits and he says, I'm sorry. But it's not just you, you know.

What do you mean, I ask him, confused, not just me?

He looks at me.

What I said — it's not just you.

What?

There have been times, he says, when I wanted to do something, too.

Something? I say. What do you mean? What sort of thing?

He shrugs in a horrible, hard way.

Something bad, he says. Something to cause — damage
— to our relationship.

I look at him and taste fear in my mouth.

But — why? I ask him.

He shrugs. His eyes are cold.

Just to see.

See what?

His face is hard and tight.

See if our marriage survives it.

But, I say, you wouldn't do that —

Wouldn't I?

I mean, what about the children?

He looks at the table.

What about them?

I stare at his face and don't recognise him, the look on
it, the look of a stranger.

If you want the truth, he says, there have been times
when I didn't really think very much about the children.

Oh.

Does that shock you?

I don't know, I say.

Seconds pass. I'd have thought it would be impossible
to think, but it's not. Just that each thought I have comes
wrapped around a picture of Rosa.

When Lennie died, I tell him, feeling around carefully for
words that seem true, I felt — well, I suppose — a little mad.

We all did, he says flatly.

I take a breath and look at him.

But —

No, he says, I mean it. You aren't the only one, Tess. All this time — it hasn't just been you —

I don't listen to this.

I had to find out, I tell him, I had to see whether I could be different without you. It's been so long and —

He waits.

We are so much a part of each other. Or we were — until Lennie had this — thing — done to her —

He seems to think about this for a moment. I hold my breath. He waits.

And were you? he says, a little coldly. Were you different without me?

I can't lie. I think of Lacey. His hands on my head, on my body.

A little, I say and I don't look at him. Yes, a little, yes I was.

And how did that feel?

It felt — oh —

I look at him and feel afraid — afraid of Mick, of my husband.

Good. It felt quite good.

A tear slips down. Outside the bells have changed and are making a different sound.

I thought it might be the answer, I tell him.

To what? he says. The answer to what?

I don't know. To — all this.

He doesn't ask what all this is. He sighs and pushes his hands through his sleeked hair. Still he says nothing. He just looks at me.

I love you, I tell him. I haven't ever not loved you.

I hold out my hand for him but he doesn't take it, he doesn't move. I'm sorry, I tell him after a moment or two.

What for?

That I've been so bad to you.

Have you? he says. Have you been bad?

Yes, I say. Yes, Mick, I have.

The bells are still ringing. Above the sound, seagulls wheeling and screaming in the sky. Jordan comes in. He's changed and put on his corduroy trousers, the only ones he has that aren't jeans or tracksuit bottoms, that are half smart. And a T-shirt with Homer Simpson on. Toothpaste splashes on it.

I want to go to the church, he says, looking from Mick to me and back again. Why can't we?

Nat stands behind him with his hands in his pockets and looks at us as well. I sense a rare moment of cooperation between them. You can tell by their organised faces that they've been talking upstairs.

Aren't we going? he says.

Mick hesitates.

Let's go, I say to him suddenly.

What? he says.

To the church — please, Mick, let's just go there.

She might be there, says Jordan, unblinking. Nat says nothing, looks at the floor.

I look at him. I know Mick knows — that I am thinking the things that Jordan is saying. That they are useless things to think. That she won't be there, she couldn't, she can't possibly be.

But he doesn't say that. He looks at me and says, We'd better be quick, then.

St Margaret's is packed. There are even people standing at the back. Almost the whole of our town is in that church.

We sit at the front on the left-hand side with Alex and the boys. When Alex sees us, he shakes his head at us and then hugs us both. Tears on his face. Some people try to smile at us, others are careful not to look.

Bob, hair combed, face tight and rigid, is next to Patsy. After the service he says he's going straight out to look for Rosa again. Patsy has done as suggested and dressed in red — red shoes and bag, the lot. She stays very still, facing front. There aren't many other bright outfits, but one or two are scattered, like petals among the black.

There are some press in the church but no cameras apparently, as respectfully requested by Canon Cleve. And the burial is not to be filmed or photographed.

In front of us, on a plinth, is Lennie's coffin. Alex didn't want it draped in anything. He wanted the beauty of the wood to show. So there it is, naked, gleaming, huge. Jordan stares at it. He knows not to ask me if she's in there.

In fact, our children are perfectly still, perfectly quiet. I had thought they might be restless but they're not. Even Liv stays quiet in Mick's arms, a string of saliva hanging from her soft, bunched-up mouth. Jordan sits with his small feet on the kneeler. He only glances around him when someone coughs or sneezes.

Alex holds both his sons' hands tight and stares straight ahead. I can tell that Connor has been crying, but he's OK now. He seems to be in a dream, or else he's tired, or both. I don't look at Mick. Instead I look up, at the tall, plain, light-filled windows through which you can always see sky, blueish cloud, tops of trees. Then I shut my eyes and for the first time ever in my life I pray.

Canon Cleve says that Lennie touched so many people. That was her gift. She will be remembered for her humour and generosity and her zest for life. When he makes a joke about her, a few people laugh. The laugh cracks the silence, lets everyone shift in their seats.

He says he hopes and prays that Alex and his family will be given strength to rebuild their lives, that they'll become a stronger family, bound together in love and grief by this tragedy.

Then he says, Let us pray.

A sudden memory comes to me, of Lennie making dough for all our kids in the kitchen and, when pieces of it got trampled all over the floor and the sofa and carpet, laughing and saying it didn't matter. Her face as she says it:

It's only furniture. Her fingers and the wrists of her jumper covered in flour. When she pushes the hair out of her face, she has to do it with her arm, awkward, laughing.

I feel myself trembling all over. Mick turns to me and mouths, Are you OK?

I nod.

Jordan's kneeler is embroidered with beach huts — one red, one yellow, one blue. He traces their shapes with a finger, round and round, up and down, over and over.

I rest my head in my arms on the hard polished wood of the pew and now the sea comes into view — wobbling and sparkling on a far-off day — and Rosa is hurrying up the beach, bringing me endless brown pebbles and demanding to know if they're amber. And I wish that just one of those times, one pebble could be honey-gold and light as plastic and I could just say, Yes.

Let us stand, says Cleve.

Oh no, I hear myself mutter to Mick, I can't do this.

It's the hymn Alex and Lennie had at their wedding. Patsy is weeping silently.

Mick leans his mouth to my ear.

Do you want to go out?

I shake my head.

I'm fine, I tell him.

He does not sing — Mick never sings — but stares up at the carving on the choir stalls. The minutes pass and I won't allow myself to think or look behind me. And then eventually I do, I look down at the grey flagstones and then I turn my head and see Lacey. He's right back against the far wall

on the left, standing there with a couple of uniformed officers and he's looking straight at me. His face doesn't change,
but he doesn't take his eyes away either. They are the last
thing I see before Cleve asks everyone to kneel for the final
prayers and Lennie's floury hands fly back at me again just
as the cold grey floor comes up to smack me in the face.

The grave is almost three metres deep. That's what Nat
tells me in the wide, cold porch as Sue Peach brings me a
glass of water and someone else holds a wad of Kleenex to
the cut on my head.

You got blood all over the floor, Jordan tells me as
people shuffle past and try not to look.

You might need a stitch on that, says Sue but I grab hold
of the Kleenex myself and I look at it and say no. I can tell
I'll have a hell of a bruise tomorrow but the bleeding has already almost stopped.

I'm fine, I tell them and no one disagrees. Mick takes the
children out to the graveside and tells me to stay sitting for
a moment. I tell him I'm coming.

As the last mourners leave the church, Lacey is behind
them. Up close his black suit is actually dark grey, his tie
crumpled.

He squats down next to where I'm sitting on the cold
stone bench and asks me if I'm OK and I just look at him.
That's all. I just gaze and gaze at his kind face.

The burial is just family, but this of course includes us.
We are all family. The rest of the town stands out there on

Bartholomew's Green and watches as the coffin is lowered down on its ropes and put in the ground. Max can't stop himself leaning forward a little way to see it go in. Con begins to cry loudly. Patsy puts her arms around him, hugs him close.

In a pocket of deep silence, Alex takes some earth from the undertaker's trowel and lets it fall and then, more slowly, Bob does the same. In the church, he was weeping and weeping as if he'd never stop, but now he's calm, dry-eyed. Max takes some earth and lets it fall, but Con won't do it, he refuses.

When the trowel is held out to him, he turns and pushes his face into Alex's clothes and Alex staggers back a second, caught off balance, and then takes his hand and holds him close. Patsy shakes her head. Tears start to come down Max's face. Alex gathers him close as well.

It's over, I can see him saying. It's OK, it's over.

This, I think, this is the moment. I glance hurriedly around the graveyard, at the rows of stones leaning back like teeth. Nothing. No sign of anything. Just gravel and shadows and stone.

Then Patsy leads Alex and the boys away from the grave and out through the little gate that leads to the playground. It's a funny way to leave the cemetery but there's no other, not today, not if they want to avoid the crowd. We watch them take the long route through the playground, past the swings and the slide and the big tyre with the bark chippings strewn underneath, past the rough-mown lumpy meadow where on so many taken-for-granted summer evenings Lennie and I stood in the warm wind with mugs of tea in our hands and nothing on our feet, just shouting and shouting for our five suddenly deaf kids to come in for baths, or tea or bed.

A cold late lunch is served at Alex's, but we skip it. No one expects us to go. Even Alex has to be begged not to abandon it after half an hour and rush off to join in the search.

And then, just after five, Mawhinney comes round with a piece of news. He says that Darren Sims of all people has reported seeing someone looking very like Rosa standing right on the groynes down beyond Gun Hill. Yesterday evening, just before dusk.

What? I cry. Standing actually on the groynes?

Mawhinney folds his arms and looks me in the eye.

He says she was shouting at the sea.

Christ, says Mick and he looks at me.

Mawhinney says that Darren said it looked like she was perfectly happy and talking to someone.

Talking? To someone in the sea?

That's what it looked like.

But, for Christ's sake, Mick says, who?

Half an hour later, Darren is brought round to see us. He looks bothered, pink. His sweatshirt is muddy and on inside out.

I couldn't see anyone out there swimming or nothing, he says. I'm not being funny, but it looked like she was talking to the sea.

He tells us that he yelled at her to get down off the groynes because everyone knows you don't go on them, that they're dangerous.

You were that close? Mick says and his face is pale and slicked with sweat. You could call to her?

Oh yes, Darren says. But she didn't hear a word of it. Or at least she turned round once but didn't do nothing, just looked at me and turned straight back again.

I sit. My head is bursting.

Ten minutes later, Darren's mum rings us. She sounds very upset. She explains to Mick that Darren did go home and tell her what he'd seen but she didn't believe him. She told him not to be daft and sent him off to pick up the two bags that needed collecting from the launderette.

Now, of course, she's kicking herself. All afternoon she's been in tears and can't concentrate on anything, not till she knows that little girl's safe.

The trouble with Darren, she says, is he's always coming home with these strange stories and I'm used to it. They never amount to anything, I swear they don't. I've learned over the years that the best thing really is just to ignore them all.

Livvy is crying and crying and won't settle. I take her upstairs and change her. In her nappy is the first poo made of formula milk — hard, brown, solid, of the real world. As I fold the nappy away and put it in a bag and clean her, she goes quiet and still and fascinated, following my movements with her clear, dark eyes.

Someone phones the squad to say a young girl has been seen getting into a blue van at Leiston, but from the description she is older than Rosa and Mawhinney says they're not going to follow it up, not at the moment anyway.

The six o'clock local TV news has Lennie's funeral on it and this is immediately followed by a report about Rosa. The picture they use is a school portrait, an awful one, in which Rosa — a smooth and alien child — smiles smugly at the camera against a sky-blue plastic background, her hair smooth, her collar down, her cardigan neatly buttoned.

You gave them that? I say to Mick.

It was the only one I could find.

From the tray in the hall?

Yes.

It was supposed to go back to school. You hated it, remember.

Oh, he says. Oh well.

I go and sit on the steps of The Polecat. I don't bother unlocking it and going in, I just sit there in my coat. It's all I've come for, just to sit.

It's dark. Seven o'clock. Seven or maybe half past. I don't know. I'm very calm now, unafraid. I sit there and I stare and stare at the rolling mass of the sea till the darkness comes up inside my head and I think maybe I can see right into it. As you can see into anything if you look at it for long enough.

I feel weightless, invisible, and in a strange way everything is clear to me now. I even think that maybe if I stop breathing and remember where to look, I might be able to see my Rosa.

Eventually Lacey comes to find me, as I knew he would.

Oh, I say quietly. Hello. I thought you'd come.

He stands on the prom with his hands in his pockets. There is a strong wind blowing, a wind I must say I hadn't noticed till he arrived. But I do see it now, it's impossible not to, because of how his clothes flap, how he has to hold his coat closed. His big coat, the one he's wearing, makes him seem very far away, just a tiny speck really, though I wouldn't of course tell him that.

I do want to tell him that his face looks terrible, just daunted and upset and worse than I've ever seen it look, but my heart's fighting so hard with my mouth that I can't get the words out.

Tess, he says.

I shut my eyes. I can't look at him. I daren't.

I'm sorry, he says. Oh Tess, I'm so sorry.

He puts his hands on my shoulders, which makes me feel a little sick, but I don't stop him.

No, I start to say but already it's too late.

Come on, he says. Come on.

No, I tell him, pulling away now, suddenly frantic.

I'm sorry, he says. I'm sorry. I have to take you back now.

Chapter 18

ROSA'S BODY IS FOUND BY A MAN OUT WALKING HIS DOG on Covehithe Cliffs. He spots her down at the edge of the water as he walks along the gorse path above.

He says he isn't really looking down at the beach at all, but his eye is caught by the bright purple of her sweatshirt. She is floating, face down, nudged against the rocks by the tide. At first he wonders if it's perhaps an adult, in a wetsuit, swimming. But soon he realises the body is far too small to be out there bobbing around in the water alone.

He scrambles down the steep cliffside using his stick to help him, but the dog gets to the body before he does and starts barking furiously. He never goes in, the man says, but he always gets excited when he sees people in the water.

He is still hoping at that point that he has it all wrong

and it's someone swimming. But as he gets closer, he sees it's a child, a girl. And that she has long fronds of seaweed grasped in her hands, he tells the police, her fingers wrapped tight around it, as if she's been trying to hold on.

A jutting rock is the only thing stopping her being washed back out to sea again, since the tide has finished coming in and is already on the turn. With some effort, the man pulls her out of the water and onto the beach. He turns her over. Her eyes are open and her mouth is blue. He feels for a pulse and thinks about trying to resuscitate her, but he's scared. He doesn't really know how to go about it. He can't quite catch his breath himself.

So he calls 999 on his mobile phone and then he goes a bit wobbly and has to sit down. He says it's very lucky he has the phone with him. He never normally brings it when walking the dog as he worries about losing it or leaving it somewhere. But as it happens he's expecting a delivery from Wrentham and grabbed it at the last moment, in case they arrived when he was out.

He lives up on Holly Lane, he says. Twenty-eight Holly Lane, Covehithe. That's the address. His name is Fitzgerald. The mobile phone is his daughter's but he sometimes borrows it. He wouldn't have one himself, he thinks they're a waste of money. How ridiculous, that he never learned to do mouth to mouth. He doesn't think he'll ever forgive himself. He feels terrible.

The paramedics assure him that Rosa has been dead some time — that no amount of resuscitation would have made a difference. But the man won't listen. He is terribly agitated and upset by the time they get to him and has to be given a hot sweet drink to calm him down. He keeps on repeating the detail about the phone to the police, even when they tell him they've got the point.

It's hard to tell how long Rosa has been in the water exactly but police believe it's close on twenty-four hours. It has to do with skin colour, how much water is in the stomach, how distended the lungs are. It's easier to tell with children apparently, because the changes happen more quickly and are more dramatic.

That night Lacey takes me all the way back from The Polecat to the kitchen at home.

It seems like the longest walk in all the world, that distance from the beach hut to our kitchen. Sometimes I don't think I'll make it. I walk and walk but my legs don't seem to touch the ground. But Lacey keeps his arm around me all the time, all the way up the street as we walk there in the dark, in the howling wind, the salt, the silence.

Even when we get in the kitchen, he keeps his arm around me. No one says anything. Everything's shifted and the rules have changed. There are no rules — there's only a phone call from Covehithe.

Mick is sitting there, crying. He is shaking all over and crying very hard, harder than I've ever seen him cry. Except for once — the time when Nat was born and for about half an hour we didn't think he was going to be OK and I was too out of it to care, and then once it turned out he was fine, Mick wrapped his arms around me and just sobbed.

Just like this.

Mawhinney is there and two female police officers I've never seen before. One of them is gently holding Mick's arm, touching his shoulder. The other's got Livvy who's holding her floppy monkey and gazing around at all the people.

They're bringing her, Mick says. In the ambulance. After the police have finished with her. They were going to take her to the hospital, but I said not to, I said of course we'd want her brought here right now. I told them we'd want to have her with us at home. I knew you'd want the same.

I look at him and tell him that I do and then I open my eyes and my mouth and I scream.

I had Rosa at home. Second baby, easy birth. So easy that I remember laughing all the way through it. My memory is of a high, hot summer morning, a perfect cup of tea and an even more perfect, fuzz-headed seven-pound child. And Mick having to shampoo the carpet where I, forgetting the waterproof sheet, simply bent over, crouched and slipped my daughter out, easy and certain as a flower opening.

We carry her up and lay her on her bed, surrounded by all her soft toys and her Walkman, her private diary with the padlock. Maria the kitten comes and settles at the foot of the bed, ponching and ponching at the duvet with her claws just as if it was a normal bedtime.

In the end, Mick pushes her off and shuts her out. I don't blame him but I know Rosa would have been furious.

What'd you do that for? She'd have sulked. What's Maria ever done to you?

With a pair of sharp scissors that I normally use for cutting the kids' hair, we snip off the wet clothes she's wearing. Then I get the bowl the children use when they feel sick at night and Mick fills it up with warm water and together we wash her with a flannel and soap.

I wish her small, brittle fingernails weren't all broken and torn, but at least they are clean for once. Bleached, almost, like tiny shells — I've never seen them so white. I take her coldish blue hand in mine and try to slot my own hot, trembling fingers in among hers but I can't. Already they're getting stiff and hard — and the soft pad of flesh beneath her thumb is starting to feel different and not like flesh at all but like something more solid.

Now and then, the room fades and I think I doze, but Mick nudges me awake.

Come on, he says. Clothes.

We can't decide what to dress her in. Eventually we agree that her blue jersey nightie and Gap hooded thing are best.

I don't want her to be cold, I tell Mick and I know how it sounds, but I still have to say it. All through this, he doesn't speak except when necessary and he doesn't look at me. I watch as he struggles to do up the bottom of the zip on her hooded thing.

I know Rosa likes the Gap thing, but I'm not so sure about the nightie. Being Rosa, wouldn't she have preferred jeans? Except that trousers would be almost impossible to get on her right now. Her legs are terribly swollen and no longer move so easily.

We leave the dolphin pendant round her neck. It's her favourite piece of jewellery, the only one she'll wear. Dolphins have magical powers, she says, it's like a talisman, a protection against, well, against all sorts of things.

There's a tiny graze on her forehead and another larger one on her chin — probably from the undertow of the shingle, the paramedics said. There's also a huge bruise on her shoulder but you can't see that now. Her eyes are shut, her eyelids dusted with mauve.

Before they closed her eyes, I looked. I insisted. What I saw was that they were already darkening, losing the spark and shine that is Rosa. I know she believes that your soul goes somewhere when you die. Obviously hers had already gone to that place. Knowing her, it would have rushed there, eager to be first. You could see this on her face — that her soul had spilled out of her far too quickly, leaving her somehow startled and bereft.

The police say we can keep her till morning but that then she will have to go to Ipswich so a proper post-mortem can be carried out. Though, based on the pathologist's initial examination, her death is not being treated as suspicious. She almost certainly just fell in the sea and drowned, they say.

But she was a good swimmer, I insist. I say it again and again to anyone who'll listen. But you can see they just daren't tell me what I already know: that it doesn't matter how far you can swim. Anyone can drown in a rough sea on a dark night.

*   *   *

We sit there all night with our Rosa. Sometimes we hold hands, Mick and me, and sometimes we hold onto each other, our whole bodies moving under waves of sobs, but mostly we just sit there in our separate silences. I see him gazing at his daughter, snatching his last hungry looks. I watch him doing this and I don't know what to say or how to feel.

As dawn comes and a greyish light moves over the chest of drawers, the bookshelves, the collection of ornamental cats and duck feathers, the pink dried-up glitter pens with their lids left off, Rosa's face seems to change again. It looks almost alive. A trick of the light, I tell myself — or else it's just that we've got used to it, to her, to this.

We both lean in and kiss her, first him then me, then both of us wanting to go again. Our girl. She doesn't smell bad — just of our family and of our soap and, slightly, of Rosa. Then we fetch the boys in to say goodbye. Mick says that's important, letting them see. Nat and Jordan look at her so carefully, as if the wrong sort of look could damage her. I feel almost proud of them, that they can look at their sister so gently.

Can I touch her? Jordan whispers.

Of course, I tell him and he reaches out and puts a hand on her cold, white forehead, on her smoothed hair.

Can she feel that? he says and my heart jumps as I tell him, No.

Yes, but if she was alive, could she? he says.

Yes, I whisper. If she was alive, yes.

He stands there and looks at her and thinks about this. I look at Mick. He is shuddering with sobs, his whole body moving. No noise, just shaking silently.

There is a time — I think so, it comes back to me later — when we all just stand and cry in the room together. That's the feeling I have anyway, though the moment has long slunk away, out of memory. I remember Jordan's small knuckles pressing on my face, the empty hungry smell of his breath. I remember Nat, the dark top of his head wrapped inside Mick's arms.

And when the ambulance comes, the men are so good. They creep up the stairs so quietly and carefully, as if a million babies were asleep in our house, instead of just Liv with her mouth wet and hands flung up in her cot. Fletcher barks as they come and then again as they go but I shush him and straightaway he shuts up.

As I stand there by the front door, I think I will never be able to let them take her, never be able to let her — that small blonde fast-asleep baby from that long ago summer morning — go. But in the end I surprise myself and it all happens quite easily, and I do, we let her, we do.

Chapter 19

LENNIE'S HEART IS NEVER FOUND. SOME MONTHS LATER though, something horrible is washed up in a plastic carrier bag at Dunwich. It turns out to be a heart — badly decomposed and a long time in the water. The carrier bag containing it has been sealed with duct tape — but not very well. I can't imagine what it was like for whoever had to open it.

Reporters rush to the town, only to be told it's nothing, the heart of a farm animal probably — maybe a cow, maybe a horse. Certainly not a human. No one has any idea why it was chucked in the sea in a carrier bag, but the truth is, people do strange things. Satanic ritual, one or two of the papers eagerly imply, but nothing the police say backs that up.

* * *

And no one is convicted of Lennie's murder either. The lead Mawhinney thought he had just petered out. Not enough evidence. It takes more than just a lead to get an arrest, he says, and even more to get a conviction. Mick always said that, after those crucial first days had elapsed, he didn't think the police ever really believed they'd get anyone.

The case stays open — Alex has been assured it will remain open for some time — but, though Mawhinney stays in touch, the murder squad leaves the town and the Dolphin Diner gets its storage rooms back and life returns pretty much to normal. One or two vindictive people continue to cut Darren Sims in the street and whisper about him in shops and pubs, and someone tells him he shouldn't ever bother showing his face at The Red Lion again.

But everyone knows who they are and no one supports them. Everyone agrees that Darren should be left alone. As Jan Curdell points out, since when did a low IQ make someone a murderer? Besides, Alex later admitted he could have been mistaken about seeing Darren. So the police have established for once and for all that there's nothing to link him to Lennie that night.

Actually, the knife Darren found in the ditch that time is indeed a lino-cutter. It is eventually traced back to a carpet fitter from Wangford who was laying a new floor in the Pool Room at The Anchor. How it got from there to the ditch at Blackshore is something no one has ever been able to explain. Even when the police interview the carpet man at some length — though there's still no forensic evidence to indicate this is the murder weapon — still no satisfactory explanation emerges.

Anyway, the man has a perfect alibi for the night of Lennie's murder. He was in custody in Lowestoft at the time, charged with drunken driving.

Anyone who knows Alex well knows he won't stay single for very long. After the funeral is over, after Rosa, it's only a matter of a month or so before he starts an affair with Gemma Dawson who has been helping out with the boys and who, at seventeen, is far too young for him. In the end, Gemma ditches him, but too late, Polly's furious. She never forgives him for distracting her daughter during her spring mocks.

So it's a relief when he falls for Ellie — single, thirtyish, independent and with her own business making and selling wrought-iron garden furniture. Ellie's based in London but, after only a couple of months of knowing him, she puts her flat on the market and moves in with him and the boys.

Just to see how things pan out, she tells me. Nothing, after all, is set in stone.

I agree with her. Nothing is.

What makes me smile is that Ellie is far more like Lennie than anyone will admit. She's unimpressed by Alex for a start. She's tough, she's creative, she's funny — she's good with the boys. She rides a bicycle around town and the locals take an instant shine to her because of her red hair and the fact that she's not stuck up. She doesn't mind getting wet or dirty — crucial when you live with boys. Best of all, perhaps, she doesn't seem to expect miracles. Alex told me she's even written to Bob, asked him to come over and spend the summer, see his grandchildren.

I think they may marry. I really hope so. I've barely seen them this past year — all of us have been so busy with one thing and another — but I'm hoping they'll come up and stay soon. Besides, Jordan misses Connor desperately. Jordan misses everyone desperately.

Last time I spoke to Alex on the phone, he mentioned that he and Ellie are trying for a baby of their own, but that it's taking its time to happen.

Still, she's only thirty-three, he went on. She's still got all the time in the world, hasn't she?

Yes, I agreed, surprised to feel the tears spring to my eyes.

We didn't stay in the town, Mick and me. How could we? As well as taking a part of us, the place had lost all of its magic, all of its charm. It's not that I blame it for what happened to Rosa, but I couldn't go on being somewhere that reminded me — of what? Of how I took my eye off the ball for that split second — which is, after all, all it takes to lose just about everything you care about?

Most of all I found I couldn't any longer bear to look at the sea — at that grey and pitiless expanse, sucking and shifting its shadowy weight over the cold wet sand. Or I could of course, if I had to — but only for just long enough to call Fletcher back, or for Jordan to be able to run and grab his Frisbee out of the foam. After that I'd have to look away, to turn. I'd have to run.

It took all of our strength to leave, but we knew, Mick and I, that leaving was our only chance of a future and we owed it to ourselves and the children to hang onto that.

We moved there to be safe but, in most ways, I feel safer where we live now. I'm amazed that Alex can stay there, that he loves it still. I think maybe Lacey was right. It makes you dizzy: too much water, too much sky.

Mick's new job pays him well. Silly money, he calls it. Everyone says he's fallen on his feet. He never really thought he'd go back into journalism — and he despises the paper for its bland complacency — but he sees it as a temporary measure.

The best thing is it's given him a push. Now he spends all his evenings and weekends writing his own stuff. I don't know if he'll be able to make a living at it, or even if he can write. All I know is, I love the look on his face when he's trying.

I know what will happen with Lacey. What will happen is that, sooner or later, one of these days, we'll find each other. There he'll be, standing in his dark coat on a crowded tube platform — or striding along the street among the bright lights and shop windows — and he'll touch my sleeve.

Come for a drink, he'll say.

What? I'll go, blushing. You mean now?

Yes of course now, he'll say, smiling. Why not now?

And we'll go and sit in a bar somewhere — a bar crowded with business people and their crushed-up suits and bags and phones — and in the space created by our new shyness, we'll talk and not talk and I'll remember him all over again, what I liked about him, how he confused me, threw me off course, how it felt, to have his body against mine.

I'll ask him how his life is going.

And he'll look down at the dirty, pine floor and then back at my face.

OK, he'll say.

And work?

A long story. Basically, something else came up, something I knew I could do better.

What? I'll ask him, unable to imagine what that something could be. What thing?

Not now, he'll say. I'll tell you all about it. Some other time.

And maybe I'll ask him how Natasha is. And he'll say he split up with her a long time ago, that winter actually. But that he's been seeing someone — a woman, an old friend he knew from long ago, from his student days.

It's all very weird, he'll add dismissively.

In what way weird?

I'm just — not sure it's going to lead to anything.

Well, I hope it does, I'll tell him truthfully, refusing the bait.

I suppose I hope so too, he'll say and then he'll glance at me in that way of his and I'll quickly look away and we'll both smile.

He'll be interested to hear about the move and will

seem genuinely glad about Mick enjoying his work. He'll ask how the boys are getting on and I'll tell him fine, adding that Nat now towers above me, would you believe it? and he'll say that yes, he does believe it.

And Livvy? he'll say — and it will make me feel strange, to hear him speak her name, not just because I know he has a soft spot for my baby girl, but also because she was part of it. She was with us on that long ago terrible night.

A terror, I'll say — explaining how she's up and walking now, running around like a maniac, driving Mick and me crazy, getting into every cupboard and pulling things off shelves and so on.

Maybe he'll ask me who Liv looks like now and I'll laugh and say she's got Mick's black hair and black eyes but she doesn't look like anyone really.

She just looks like herself, I'll say.

Her own person.

Exactly.

And we won't talk about Rosa, but when we discuss the other kids, I'll see a question in his eyes and I'll answer it truthfully without speaking, because that's how it is with Lacey. Not everything comes down to words.

We'll both agree it would be great to meet up.

Well, I'll say, why not come over for supper some time?

I'd like that, he'll say and I'll tell him that he could see Mick and he could see the house — though it's still a mess with builders everywhere of course — and he might if he's lucky even get a glimpse of the kids.

And I'll pull a scrap of paper from my bag and we'll write

down each other's e-mail addresses. He'll read mine aloud to check he's got it right and fold it away in his wallet, but we both know we'll never do it, we'll never e-mail. We know that, even as we write them down so carefully and as we fix on each other's faces for that one last time, we won't do it.

Maybe once or twice in my life, on a sad or shaky night, my fingers will hover over the keys. They may, occasionally, even go so far as to type in his address. But I'll always reach for the split-second safety of the delete. Mostly it will just be enough to see that scrap of blue paper with his handwriting on it stuck to my wall, to know it's there, to know it could be there, that it will continue to be there if I want it to be.

Rosa is buried right bang next to Lennie, as close under the yew as they could manage. Cleve was very good about it. Asked no questions, made no fuss, just made it happen. Leave it to me, he said and we did.

She is there and we are here and sometimes that is very hard, but that's why we still go down there, why we'll always go. Apart from Alex and his family, Rosa is what pulls us forever towards the town. She lies there and maybe one day we'll lie there too. I hope so. I used not to care at all about where I ended up, but I don't think I could leave my little girl there forever on her own.

Though she's not alone of course. When I'm there, I'm amazed at how I see the place through their eyes — Rosa's and Lennie's. Lennie used to say that the countryside around there scared her — that it had an energy that sucked you in, that snared you, whether you wanted it or not. I think Rosa understood that. And now I too am beginning to understand what she meant.

Because I know that, if you walk along past Blackshore and the ferry to the marshes, something strange happens. Sound and texture dissolve and all signs of human life recede and silence crashes into your ears. And that, once you're past a certain point, the cow parsley grows as high as your head and the sky clots to a palish green and the horizon dips and swerves and falls away.

And then, when you can no longer see a single soul or any sign of life save, to your right, maybe one small dark sail out at sea and, to your left, crowds of terns alighting in slow motion on the flats beyond Buss Creek, you can convince yourself that you're truly alone on the planet, that everyone's gone and there's no one out there but you.

Knowing this can cause a person's breathing to sharpen and their heart to tilt. Because, with or without the friendly souls of the dead, this place can seem like the loneliest and forlornest on earth.

And then, despite the crackle of insects in the gorse, the cry of the bittern, the brown gleam of the saltings, the eerie, mauve light that creeps in just before rain, you shiver. Because — smelling the coltsfoot coming off the dunes, feeling the sharp breeze that lifts your hair — you sense the truth. That there's no one at all out there to save you, should something happen.